THE
DROP
ZONE

A T.J. PETERSON MYSTERY

BOB KROLL

ECW PRESS

PUBLISHED BY ECW PRESS
665 GERRARD STREET EAST
TORONTO, ONTARIO M4M 1Y2
416-694-3348 / INFO@ECWPRESS.COM

COVER DESIGN: CYANOTYPE
COVER IMAGES: SKYLINE © JAMIE FARRANT / GETTY IMAGES INTERNATIONAL, BRIDGE © OLGA LARINA / SHUTTERSTOCK
AUTHOR PHOTO: J. WILLIAM JOHNSON

LIBRARY AND ARCHIVES CANADA CATALOGUING IN PUBLICATION

KROLL, ROBERT E., 1947-, AUTHOR
THE DROP ZONE : A T.J. PETERSON MYSTERY / BOB KROLL

ISSUED IN PRINT AND ELECTRONIC FORMATS
ISBN 978-1-77041-244-6 (PBK.)
978-1-77090-724-9 (PDF)
978-1-77090-725-6 (EPUB)

I. TITLE.

PS8621.R644D76 2015   C813'.6
C2014-907598-7 C2014-907599-5

THE PUBLICATION OF **THE DROP ZONE** HAS BEEN GENEROUSLY SUPPORTED BY THE CANADA COUNCIL FOR THE ARTS WHICH LAST YEAR INVESTED $157 MILLION TO BRING THE ARTS TO CANADIANS THROUGHOUT THE COUNTRY, AND BY THE ONTARIO ARTS COUNCIL (OAC), AN AGENCY OF THE GOVERNMENT OF ONTARIO, WHICH LAST YEAR FUNDED 1,793 INDIVIDUAL ARTISTS AND 1,076 ORGANIZATIONS IN 232 COMMUNITIES ACROSS ONTARIO, FOR A TOTAL OF $52.1 MILLION. WE ALSO ACKNOWLEDGE THE FINANCIAL SUPPORT OF THE GOVERNMENT OF CANADA THROUGH THE CANADA BOOK FUND FOR OUR PUBLISHING ACTIVITIES, AND THE CONTRIBUTION OF THE GOVERNMENT OF ONTARIO THROUGH THE ONTARIO MEDIA DEVELOPMENT CORPORATION.

PRINTED AND BOUND IN CANADA   PRINTING: FRIESENS 5 4 3 2 1

TO MY CLUTCH HITTER.

CHAPTER
ONE

Skype image. No one on the screen, just an angled view of an unmade bed in a crummy corner of a fleabag room with peeling wallpaper. No hello. Nothing said — not by her, not by him.

He squirmed at the silence, knowing she was on the other end listening to his nervous breathing. She had been calling him like this almost every day for more than a year. And like all the other calls, this one had him wincing, as if the Skype image were pressing on a sore spot.

Then she hung up and the screen went white. He set the cell phone on his desk, snapped his head back, and stared at the cold fluorescent lighting. He sat that way for several minutes, then he pulled a pint of Johnnie Walker from the pocket of his green jacket, the one with a pack of wolves stencilled on the back, and held it to the light to see how much was left.

The room was large with wall-to-wall desks, and a woman at a desk three away from his broke into his thoughts. "You stare at it long enough, Peterson, it'll disappear."

He knew the wide smile that went with that voice. He'd recently seen her flash it in an interrogation room to entice a suspect into telling her what she wanted to know. Her name was Detective Grace Bernard, but she preferred being called Bernie.

"It'll disappear whether I stare at it or not," T.J. Peterson said without turning her way. "And no splitsies," he added, dressing the comment in a dollar-store laugh. He swivelled his chair and looked at her. "There's just enough to top up my coffee."

Bernie's husky voice didn't match her sweet face and thin frame, but it had worked wonders for her as a uniform cop whenever she'd ordered a street seller or gangbanger to go up against the wall and spread 'em. And the voice was only one of her deceptions. Her easy manner was another. He had seen her in action, smiling an aggressive six-foot, two-hundred-pound suspect off balance, then taking out his knees.

He slipped around the desks to reach hers. "I'm on the coffee run, you want a cup?"

"Thanks. But I'm going home. Sleep does wonders, Peterson. You should go home and try it sometime."

"I did once, Bernie. Overrated!"

She smiled that big smile of hers and asked, "Do you even have a home?"

Peterson ducked the question the way he ducked most questions about his private life — especially the one about what the T.J. in T.J. Peterson stood for — with a shrug. He was out the door and halfway down the hall when he heard Andy Miles holding court in the coffee room.

"Don't talk to me about justice," Miles said. He was fifty-eight, a detective, a has-been on the front line. A cover-my-ass complainer with a Rolex that didn't match his pay scale. He slashed his hand under his chin. "I've had it right up to here."

"The guy's waiting for her to come home," he continued. "He's watching TV with the Remington across his lap. Loaded. She didn't even get to close the door."

Sitting with Miles at the Formica table was Jamie Gould, midthirties, hair gelled and combed for a Thursday night in the downtown bars. Gould had the newspaper opened to the crossword. A smartass to most other cops in the Investigation Unit. He cupped his hands over his ears. "We going through this again?"

"A hundred times, asshole," Miles said.

"In your face!" Tommy Amiro shouted, cocking his fingers into a gun and blowing off the smoke. Amiro, an acne-scarred hotshot, was sitting on the side counter. He had squinty eyes, like he was perpetually in a room full of smoke, and a squealing voice that must have driven his mother mad.

Peterson walked in and made straight for the Mr. Coffee, doing his best to ignore the conversation. But Miles saw him and piped, "How'd you see it, Peterson? Justifiable homicide or what?"

Peterson poured a mug half full, showing Miles his back.

"From your point of view," Miles insisted. "Give us your inside take on the drug head out in Hardwoods smoking his old lady for body packing another man."

One swing, Peterson thought, one swing to shut him up. Bad blood had been between them for years, ever since they had squared off at a Christmas party, both drunk, both belligerent, and both wanting the other to start what each believed they could finish. But one swing now would bring the house down around Peterson's ears.

"The lawyers did a sit down and got a plea bargain," Gould explained.

"Lawyers get involved and everything goes to rat shit," Miles said.

Peterson pulled the pint of Johnnie Walker from his jacket pocket and topped up the coffee. He looked at the door like he wanted back out.

It was show time in the coffee room, with Miles acting the stand-up guy for an audience of fellow cops. "We don't nail a confession with the punks, shitters, and show runners, and the case goes behind closed doors. They plea-bargain a murder rap down to five on the inside and he walks in two. And then you know who they blame? They blame us. They blame you, me, and every cop on the street. So don't talk to me about justice."

Peterson rolled his eyes.

"Fuck you and the uh-oh eyes!" Miles said. "How many times, right here, right in this fucking room, I hear you complain about back-room deals that keep a perp from doing time?"

Peterson took a big slurp of coffee-plus. "We do the job. We put a case together." He stared hard at Miles. "What's personal stays on the shelf. We fix nothing, and the rest we leave to judges and lawyers."

"And you know how far that goes," Tommy Amiro said.

"It's the fucking lawyers," Miles said. "I work a case and it gets shafted by two lawyers over a dry martini. I wish I'd never brought it in. I should have fixed it so it looked like suicide or self-defence."

Peterson shook his head and started for the door.

"Don't tell me you never felt that itch," Miles pressed.

Peterson stopped but didn't answer. He backed up a few steps into the room.

"You know it, Peterson! Don't tell me if you had a perp in cuffs and enough evidence to prove it, and the Crown and defence take it sideways, don't tell me you never wished you'd had one loaded in the throat for a head shot. You shake your head, but you're no better than the rest of us. You get the itch to settle things yourself, just like me, just like Tommy and Jamie here, and everybody else with a badge and nine mil Sig to go with it."

Peterson was about to turn on him when Bernie's voice snagged everyone's attention. "The Airport Road homicide. That's you, Peterson."

Peterson wheeled her way. "Ice cold."

"Someone doesn't think so."

He followed Bernie into a glassed-in room where two cops, male and female dispatchers, sat before a semicircle of computers and digital audio boards. Both wore headphones. This was Central Messaging and Dispatch.

The female dispatcher saw them enter, jotted a time code number on a yellow pad, and played her fingers over a keyboard. She listened for a moment. Once she heard what she wanted, she moused over the timeline to cue the recording. She pulled the headphones down around her neck.

"This came into 911 less than ten minutes ago," she said. "A cell phone call. The caller hung up. It could also be a prank call."

"Like the other night," Peterson said with a smile in his voice.

"You heard about that?"

"The guy in a Burger King drive-through."

"It takes all kinds," she said.

"All what kinds?" Bernie asked.

"A guy calls 911 from the drive-through," the dispatcher said. "It's past one in the morning, and he complains he's not getting any service. He sees staff inside mopping floors, but nobody's answering his order. He considered that an emergency."

"C'mon?" Bernie said.

"He was yelling his order at the 911 operator," the dispatcher said. "'Whopper, fries, extra large Coke.' True story."

"What about this one?" Peterson asked. "Prank or not?"

"Judge for yourself. A screener at 911 picked it up right away. We usually don't get it that fast, but the Airport Road thing caught her attention and she thought we should have a listen." She transferred the output to the speakers and clicked the mouse.

There was a scramble of noise then a male voice said, "911. State your emergency."

"I saw something," a young woman said, her voice jittery.

"Go ahead."

"Not this!" The woman was suddenly frantic. "To talk to . . . I got to tell them."

"Tell them what?"

"About it."

"Please?"

"You know."

"What would you like to tell someone?"

"What they did!"

"Did? Did what?" His voice was calm, encouraging. "Who are you talking about?"

"Tee fie!"

"I don't understand what you're —"

"Body!"

"What body?"

"Took it away and then the Airport Road!"

"Was there an accident? Are you reporting a car accident on Airport Road?"

"No!" The girl screamed. Then her voice became distant, hollow sounding, as though she had lowered the phone. She was muttering a battery of unintelligible words. Then she said, "Drop Zone!" and something else that was another wild ramble of broken words.

"The Drop Zone?" the male voice asked.

"Midnight or . . ."

"I'm not following you. Can we start over please? What is the situation there?"

"No!" She was angry now, shouting, moving the phone away from her mouth then back again. Disjointed words.

"But I'm not following you. Hello? Hello?"

Peterson slid the yellow pad closer and pulled a pen from his breast pocket. "Can I use the headphones?"

The dispatcher removed them from around her neck and passed them over.

He signalled her to play the recording again. This time he took notes, telling her when to stop and start. Bernie read them over his shoulder. "Diesel truck idling nearby. Major intersection? People talking. Moving away. Traffic light? Crosswalk? Bus pulls up. Doors open."

He had the dispatcher replay it, and he underlined a few words on the notepad. Then he removed the headphones. "People are talking in the background," he said. "Any chance we can brighten up what they're saying?"

"Not here. Communications probably can, but not until tomorrow morning."

Peterson checked his watch: 9:38 p.m.

"What's your verdict?" the dispatcher asked.

Peterson rubbed his face. "She could be spiced. Definitely scared. But I don't think it's a prank."

He and Bernie returned to the Investigation Unit. He opened his desk drawer and finger-walked the active files. Pulled one out and opened it flat on his desk.

"Are you going?" Bernie asked.

Peterson nodded.

"Want company?"

"I thought you were going home."

"I can hang in."

"Thanks, but I'll call Danny," he said, shaking his head. "If this turns into something, he'll want to be there."

"Why the Drop Zone?"

His eyes went distant, and his face seemed to sink with sadness. Then he looked up from the file. "Out of the way, maybe. Abandoned building. It used to be the first stop for teenage runaways. The caller could be in there hiding."

"I heard it's the next in line for demolition."

"It won't be missed."

"Sure you don't want me to hang around?"

"You got your kid to go home to. But thanks."

"I hope it's something," she said. She started to leave, then turned back. Wide smile. "How long have you been camping at your desk?"

Three months with her detective's badge and the inside buzz about him had finally piqued her curiosity.

His voice flattened with disappointment. "Hearsay evidence is inadmissible," he said.

"We haven't worked together," there was an apology in her voice and eyes, "so I only know . . ."

"What you hear."

She tried shrugging out of it.

"You're a detective aren't you?" he asked.

"Maybe that's why I'm asking."

Peterson cut her some slack. "Most of what's said about me is true. Not all."

Her eyes filled with curiosity, but she let it go. "Goodnight, Peterson."

He nodded, waved, and opened the two-week-old file.

White female, late teens or early twenties, buried in the woods off Airport Road. Shallow grave. Ten months in wet soil. Body largely decomposed.

He remembered how the body was discovered. A nearby resident had called it in. Her black lab, off leash, had dug for something rich to roll in.

When he read his handwritten note in the margin, he again felt disappointed with the forensic report. No missing person match with dental records or DNA. Nothing to go on but the body of a murdered girl whom nobody had bothered to report missing. Exact cause of death: Blunt force trauma, skull fracture.

He picked up his cell phone, speed-dialed Danny's number and got voice mail. After seven days on the clock and a successful collar in a drug hit, Danny had booked off until the following afternoon. A hot date. Who could blame him? He was midforties, good looking, and, according to a few female cops and the girls working in administration, a dead ringer for some heartthrob who played the casino circuit with a rockabilly band.

Peterson waited for the beep and left his own message. "Midnight in the Drop Zone, Danny Boy. Face to face with someone playing Deep Throat about the Airport Road homicide. Possibility, but a long shot. If you don't show, I'll call it a lucky night."

He checked his watch again, saw he had two hours to kill in a pub on the way.

CHAPTER
TWO

There were more potholes than pavement, and Peterson felt like a bobblehead doll as he eased the black Jetta down the back road to the waterfront, his brake lights pulsing. His eyes widened in the dark, searching for the foot-deep craters. Then the road gave into a dirt track with caved sections along the shoulders. The car scraped bottom where runoff from the upper streets had scoured a two-foot-wide gully that snatched the back wheel on the driver's side and jammed it tight.

Peterson got out and looked, scowled, and got back in and rocked the car until it pulled free. Then he crept it forward, past what had once been a three-storey red-brick tenement. The multicoloured graffiti on its crumbling walls sizzled under the high beams. Painted red waves exploded into orange tongues of fire, and black ooze dripped from dark blue scrolls.

He drove by empty lots that had turned into junk-littered fields overgrown with weeds. Then he pulled up before the Drop Zone, a condemned dockyard warehouse, its grey walls scoured by the sun and wind. Glassless windowpanes. Doorjambs hanging free. He cut the lights and engine. Checked his watch, 11:35 p.m., and reached for the pint of Johnnie Walker on the shotgun seat.

As he pulled at the mickey, his eyes wandered across the dark harbour to the downtown lights of this port city on Canada's east coast, his city, rolled out and ripe for the Thursday night crowd to drink the bars dry, and with a dockyard ramped up for shipbuilding, five universities, and half a dozen hospitals, there's a lot of drinking going on. And that has people using and abusing each other and picking fights and taking them to the streets, and lacing down cops to foot patrols that corralled young drunks and pipeheads and crammed them into caged vans.

He shook his head then capped the bottle and returned it to the shotgun seat. Emptied his mind. Closed his eyes. Opened them. His watch read 11:54. He punched Danny's number again and left another message, "Hey Dan! I'm going in."

He grabbed the Maglite flashlight from the back seat. Then he climbed from the car and reached back under his seat to retrieve a twelve-inch nail puller, a cat's paw. He shoved the cat's paw up his jacket sleeve and cupped it in place. Holding the flashlight hip high, he kicked through trash and smashed glass and the high weeds growing up around broken bricks and chunks of concrete.

He stepped over the yellow No Trespassing tape and squeezed through the space between splintered boards nailed over the entrance. He caught a soft spot in the floor and stumbled. The flashlight flew out of his hand as he grabbed the edge of a stack of wooden pallets and held his balance. It landed a few feet away and its angled beam transfigured a burlap roll into a shadowy, outstretched body.

Peterson stared at it. Moved closer, grabbed the flashlight, and continued staring, thinking about the last time he was in this place, the time he came here to search for his daughter.

He ducked under a sagging beam and stepped between the burlap roll and a pile of rubble. His senses reached into the darkness, and he heard water dripping and felt the confines of a large room shrunk by walls of shadows.

"I'm Detective Peterson," he shouted. "You called 911."

The brick walls flung back his voice and the high ceiling hollowed his words into meaningless sounds. He listened, flicked off the light, and listened. Heard only the unnerving quiet. For the next few moments, he stood unmoving, hating and loving the darkness for how it conjured a sense of being alone. Isolated.

Then he turned on the light and played its beam slowly across graffiti-scarred walls. Indecipherable names. Ms and Ns and large Os like solar disks; Ss like shepherds' crooks. Tags and phrases in quotations. Circles and bent lines with curlicues on the ends. An almond shape divided by intersecting circles. An enormous T, like a double-headed axe. Zigzags and wavy lines twisting into spirals and plaited with meanings. Triangles with snakes coiled up the sides. Happy faces. Sad faces. "Fuck" scrawled a dozen times and by a dozen different hands.

He studied them all, searching for and finding the one that had jumped out at him the last time he was here, the one that had stripped his nerves raw. Large block letters: "Fuck You Dad / Katy."

He passed through an archway with a sliding door that had jumped its rusted iron rail and lay caved and twisted on the floor. This room was smaller, and the light beam reached from wall to wall. It was even more filthy and littered with torn mattresses, broken bottles, and empty food cans. He inhaled dampness and rot and the stink of abandonment. He kicked through a decade of dust, shooing shadows against the walls and seeing where a campfire had been fuelled with baseboards, with door and window frames.

Again he hollered, "Hello! You wanted to tell me something. You said midnight, the Drop Zone."

He stepped through plaster and rubble. Stumbled again. Cursed under his breath at something other than his misstep. Then he played the light down a long hallway to a closed door. Again he hesitated before advancing, threatened by the narrowness of the hallway and by the spongy, saggy look of the floor.

He reached the closed door and leaned against the jamb, sweaty faced, heaving for breath. He tried the door but it was swollen and crusted shut. He doubted anyone had been beyond it in years. Then he stepped back and shouldered it, riding the rusted hinges into the room.

A mountain of bricks and mortar confronted him. The ceiling drooped from the inward collapse of the far wall. Through the opening, he saw city lights twinkling in the wake of an outbound container ship. For a moment or two, he watched the ship glide toward the harbour mouth, almost wishing he could hire on and just sail away.

Then he turned and swept the room with his flashlight, wondering about the 911 call, about the anxiety in the voice and the direct reference to a body on Airport Road. And he wondered why the no show. Who the hell was she?

He checked his watch again: 12:16 a.m. Then he pulled out his cell phone. As he dialed Danny's number and waited for the message, he played the 911 call in his head and rummaged through the caller's words: *What they did. Tee fie. Body.*

He heard the beep and said, "You didn't miss much, pal. I'll tell you about it."

Then, just in case he had heard the time wrong, he found a flat chunk of mortared bricks to sit out the hour, suddenly wishing he had brought Johnnie Walker along for the wait. Then he settled himself and flicked off the light to let the darkness have its way with his thoughts.

Peterson was two beers deep at a dive with no closing time, the Drop Zone still bile in his throat. Alone, yet sitting among diehards at the bar — them talking and him not listening. His eyes were on a nearby table, where a drunk was sorting change. Another drunk at the same table had passed out, his arms outstretched, his mouth leaking drool onto the chipped laminate tabletop.

The bald bartender took Peterson's empty and returned a few moments later with a refill. He saw the badge when Peterson reached for his wallet. The bartender nodded and retreated down the bar, fingering Peterson for another off-duty cop drowning his thoughts and measuring his life by the wet rings on the polished oak.

Then a guy who was all elbows and knees, with short grey hair and wrinkled shirt and pants that hung from his thin frame, entered the pub. He caught Peterson's eye and head-signalled to a table at the back where the light was low. Peterson ordered another draft and carried it and his own beer to the table.

"Long time," the guy said, offering Peterson a broad smile as a handshake. The smile ran cracks across the guy's leathery face.

Peterson nodded and returned the smile. He passed the guy the draft. "You losing weight?"

"Since I was twelve. Lose any more and they'll mark me absent. So what's it been, Peterson, two years at least?"

"Must be."

"Sorry about your wife."

Peterson flinched, but he knew the words were genuine.

"I heard it's taking its toll," the guy said.

"The grapevine never stops."

"Not for you and not for me."

"And what's it telling the Bone Man now."

The Bone Man took a gulp of beer. "You're getting even rougher than you used to be, sometimes with people you used to like."

Peterson's face softened and he started to say something, but the Bone Man held up his hand like a traffic cop.

"No excuses, Peterson, not with the Bone Man. I buried one too. Took it out on my son."

"You make up?"

"We get along," the Bone Man sighed.

"How's he doing?"

"Community college, studying computers. Imagine that, a dumb alley rat like me with a kid going to college."

"Not too dumb."

"You don't think?"

"You've been odd-jobbing how long?"

"All my life," the Bone Man said.

"No government handouts. No warrants. And I doubt you ever been shafted."

The Bone Man shrugged. "Not enough to worry about."

"Probably picking up the kid's tab."

"Some of it."

"You think that's a dumb guy's life?"

Again the Bone Man shrugged.

"We see the same thing from different sides of the street, Bony Walker. Thanks for thinking about my wife."

They each settled into silence and into their beers. Then Bony said, "So what brings you out to see me?"

"An anonymous 911 call," Peterson said, "about the Airport Road body. Girl's voice from a cell phone at a busy intersection. She threw a name — at least I think it was a name: Tee Fie."

"Tee Fie?"

"Something like that. I think the caller knows who did it and wanted to spill, but . . . I don't know, afraid I think."

"A hooker? Junkie?"

"Could be. She mentioned the Drop Zone. Said a time, midnight. I thought she wanted to meet, but she never showed."

"Not much to ask around about."

"Asking too much might make someone jumpy. I thought you might just keep an ear open."

"Two ears for you."

"What do you need?"

"Nothing. You did plenty for me already."

Peterson's cell phone rang and he cringed before he realized the ring tone was "Auld Lang Syne," his cop ring.

"Peterson," he said.

"Central Dispatch," a woman's voice said. "We have a possible homicide in St. Jude's Roman Catholic Church, on Westphal Street."

"I'm short one partner," Peterson said.

"Detective Little booked in half an hour ago," the dispatcher said. "He'll be at the church."

Peterson grumbled, hung up, and pushed what was left of his beer to the centre of the table.

"Must be important," Bony said.

"Homicide at St. Jude's."

"You like doing this?" Bony asked before draining his beer.

Peterson let it go.

Peterson drove with his head on a swivel, searching through the chase lights and flashing signs that blistered both sides of the Strip, a six-lane through the commercial section of a rundown neighbourhood. He passed one joint after another: pizza, falafel, souvalaki, then a dollar store, porn store, empty lot, used-car lot, realtor, barber, gas bar, pawn shop, then more of the same. The Strip was churning with sleaze. Prostitutes with blank eyes hustling the corners, and pipeheads and brick-faced buyers hounding the sidewalks like ants on a sugar cube.

Peterson slowed past a cluster of half a dozen cars in a strip-mall parking lot, each car a mini-mart for self-abuse, with sellers operating from open trunks or from open windows on the passenger side. Muscle on the driveways screened the flow of customers like security guards at a Walmart.

Useless to crack down, he thought. Bust them, jail them, hide the key where the sun don't shine, and they still wouldn't go away. Others would take their places. Need and greed, the free market system.

Peterson hung a left and drove into the tangle of side streets bordered by shabby track housing and dilapidated high rises. He turned into the empty lot at a closed elementary school and parked beside a blacktop basketball court, where T-shirted teens were still going two-on-two in a streetlight's dull glow. They must be better off here than home, Peterson thought, and clicked on the dome light. He checked his haggard face in the rear-view to see if his eyes were as bloodshot as they felt. Then he reached for mints in the glove box, popped one, and dug into the back seat for a tan cloth bag containing blue forensic booties and latex gloves. He took what he needed, climbed from the car, and walked half a block to St. Jude's Roman Catholic Church.

The heavy front door squealed on its thick iron hinges. In the vestibule, he hesitated before the holy water font, remembering a habit that now grated against his frame of mind. He slipped booties on his feet, pulled on gloves, and entered the nave.

The church smelled of burnt offerings. The light was

dim and moody from the flicker of devotional candles in metal racks set before statues of the Blessed Virgin and of St. Jude reaching down a hand to help lost souls.

As Peterson walked down the centre aisle, the shadows, the candles, the hint of beeswax, and the lingering smell of incense insinuated an urge to pray. He ignored it and dug his hands into his jacket pockets.

Detective Corporal Danny Little, still dressed for a night on the town in a brown bomber jacket and loosened tie, stood beneath the vigil light. He was looking down at Janet Crouse, who was squatting at the centre of the transept before a circle of votive candles. Danny saw Peterson and pounded up the aisle to meet him.

"Drunk or sober?" Danny asked. His voice was thick, his tongue digging out the words.

"Does it matter?"

"Not to me," Danny said. "You want me to do this?"

"I'm good," Peterson said.

"Your last message said I didn't miss much."

"Stood up."

Danny laughed. "That's better than being shot down. But don't ask."

Peterson fingered his partner's tie. "She must have left in a hurry."

"What'd I just say?" A sheepish grin. "I ask you to leave it and what'd you do?"

"You're going to tell me anyway, you might as well do it now."

Danny frowned then tossed it like he didn't care. "So what's with the Drop Zone? You chasing ghosts?"

Peterson offered a tight smile.

Danny caught it. "Was the caller definitely a woman?"

"A girl," Peterson said.

"And she knows something about the Airport Road?"

"I think she does."

"But unwilling to show up and tell us what it is."

"You know what they say about cold feet," Peterson said. "Maybe she had a reason."

Danny looked back at the altar. "You sure you want to do this?"

Peterson nodded. "Who's dead?"

"Old priest got whacked from behind," Danny said and led Peterson down to the transept, where Peterson sidled into the front pew and saw that inside the circle of candles the letter Alpha was pasted to the floor.

"Whoever did this cut it from the altar cloth and stuck it down with blood," Janet Crouse said, sweeping her flashlight beam over the altar to show the ragged hole in the green cloth.

Crouse worked forensics. She was a big-boned woman with big hips who wore her long dark hair coiled and pinned on the back of her head like a cinnamon bun. She wore blue coveralls, blue booties, and latex gloves.

Danny Little asked Peterson, "Any idea what it means?"

"Book of Revelations," Peterson said. "God said, 'I am the Alpha and the Omega,' the beginning and the end."

Crouse looked up with a quizzical expression.

Peterson shrugged. "Altar boy."

"*You!*" Crouse cried. She almost laughed.

"My mother wanted a priest, my father a lawyer."

"So they end up with a cop. Some compromise," Danny scoffed.

Peterson gestured to Crouse's flashlight. "No bright lights?"

"They're on their way from the suburbs," Crouse said and held the flashlight under her chin, angled upward to make herself look ghoulish. "Double murder out there. Looks like the husband did his wife and then himself. Busy night."

Peterson shook his head. "Where's the body?"

Crouse struggled to her feet and led him up the steps and across the altar, avoiding the small orange plastic pyramids that marked blood splotches and bloody footprints. They entered the sacristy.

Peterson closed his eyes to settle himself. Then he looked down at the body lying in a large pool of blood. He looked away, swallowed to hold down the claw in his stomach, and then looked back.

The dead man wore a black cassock. He was lying on his front, his head turned to one side, and appeared to be in his late sixties or early seventies; grey haired, of slender build.

"Smashed skull," Crouse said. "Someone was angry."

Peterson nodded. "Died where he fell?"

"Pretty much," Crouse answered. "It looks like he was moving forward when he was clubbed from behind. Then hit a few more times."

Off Peterson's questioning look, she added, "All on the right side."

"Parish priest?"

"Father Andre Boutilier," Danny said. "He shares the rectory next door with Father Ronny — Ronny Eisner. Father Andre worked this parish and St. Patrick's; Father Ronny worked St. John's and St. Martha's across town."

"Who found the body?" Peterson asked.

"Father Ronny," Danny said. "He's in the rectory."

Peterson turned to Crouse. "How soon for a post-mortem?"

"Take a number," she grouched.

"New federal crime bill," Danny said. "Forensic tests go to Ottawa."

Peterson looked around the sacristy. There was a clothes tree hung with a long white alb and green vestments for daily mass. Beside it stood a small table holding a silver finger bowl and glass cruets for holy water and wine. Running the length of the opposite wall was a built-in cupboard with a grey laminate countertop, and on this were a breviary and a gold-plated chalice, paten, and ciborium.

Peterson stepped around the body to the counter and lifted the lid on the ciborium. It was empty. Then he fingered the top, where some adornment had been broken off.

"I thought the same thing," Danny said. "Someone killing the priest for the Holy Eucharist. But that thing's a dust collector."

Peterson's eyes again swept the room and landed on a tall staff hung with a banner used in religious processions. The crimson pennant bore the depiction of a lamb and a cross, and the motto "By This Sign Conquer."

Peterson retraced his steps around the body and went over to the flagstaff. By the discoloration on the floor where the tripod base had been standing for years, he noticed it had moved. Then he looked closely at its brass top.

"It's blood," Crouse confirmed.

Peterson nodded. He pretended to grab the flagstaff and use it to strike forward.

"That's my guess as well," Crouse said. "The murderer

hit him from behind, then stood over him and swung a few more times."

"Why would the killer set it back down almost exactly where he had grabbed it from?" Peterson asked. "Self control? Shock? Overcome with guilt?"

"Maybe the killer just likes things neat and tidy," Crouse said.

"What's out front?" Peterson asked.

Crouse led them from the sacristy. As the three walked over to the candlelit statue of the Blessed Virgin, the four-member forensics team came in through the front doors. Crouse left Peterson and Danny to direct the team to the body in the sacristy. When she returned, Peterson was staring at the blackened face of the Blessed Virgin.

"Someone burned a prayer book and wet the ashes with holy water to smudge it like that," Crouse explained. "And someone left that bundle at the statue's feet."

Peterson stepped in to get a closer look. It was a bundle of cloth cinched with a string to form what appeared to be a head. "A rag doll?"

"Looks like it," Crouse said. "The cloth is still damp. Someone soaked it in water."

"Or baptized it," Peterson said. He followed the Virgin's downward gaze to the vigil lights surrounding the letter Alpha and a small pool of blood on the floor at the statue's feet.

"The priest's?" Peterson asked Crouse, gesturing with his head toward the sacristy.

"We'll know when we analyze it. There's something else."

She led Danny and Peterson to the baptismal font. On the floor beside it was a pool of blood-spotted liquid.

"I'll confirm it in the lab, but my first thought was amniotic fluid."

Peterson stroked his brown hair. His eyes narrowed as he looked back toward the pool of blood, thinking it through, questioning his own conclusion. "Someone gave birth?"

"I'm not sure," Crouse said, uncomfortable with the evidence. She walked back to the circle of votive candles and the pool of blood on the floor before the statue of the Blessed Virgin. "There's lots of blood but no placenta, no traces of a fetus."

Peterson looked beyond Crouse to the altar and to the crucifix that towered over it. "It's a ritual of some kind. She gave birth or maybe just pretended to with the rag doll. Maybe dunked it in the baptismal font. A make-believe sacrifice or a real one?"

Crouse met his eyes and saw the hollowness in them. "I'd just be guessing," she said.

Peterson looked back at the baptismal font, then at the statue of the Virgin. He thought for a moment then turned to Crouse, "Time of death?"

"Not long ago," she said. "Three, maybe four hours."

Peterson checked his watch: 2:35 a.m. "And the call?"

"Midnight, give or take," Danny said.

"Let's hear what the priest has to say," Peterson said.

The two of them left Crouse to the forensic investigation and made their way up the centre aisle, out the heavy front door, and toward the rectory.

"You want to know, right? I mean, I'll tell you if you want to know," Danny said, as they descended the church stairs.

Peterson creased a smile Danny didn't see. "I don't want to know."

"You want to know. Who you kidding?"

"You got something on your mind?"

"You know what you are?"

"Yeah, I know. So tell me." Peterson nudged Danny to cut across the lawn to the rectory.

"Waterfront restaurant," Danny said. "Harbour view. I drop near a hundred bucks on dinner. Then it's a couple of Grand Marniers up the street, and she suggests I take her home. You know what I'm thinking. Then my cell vibrates in my pocket, but I don't answer. I'm booked off for the night, so I don't answer. So we grab a cab, and we're in the elevator to her condo, and I can tell she's having second thoughts, you know, by the way we're standing two feet apart and she's watching the floor numbers clicking off. Looking worried. So I said, 'If this is a bad idea, I'm okay.' And she said, 'I was underwater and I'm resurfacing. Right now, I just need to breathe.' Talk about ice water, huh?"

They climbed the stairs to the rectory. Peterson took a deep breath for Danny's drowning date.

"I like her," Danny said. "If she needs to breathe, let her breathe. No push back. No rush. Crazy, huh?"

Peterson opened the rectory door, but Danny had something on his mind and held back from entering.

"I'll tell you what I'm tired of, Peterson," Danny said. "I'm forty-six years old, I'm tired of going home and there's no one there, no one to talk to, about the job, about anything."

"You wouldn't talk about the job even if there was someone there."

"Maybe not you."

Peterson was expressionless. "Yeah, maybe not me. But

what's there to talk about, a hit and run, or Father What's-His-Name with a smashed skull?"

"You don't make it easy for someone to say something."

Peterson gave him the fake nonchalance — a squeezed laugh and raised shoulders.

"I never thought about it before," Danny said, "not until I started feeling it myself, but the empty house would've been the hardest part for you, right? I mean after how many years and all of a sudden there's no one there."

Peterson looked past Danny into the shadow of the church, struggling with a memory. Then he shifted his eyes back to Danny. Stony. "You done with the heart-to-heart?"

Father Ronny, a pudgy, balding, middle-aged man in a grey tracksuit, met them at the door and led them to a quiet parlour with understated furnishings. A large icon of St. Jude broke up the monotony of a long beige wall.

Father Ronny was visibly shaken. His eyes kept drifting past Peterson and Danny, staring into space.

"What time did you find the body?" Peterson asked.

"Close to midnight," the priest said.

"You always roam the church late at night?"

"I was looking for Father Boutilier."

"Why was that?"

"He wasn't in the rectory. When I left earlier, he was going to the church for holy oil and the Eucharist. A parishioner was dying in hospital. Last rites."

"What time did you leave?" Danny asked.

"After nine."

"You thought he'd still be in the church three hours later?" Peterson's tone was harsh.

Father Ronny became defensive. "He wasn't back yet. That wasn't like him, so I called the hospital. He never got there. I thought something had happened."

"Like what?" Still Peterson.

"He's sixty-seven and has a heart condition."

"And where were you all this time?" Danny asked.

Father Ronny hesitated, and Peterson caught it. "I returned a shawl to Mrs. Harding. Angela Harding. She left it behind in church after mass."

"You said mass this evening?" Peterson asked.

"No. Father Boutilier did."

"So he found the shawl?" Peterson persisted.

"No. I did. I went into church after mass . . ."

"To find the shawl," Peterson added.

Father Ronny avoided looking at him. "To check the doors were locked."

"Why didn't you get the Eucharist and holy oil while you were in the church?"

"The hospital didn't call until I was back in the rectory."

"Why didn't you go to the hospital?" Danny asked.

"The dying person was his parishioner."

"You delivered the shawl, then what?" Peterson asked.

"I came back here and went to the church to look for him."

"Three hours to deliver a shawl?" Peterson's question had an edge to it.

"We had a glass of wine."

"Big glass," Peterson asked, "or are you a slow sipper?"

Father Ronny buckled, "What does this have to do —"

"You said you checked the doors," Peterson interrupted.

"Yes. I picked up the shawl and checked all the doors." Then off Peterson's questioning look the priest added, "Father Boutilier sometimes forgets."

"Did he?"

"Did he what?"

"Did he forget to lock the doors after mass."

"No. They were all locked."

"Every door?" Danny asked.

"You know the neighbourhood," the priest said.

"When you went back for Boutilier was the front door locked?" Peterson asked.

"No. That's why I thought he was inside."

"So someone could have followed him in," Danny said.

"Maybe," Peterson said.

"No broken windows," Danny said. "No forced locks."

"The church is only open for mass and confession," the priest said. "We open the front door a half-hour before mass and lock it after."

"Could they have come for mass and stayed?"

"I don't know. The congregation is small, a few more than fifty, and we only get eight to ten regulars for daily mass. More on Sunday. And there's always someone from the neighbourhood looking for comfort."

"Any of the fifty hold a grudge against Father Boutilier?" Danny asked.

Father Ronny shook his head. "He was a gentle man. Easy going."

"Someone didn't think so," Peterson said. "Anyone in the neighbourhood not like him?"

"I doubt it," Father Ronny said. "He understood poverty."

"Which means what?"

"He didn't blame people for being poor. He accepted them whatever their lot in life."

"That include drug heads and pimps?"

Father Ronny met Peterson's eyes with a look that was as cold as the cop's. "They don't attend mass very often."

"That leaves you," Peterson pressed, holding the priest's gaze. "Did you get along with Father Boutilier?"

"We had our differences."

"You didn't like him, or he didn't like you?"

Father Ronny searched Peterson's face. "Am I a suspect?"

Peterson smiled. "Everyone is suspect. It comes with Original Sin. Guilt and suspicion. Now what kind of differences?"

Father Ronny looked past Peterson. "I was too liberal minded for Father Boutilier. He was a strict conservative. I want the priesthood open to everyone, and he didn't."

"You argued over religion?"

"Not religion," Father Ronny said, "church rules and regulations. And we didn't argue. Discussed. And not in a while. Our discussions ended long ago. I suppose we agreed to disagree. We went about our duties and spoke when necessary. He lived a life devoted to the church."

"And you don't," Peterson said, and the priest glared. "Did you argue about that?"

"It's not what you think."

"And what do I think?"

Father Ronny looked away again, unwilling to answer. Then he faced Peterson. "We have fifty parishioners. The other three churches, not much more than a hundred among them. In the modern world, a conservative Catholicism is irrelevant."

"Yet you're still a priest," Peterson said.

"Yes, I am still a priest." His voice was low.

"Just going through the motions?" Danny asked.

Father Ronny held up his hands. "My hands were consecrated to change bread and wine into the body and blood of Christ. That is what makes me a priest."

"That's like saying the badge is what makes me a cop," Peterson scoffed.

Father Ronny lowered his hands to his lap. His face reddened. "I would have thought the gun is what makes you a cop."

Peterson shrugged. "Sometimes it comes down to that. Tell me about the Holy Eucharist. Any signs of desecration?"

"It hadn't been touched," Father Ronny answered.

"You checked?"

"After I called 911."

"You called from the rectory?"

"My cell."

"Then what?"

"I went into the nave. I couldn't be in the sacristy, not with Father Boutilier lying there. I saw the torn altar cloth, the blood, and the candles. Satanists was my first thought, so I checked the tabernacle and it was locked."

"You have another ciborium in the sacristy," Peterson said.

"For a time when the congregation was larger and we needed two priests serving Holy Communion."

"How long has the top been broken off?" Danny asked.

"I didn't know it was. We would have used that ciborium

last Easter when the church was full with those making their Easter duty. It wasn't broken then."

"It's broken now. What are we looking for?"

"The top had a Chi-Rho. It looks like this."

Father Ronny borrowed Danny's notebook and pencil and quickly drew an X superimposed by a P.

"I doubt someone stole it. It's not valuable," Father Ronny said.

"Maybe they thought it was," Danny said.

"Then they would have taken the ciborium and chalice," Peterson said.

"Is anything else missing?" Danny asked.

"I'm not sure," Father Ronny said. "I haven't really looked."

"If the only thing missing is the top to the ciborium, the Chi-Rho," Peterson said, "then whoever killed the priest didn't come here to rob the place."

CHAPTER
THREE

Danny followed Peterson into the dead priest's bedroom. It was ascetic: a single bed pushed into a corner, covered by a grey wool blanket. The wall opposite it had two large windows that overlooked the south side of the church and the side door to the sacristy. The furniture was all dark oak: a small desk and chair, a matching dresser, and a cushioned armchair with a floor lamp beside it. Several books were neatly stacked on the desk. There was no computer. A crucifix hung on one wall and a cork bulletin board on another.

Danny scanned the notices on the bulletin board. Peterson examined the desk. The books included a Bible, *The Dictionary of Christian Lore and Legend*, *The Bestiary of Christ*, *Harper's Bible Dictionary*, a personal diary, and an appointment book. Peterson thumbed through the appointment book. The last entry was a week ago, for a Mrs. DeMilo.

Peterson set aside the diary and appointment book to take with him. Then he flipped through the books for marked passages and loose inserts. A folded paper fell out of *Harper's Bible Dictionary*. The handwritten note was in French. Peterson struggled to translate it then gave up.

Danny moved on to the dresser. On top was a tray with a water glass, a coffee mug, and an empty plastic pitcher. The drawers contained the usual assortment of clothing.

Peterson was now combing through the closet, feeling each article of clothing for something in the pockets. Priestly garb comprised the most of it, with a few sport shirts and casual slacks mixed in. Nothing hidden.

Then Danny whistled at finding a half-dozen old black-and-white photos in the bottom drawer, hidden under carefully folded sweaters. Peterson looked at the photos. All pictured early teenage girls, mostly undressed.

Danny pulled out a Kodak Instamatic camera from behind the sweaters. The little window on the back showed the number one, which meant there was film in the camera, with one frame exposed.

"An Instamatic must be thirty years old at least," Peterson said. "These girls would be women by now. Some with children of their own."

Peterson took another look at the photos, then crossed to the window that looked out on the darkened mass of the church. He turned back to Danny. "A film cartridge left in the camera and only one frame exposed. Then the camera is tucked away in a bottom drawer with the five photos. What does that tell us?"

"He never got around to taking more pictures," Danny said. "Maybe he never got the opportunity?"

"For over thirty years?"

"It's possible."

Peterson looked back out the window at the church in shadow. He spoke to his reflected image. "The camera and photos were too neatly stored," he said. "Trophies? Maybe. Or maybe they were a form of penance, a way to punish himself for what he had done."

"You believe that?" Danny asked.

Peterson turned from the window. "I want to. I want to believe we're more than just goddamn garbage collectors."

Later, Peterson stood on the stone steps of the church looking at a closed-down school and a corner store with riot gates over its windows. Looking at the crummy neighbourhood. Looking in a mirror. Not fully conscious of the wind, of the newspaper waving in the gutter, of the traffic and the pedestrians on the sidewalks, of the shadows boxing with telephone poles and drifting along the sides of buildings, of the blurred swimmings of his own brain.

Crouse joined him on the stone steps. She lit a cigarette. Inhaled deeply. They stood together in silence for a long time then she said, "Sometimes I wonder what the hell is going on, what's happening out here. What makes people do the things they do?"

Across the street a light went on in an upstairs room. They both looked up at the same time and watched a man pass before the window. Then the light went out.

Peterson shrugged. "Catholics believe we're born with it. The evil that we do. Bad to the bone."

"Do you believe that stuff?"

"I used to."

"Now?"

"Who knows what to believe?"

Peterson started down the stone steps.

"Keep yourself human," Crouse said.

Peterson stopped and turned back.

"That's what you told me ten years ago," Crouse continued. "'Don't let yourself get used to it.'" She flicked her cigarette to the sidewalk. "So what happened?"

"You tell me," Peterson said.

CHAPTER
FOUR

The deputy chief's office looked out on a grid of narrow paths and crowded desks that hummed with constant chatter and ringing phones. Through the glass wall, Deputy Chief Fultz could watch his staff, and his staff could see him. They could see Peterson standing before Fultz's desk, one hand toying with his waistband, like a delinquent child awaiting the punishing end of a belt.

Fultz finished reading the report, carefully placed it on his desk, and folded his arms on his chest.

"What is it, Peterson? What gets inside your head?"

Peterson flinched but did not blink.

Fultz studied him. He took in the detective's dog-eared face. He saw something else too, but he couldn't put a finger on what it was. He nodded at the report. "Don't you ever sleep?"

"I sleep."

"Not last night. You were here until after nine, then you hit a pub on your way to the Drop Zone for a meet with a possible witness. Then you drank away the next hour at a hole in the wall. Investigated a murder of a Roman Catholic priest, after which you closed another bar, had half-a-dozen shots one after the other, and then you walked around downtown alone, hassling people, picking fights. You're six months off probation and you're at it again. What is it this time? What triggered it?"

Peterson didn't answer.

Fultz checked the report. "Officer Sperry found your car in a pub's parking lot and you sleeping on the front steps of the church where the priest was killed. What's that all about?"

Peterson avoided the deputy chief's eyes.

"You said you were over it," Fultz said. "But you're not over it."

Peterson's eyes roved the room until they found a lion's head carved into the apron of a rosewood side table. He stared at it to avoid Fultz's gaze, his questions.

"You're a good cop, Peterson, but you're falling apart."

Peterson's eyes darted to a painting of old-time baseball players in a farmer's field that seemed chromatically endless.

"You know she's not here," Fultz continued, "yet you still roam the streets looking for her. You still hit the bars. You think I don't keep tabs on how you're drinking yourself crazy? You're a cop for Christ's sake! You know where your daughter is. You had half the department tracking her down. So why don't you go look for her in Vancouver? Take

42

a vacation. You haven't had one in years. Take a fucking break, and give me a rest."

Peterson searched the weedy base paths for a place to hide. Slipped over the painting's horizon into an ugly shade of blue.

Fultz sighed in frustration. "I want you to go back to Carmichael. You still need help, probably more now than ever. That's an order! And no cutting it short. Not this time. You don't miss a session. You don't leave early, and you don't show up late. You're lucky I don't have you riding a desk until Carmichael hands me a clean bill on your mental state. You're back on probation, Peterson. Screw up with the shrink, screw up with anything, and I'll suspend you."

Peterson turned to go, but Fultz wasn't letting him off just then.

"And here's another thing. One word that you're not doing the job, and I'll have you walking a beat. And that includes your partner if he so much as waltzes in here with some goddamn line about the two of you being the dynamic duo."

Peterson nodded. He could tell Danny a hundred times not to stick up for him, but Danny still would, no matter what. They had a history together.

Peterson left Fultz's office. Andy Miles was waiting for him to pass by. He moved from behind his desk as Peterson neared, put on a smile, and said, "There it is, Peterson. You run with the stray dogs, sooner or later you're pissing with them."

Bernie saw it coming and was around her desk and between the two of them as Peterson's fists balled and anger flashed across his face. She saw his right arm cock at the hip. She looped her arm into his, as though they were out for a Sunday stroll, and ushered him around a couple of desks toward the back-to-back he shared with Danny.

"Don't add to it," she said, offering Peterson a dusky, sympathetic smile.

When they reached his desk, she unhooked her arm. "This belong to you?" she asked Danny.

Danny looked at them both and shook his head. "Mental health is two desks over." Then, feigning a second thought, he added, "But what the hell. Dump him here! I'll see he gets a straightjacket and heavy chain."

Peterson slumped behind his desk.

"So?" Danny asked.

Peterson scowled. Danny left it at that and passed him a handwritten sheet of paper. "Fifty-five members of St. Jude congregation, not counting the riffraff that wander in to get warm."

"Many of those?"

"Daniel Hearn thinks so. Seventy-eight years old, head of the Holy Name Society. He said half of the regulars at mass aren't on that list, and they change with the weather."

"That means we scour the street."

Danny raised his shoulders, pretending defeat.

"Anything from Crouse?" Peterson asked.

"Fingerprints and blood. The prints she'll run through the database, but the blood analysis and everything else are days away."

"How about the film cartridge?"

"Dated 1962."

"The undeveloped film?"

"Waiting on it."

"So where was Father Boutilier in 1962?"

"We're working on it."

Peterson frowned. "The blood ritual confuses it."

"You're not buying Satan worship."

"I'm not writing it off. We check out satanic groups, witch covens, every weirdo group in the city."

Danny smiled. "That include Masonic Lodges, Knights of Columbus, and every holy-roller church we can track down?"

"The usual weirdos will do. You got an address for Mrs. Harding?"

Danny flashed a shit-eating grin. "Like you don't know Mrs. Angela Harding?"

"Too upscale for me."

"Yeah, well, you should shower and shave before you go calling, otherwise neighbourhood watch are likely to think the street lice are back."

CHAPTER
FIVE

Swanky south-end neighbourhood. Crescent-shaped driveway. Red paving stones. White two-storey with Doric columns and a bevelled-glass front door. A house built to show off wealth. So it surprised Peterson that the lady of the house answered his knock herself. He recognized her right off: big woman behind a big smile, pretty, blossoming beneath a dark blue wrapper, an extra large size that fits all.

He held up his badge.

"Mrs. Harding?"

"Yes."

"Detective Peterson. Can we talk?"

"Yes," she said, not sounding surprised a cop had come calling. She led him to a front sitting room, furnished for several small groups to gather for conversation. They sat in matching pink damask armchairs.

"This is about Father Boutilier, isn't it?" she asked. She had a whispery voice fit for a commercial.

"How well did you know him?"

"Not at all. I attend mass three evenings a week and on Sunday. He said mass, served Communion."

"Did you like him?"

"I had no reason to like him or dislike him. I attend mass. It comforts me. We never spoke. He made no effort, and neither did I."

"Why not a church closer to home?"

Her eyes brightened. "You mean a church more appropriate for my social standing."

Peterson shrugged.

"I get that all the time. I grew up in that parish, at a time when the neighbourhood was more respectable. My husband did as well. Call it a debt of gratitude, if you like."

"Open wallet?"

"I contribute handsomely."

"Last night at mass, did you notice anyone unusual, someone not a regular?"

"They're all unusual, Detective, at least to me. I started back at St. Jude's a few years ago, and I always sit in the same pew, second from the front, on the left. I have learned not to take notice."

"You go there alone?"

"You mean in that neighbourhood?"

"It does get rough."

"I don't drive and I refuse to have a regular driver. My housekeeper goes with me. Not Catholic. She sits in the back."

"A housekeeper?"

47

"Agnes DeLorey."

"A long time?"

"Nearly twelve years."

"Devoted?"

"What are you getting at, Detective?"

"Protects your privacy?"

"That goes with the position."

"Did she ever notice that you often leave your shawl behind?"

She locked eyes with him and offered a tired smile. "The confessional serves those without resolve. And as to your next question, yes, last night I left my shawl for Father Ronny to find. And he paid me a visit shortly after."

Peterson rose to leave. "For three hours?"

She smiled again, this time for her own benefit. "Does that surprise you?"

She did not see him to the door.

CHAPTER
SIX

Peterson and Danny sat opposite each other across a table in a cramped meeting room.

"Most in the congregation are no-shows for daily mass," Peterson said, flipping through his notebook. "They contribute to the church out of charity, for old times' sake. And those that do attend don't have a bad word for Boutilier. Some thought he was too strict. But over all he came up roses."

"Father Ronny?"

"The jury's still out. Some think he's likable, others too liberal. Because he works other parishes, most don't know him that well."

"Prime candidate, then."

"He screws another guy's wife," Peterson shrugged. "If that makes him a killer, half the male population would be up on murder charges."

Danny leaned over the table. "Love usually brings out the worst in us."

"You got that first hand?"

"You never know. I may have found the one I'd kill for."

"You think Father Ronny found his?"

"Maybe," Danny said. "And maybe Father Boutilier threatened to blow the whistle."

Peterson acknowledged the possibility then shook it off. "It doesn't explain the torn altar cloth, candles, black-face statue, the blood, and possibility of amniotic fluid."

"A way of throwing us off," Danny said.

"Yeah," Peterson scoffed, "he got forty-year-old Mrs. Harding pregnant just to throw us off."

"If it's amniotic fluid."

Peterson stood to stretch his neck and back. "I think Father Ronny isn't long for the priesthood, and Boutilier going public would only hasten his departure. No threat there."

"I doubt she'd want her rich hubby finding out."

"Still too elaborate a cover-up."

"Priests would know about weirdo rituals."

"All right," Peterson conceded. "He stays on the list. But my gut tells me it's something else. Someone was in the church performing some sort of ritual, and Boutilier caught them."

"Satanists then," Danny said. "Or witches. The black arts. Some weirdo group using the church for a ritual."

Peterson sat down. "But they didn't break into the tabernacle for the hosts," he objected.

"Do they have to?"

Peterson fell silent. After a moment, he lifted his eyes. "You've talked to some of these people, what do you think?"

Danny threw back his head. "Post-grads from a ring-around-the-rosy class playing evil."

"The game could have gotten out of hand," Peterson said.

"There's one guy, named Fisher, that takes it for real. I didn't talk to him, but two girls that work for him made Fisher out as over the top."

"Fisher?"

"Midfifties. Owns a hair salon. Lives in back. You want weird?"

"Previous?"

Danny flipped a few pages in his notebook. "Beat up his girlfriend two years ago. Did a month of community service and one year probation. And he's been into this Satan shit for a while. At eighteen, he and a girl dug up a grave in Burton, New Brunswick. They took the skull."

"Do time?"

"Are you kidding! The prosecution thought it was a lark, and the judge slapped their hands and told them to be good."

"What happened with the skull?"

"The record doesn't show. But this is good. A woman I talked to, Janis Low, was a member of Fisher's cult until two years ago. Then the rituals got extreme. Screwing on demand. Offerings of menstrual blood. That kind of stuff. She said Fisher once said human sacrifice was the ultimate. A black mass in a church."

"Bragging turns to action," Peterson suggested.

"And the priest catches them playing with their lucky charms. Should we bring him in?"

Peterson shook his head. "I'll go to him. I like weird places."

The door opened and Crouse came in. She sat down beside Peterson.

"Father Boutilier and Father Ronny's prints were everywhere," she said, "including the baptismal font, the altar, the tabernacle, and throughout the sacristy. There were two sets of unidentified prints in the sacristy. One presumably belongs to the altar boy."

"We can clear that up pretty quick," Danny said.

Crouse continued, "The other unidentified prints were on the baptismal font, the statue with the blackened face, and on the floor beside the body."

"What about the flagstaff?" Peterson asked.

"They were on that too — the only ones. It looked like the person held the shaft with both hands. The same prints were on the ciborium," Crouse said. "We still have to do an autopsy."

"When is that?"

"Yours is second in line." She rotated a page from the report so they could read it. "The blood in front of the statue was not the priest's."

"That complicates it," Peterson said.

"When is it ever neat and tidy?" Crouse smiled, then she rotated another page. "And the puddle beside the font was not amniotic fluid."

Peterson shut his eyes.

"You were hoping it wouldn't be," Crouse said.

Peterson looked at her. "Weren't you?"

CHAPTER
SEVEN

The oak door whispered open, and Peterson walked into David Carmichael's office, already on the defensive. From their previous sessions, Peterson knew Carmichael was the kind of shrink who tried to slip through the cracks in his patients' psychological defenses and look behind their many disguises.

There was nothing mood settling about the office. The windows on the exterior wall were heavily curtained, darkening the room even during daytime and accentuating the puddle of light in the centre, where two overstuffed armchairs faced each other. A floor-to-ceiling bookcase, the shelves heavy with books, lined the wall opposite the windows. A desk was set diagonally in one corner, the flanking walls bearing framed diplomas and certificates.

Carmichael sat in one armchair. Peterson squirmed in the other.

"Are you still dreaming?" Carmichael asked. His casual tone matched the casual way he was dressed: checked sport shirt and chinos. Midfifties, youthful spirit, and liberal minded.

Peterson shrugged. He was bored, tired, disconsolate.

"Is it the same one?" Carmichael pressed, studying Peterson's reaction. "You were fitting together different pieces from different puzzles. And crying."

"I don't cry," Peterson protested.

"I meant in your dream. You are crying in your dream."

Peterson got up to avoid answering. He circled to the back of the chair, then stopped at a curtained window and peeked out.

In the sliver of light through the cracked curtain, Carmichael could see the futility written on Peterson's face. He watched and waited. Picked his moment.

"What was it that made you cry?"

Peterson fixed a smile on his face. He knew the game of interrogation — ease around a confidence for a trickle of truth. He made his way back to the stuffed chair in the puddle of light and leaned over its back. "Do you always ask questions you know the answers to?"

It was Carmichael's turn to smile. "Sometimes. It helps me understand what you say."

"Then you know I buried it."

"Is that what you think you did, buried it?"

The sarcasm felt like a fingernail ripping through a scab.

"Stop me if I'm wrong," Carmichael said, "but I remember our last sessions ended with you walking out the door. Slamming it. If I check my notes, I'll give you ten to one I can find the question that set you off. Should I look? Should I ask it again now?"

Peterson flushed, straightened, and turned away from the psychiatrist. He made his way along the wall of books, scanning the titles. He wanted to bolt, but couldn't. Deputy chief's orders.

Carmichael broke the silence, "Why don't the puzzle pieces fit?"

"I don't know."

"Of course you do!"

"Different puzzles. The pieces come from different puzzles."

"And you try to make them fit, force them to fit?"

Peterson nodded.

"The way you tried to stuff all your wife's dresses into one suitcase."

"That was different."

"How was it different?"

"I had to get rid of them. What the hell would you do? They were just hanging there, on her side of the closet. I kept seeing them. Seeing her."

"And when they wouldn't all fit, what did you do?"

"What the hell difference does it make?"

"Tell me."

Peterson avoided Carmichael's eyes. "I hung them back up."

Carmichael said nothing, let the silence stretch. He watched Peterson stir uneasily. A minute passed. Two. Then Carmichael said, "Tell me about the puzzle."

"Forget the puzzle!"

"Was it a picture of something?"

"I said they were different puzzles!"

"But you tried to make them fit."

Peterson closed his eyes. "They seemed to go together."

Carmichael waited.

"One was a road," Peterson said. "A dirt road. Country road."

"A familiar road?"

"It was a long time ago," Peterson kept his eyes closed. "There was a path that led from the road to the river and a big rock and a deep pool reflecting the overhanging trees."

"Another puzzle?" Carmichael asked.

Peterson nodded. "I wanted to go out on one of the branches and drop into the pool."

Peterson fell silent.

"But you didn't," Carmichael coaxed.

Peterson shook his head and opened his eyes. "I was afraid."

"Afraid of what?"

"Afraid of nothing. It doesn't matter. I don't dream it anymore."

Carmichael watched Peterson. Waiting.

Finally, Peterson said, "What do you want me to say?"

"What do you want to say?"

"You want the truth?"

"Always."

"This is bullshit. I had a dream. So what? Everybody dreams. I stop dreaming one dream and start dreaming another. What's so different about that?"

"You tell me what's different about it."

Peterson clammed up.

"You've been dreaming a new one, you said."

Peterson said nothing.

"How often?" Carmichael pressed.

Peterson locked his hands behind his head. "Sometimes I'm too drunk to dream."

CHAPTER
EIGHT

New Look Hair Design took up the ground floor of a four-storey condo complex in an upscale neighbourhood, not far from where Mrs. Harding lived. The building faced north, and that orientation held its facade in shadow.

Peterson was parked three doors down and across the street. For more than half an hour, he had watched the comings and goings at the hair salon. He had wanted to get a read on the clientele.

He had allowed his prejudice to shape his expectations. As it turned out, none of the half-dozen women he saw were young tattooed damsels draped in chains and wearing heavy black coats cinched at the waist by belts with metal studs. They were mostly middle-aged and upper-middle-class devotees of low-fat menus and gym workouts.

He climbed from the car and went in.

The receptionist gave him a double take. And another when he flashed his badge. Then she suggested he take a seat until Mr. Fisher finished with a client.

Peterson looked the place over. Bright lights and mirrors made up for the lack of sunlight. Rose-coloured walls had a settling effect. And the three female stylists in pastel tunics further brightened the room with their light-hearted chatter about the everyday of life.

Fisher was the odd one out. He was thin, almost frail-looking, and dressed completely in black. Though easy in his movements, there was something stiff about the way he held himself, as though he had a board strapped to his back. It was not until Fisher repositioned himself on the far side of his middle-aged client that Peterson saw his face — pasty and solemn, perhaps even joyless, with a pencil-thin beard that must have taken him a long time, certainly a steady hand, to trim with a razor.

With an exaggerated flourish, Fisher tore away a sunburst apron covering his client and released her to her new hairdo. Then, at the receptionist's gesture, he made for Peterson. Fisher offered his hand, and Peterson showed his badge. And that brought about a hasty retreat to Fisher's office and living quarters.

This was more to Peterson's expectations — black walls in a backroom closed to the little daylight that entered the building. A spot of incandescent light over a computer desk and monitor. The monitor had a screen saver of an astonished-looking gypsy woman decked out in bangles and beads, endlessly pouring brown liquid from a flagon into a flaming brazier. On the wall behind the desk was an elaborate drawing of a three-headed bat. And on the one behind Fisher was a shelf with a few books prominently displayed — among them *The Confessions of Aleister Crowley* and Crowley's *Holy Books of Thelema*.

Fisher lowered himself into a high-tech desk chair that had more knobs and levers than the body had contortions. Peterson finished giving the room the once over and sank into a straightback side chair. He stared at Fisher.

"The word is you're in a satanic cult," he said.

Fisher smiled. He spoke softly, each word distinct. "Not even time to offer a cup of tea."

"I saved you the effort."

"Who says I am?"

"We asked around."

"Not quite."

"How quite?"

"We don't worship the devil. We are beyond good and evil."

"Free for all? Anything goes?"

Fisher clasped his hands in front of him. He wore the smile of someone tired with the same run of questions and with delivering the same pat answers.

"We recognize the sustaining force of human will," Fisher said. "We do not think in duality but in oneness — two sides of the same coin. Most cults worship one side or the other. We worship both."

"Straddling the moral fence," Peterson said. "Sounds like corporate Canada."

Fisher gave him a disdainful look.

"Worship must be fun," Peterson said, "half praising the Lord, the other half calling him a wrathful old bastard."

Fisher ignored the cynicism. "We hold ceremonies at

sunrise, celebrating the birth of nature, and at nightfall, welcoming the death of it."

"Beginning and ending," Peterson said. "Alpha and Omega."

Fisher nodded.

"What kind of ceremonies?"

Fisher shifted his weight, and Peterson realized the man was in pain. "We pray, sing, dance, and make offerings to the forces of light and darkness."

Peterson pointed at the high-tech chair. "Do much dancing?"

"I broke my back in a skiing accident six years ago. But I can sing and pray."

"And make offerings?"

The sarcasm was not lost on Fisher.

"Already down to the nub of it," Fisher said. "No beating about the bush."

"Does the bush need beating?"

"Only if you don't know what you're looking for. I suspect the crime rate is up."

"As of two nights ago it is."

"And we're the ones you blame."

"Who's we?"

Fisher curled his lower lip. "If Christians had not come to dominate the world, they would be the ones under the microscope, with their eating and drinking the body and blood of the man called Jesus."

Peterson let Fisher have his little harangue. He stayed impassive — the look he used in interviews — unemotional, uninterested.

"Are we talking sacrifice here?" Peterson asked with just

the right touch of innocence. "Is that what your offerings are all about?"

Fisher saw through Peterson's act. He shook his head. "Not the hocus pocus of the bread and wine. And we don't sacrifice animals, if that's what you are getting at."

Peterson leaned forward. "What about menstrual blood? Is that part of the offerings?"

Fisher flinched then recovered. "That would be Janis Low telling tales out of school."

Peterson's face gave nothing away.

"We don't believe a menstruating woman should be abhorred," Fisher said. "Her monthly blood is a symbol of nature's endurance. To sacrifice what is freely given is a sacred act."

"What about washing church floors in blood?"

Fisher suddenly looked as nervous as an old man in need of a toilet. His voice crept up a note. "Do you want to tell me what this is about?"

"It's about ceremonies and rituals and whether you performed one two nights ago?"

"We hold ceremonies every night."

"And where was the one two nights ago?"

"In a park in the north end. There's no law against it. We're allowed in the park until a half-hour after sunset."

Peterson pulled a photograph from his hip pocket that Father Ronny had provided. "Do you know this man?"

Fisher took the photo. "A priest, I take it."

"Do you know him?"

"No," Fisher said. He returned the photo.

"Ever seen him before?"

"No."

"Many people doing the mumbo jumbo the other night?"

"That's offensive."

Peterson shrugged. "How many?"

"I don't have to tell you anything."

"No you don't. But I can ask it again in a more confined space."

"On what charge?"

"I have twenty-four hours to think one up."

"You give a farmer a badge and he is still a farmer."

Peterson let it go. "I only ask once."

Fisher glared. "About forty."

"That's more than a lot of Christian churches."

Now it was Fisher's turn to be stone faced.

"Of course, they'll confirm you were there?" Peterson asked.

That question pricked Fisher a bit. "What is this about?"

"Just answer the question."

"Yes! I officiated the ceremony. I always do."

"You were there between what hours?"

"We gathered around six thirty, and sunset was about an hour later."

"And after that?"

"A group of us went to a downtown pub. It must have been one in the morning when we left."

"Come straight home?"

"No. One of the women invited me to her place."

"She have a name?"

"She does. But unless you tell me what is going on, I will not involve others in whatever it is you think you are doing."

Peterson returned the photo to his pocket.

"His name is Father Andre Boutilier, a Roman Catholic

priest. Someone killed him in St. Jude's church the other night."

Fisher showed his indignation. "And you think it must be the occult?"

"They desecrated the altar and a statue and laid out candles on the floor."

"Satanism! That was your first thought!"

Peterson shrugged. "No, my first thought was weirdos; the ones who take whatever they believe too far and start hurting other people. Those are the ones that land on my desk."

Fisher shifted uneasily and caught his breath at a spasm of pain. Then he released it. He took another long, slow breath. His faced relaxed.

"We do not use churches. We celebrate in the open air, rain or shine, summer and winter. Because we are not Christian or Muslim or Hindu or Buddhist, you call us 'weirdos.' Well, we are not much different than any other spiritual sect. We are law-abiding people with regular jobs and businesses. We worship forces beyond ourselves just like every other religion. We do not engage in blood sacrifice and we do not murder priests. Will there be anything else?"

Peterson nodded by way of compliment. "Did that just come off the top of your head, or did you practise it?"

The cords in Fisher's neck tightened. His face reddened. But his voice remained calm. "I believe it is time you left."

Peterson rose. "You once claimed human sacrifice was the ultimate sacrifice. And you said it should be done in a church."

"That would be Janis Low again making false accusations."

64

"Why Janis Low?"

"Because anything negative said about us usually comes from her."

Peterson liked the quick response, so he tried again. "And of course there's that little thing about digging up a human skull from a grave in New Brunswick."

Fisher gasped, either from the pain in his back or the verbal shiv slipped between his ribs.

"That was a long time ago," Fisher said.

"Yeah," Peterson said, "but it helps paint a picture doesn't it? One you wouldn't want hanging on a wall out front."

CHAPTER

NINE

At the upper end of the Strip, just before the railway under-pass, where the boulevard changed gears into a six-lane highway speeding out of town, far enough from the action but not too far to miss the fun, there was a 24/7 coffee shop spilling homey yellow warmth from its windows.

Peterson and Danny sat in a blue vinyl booth at one of the windows. They took turns looking out across the six lanes at the Broken Promise country bar, a stand-alone cinder block bunker with frosted windows, a heavy steel door, and a blinking bar sign with the word "Promise" looking as though it was cracked and the last three letters were falling off.

"Did you believe him?" Danny asked.

Peterson nodded. "His answers stacked up, and he has

an alibi, but he's no innocent. We keep his name at the top of the list. Circle it."

"You think the old priest caught him in the church."

"Someone was in that church performing a blood ritual. Whether killing the priest was part of that ritual, I don't know. We have no hard evidence that links anyone to the murder. All we have is supposition and our own prejudice. We don't like Father Ronny, and I don't like Fisher."

"We also have the five girls the priest took photos of."

"And how close are we to finding out who they are?"

Danny smiled. "The archdiocese couldn't help us enough. Pedophilia scares the hell out of them. In 1962, Father Andre Boutilier was right here, at St. Jude's. He got transferred to Barrie, Ontario, a year later. He was there over five years. He had three more transfers before being sent back here three years ago. And you know who was in his congregation in 1962?"

Peterson toyed with the rim of his cup. "I wonder if she's in one of those photos."

"We have a motive if she is?"

"We have a motive for each one of them," Peterson said. "What about the undeveloped one?"

Danny withdrew a photo from a file folder and passed it to Peterson. "Another girl. This one is crying."

Peterson studied the photo. "This is why he stopped taking pictures." He held the photo out for Danny. "Look at it! She's scared to death. Bawling her eyes out. And the photo is blurry. His hands are shaking."

Peterson's cell phone rang. He pulled it from his jacket pocket and checked the number. He let it ring.

Danny didn't miss how Peterson's expression weakened and the way he shut his eyes to close himself off from the ringing phone.

"How often is she calling now?" Danny asked.

Peterson didn't answer. The phone stopped ringing, and he set it on the table and leaned back in the booth.

Danny checked his watch and got up to go. "Do you want to ask Angela Harding about the photos or should I?"

Peterson forced a smile. "I'll go first thing in the morning, before she has time to make up her face."

Danny left Peterson stirring his coffee, stirring his thoughts.

Ten feet away, a middle-aged woman in a beige blouse with a wooden crucifix around her neck sat in another booth, slouched in thoughts of her own. The space between her and Peterson was accentuated by the similarity of their distant and trapped expressions and by the way they took turns lifting their eyes and fixing them on the blinking bar sign.

The waitress was boxing donuts and filling a Thermos for a truck driver who was too tired to give her the time of day. The truck driver left and she made the rounds topping up coffee. She caught Peterson by surprise, staring out the window at the Broken Promise bar sign.

"That sign tells the story of my life," she said.

Peterson covered his mug with both hands to stop her from pouring. "Nobody keeping them?"

"Nobody making them. Not anymore." She stepped back from the table and flared out her arms in a sensual gesture to mock her widening girth. "Sooner or later it catches up."

"Sooner or later it does," Peterson said and turned

toward the middle-aged woman, but she was on her feet and making her way to the cash to pay her bill.

His cell phone rang again. Unknown number. He tensed and clicked for the image and saw the fleabag room with badly stained walls and an unmade bed.

"Katy?" No reply.

The woman fumbled for the exact change. She could not help overhearing Peterson.

"Say something. Anything."

The woman saw his face strain under the silence.

"Why do you call if you don't want to talk?" Peterson begged.

The woman turned from the waitress to leave the coffee shop and heard his brittle words like notes bent and broken off a violin.

"Say something. Don't make me hang up. Katy?"

A while later, Peterson still sat in the window booth, nursing what was left of his coffee, cell phone on the table. His feelings ran a four-minute mile at memories that hung in his mind like his wife's dresses on her side of the closet. His daughter's room behind a door he never opened.

He mindlessly watched a teenage girl walking in the halo of passing headlights along the dirt path that ran between a chain-link fence and the highway. She had come from the direction of the highway exit for a low-rent suburb and a trailer park, carrying a jacket in her hand. She moved sluggishly as though her knees were locked and her feet each weighed a ton. She was slouchy too, and tired looking, but not her eyes. Her eyes were knife points in a thin face, and they were fixed on the bright lights of the Broken Promise.

A horn blast from a semi made Peterson pay closer attention. The girl was crossing six lanes of traffic. Awkward in her movements. Not checking the oncoming vehicles.

Dropping a five spot on the table, Peterson quickly made for the door, watching the girl on the highway, expecting the worst and feeling helpless to prevent it, like the helplessness he felt during the Skype calls from his daughter, or when he'd heard the dispatch for the Rescue Team to the shore road for an accident involving an overturned cement truck and a blue Buick.

The girl kept walking, her steps unsteady on the pavement, crossing over the double yellow lines. Headlights swirled by. Horns honked. Brake lights blazed on and off.

Peterson was on the street with his own barrier of traffic to cross. He watched her in the gun sights of an SUV that swerved in time to pass her by. The driver gave a finger that she didn't see. Her eyes were fixed straight ahead on the flashing bar sign. A moth to a flame.

Two guys hanging outside the bar were smoking joints and watching the girl on the highway. Neither moved a muscle to help. They were juiced and squirming to see her smeared on a windshield like a bug. Horny as hell when she made it across. They both laughed and imitated the awkward way she walked, feigned grab ass as she went by. They followed her into the Broken Promise.

Peterson couldn't find a break in the constant traffic and gave up the idea of crossing the six-lane. He hurried to the coffee shop parking lot and climbed into his car. He swung down a service road to the overpass that would take him to the opposite side of the highway and to the Broken Promise.

Inside the bar the music was hard and crusty. And it was loud, so loud the bass ached in the bones of the two dozen people scattered through the place. It had them shaking and tapping with the beat, drinking and blowing their minds on the fantasy images powered from a video wall. Two girls gyrated on barstools. One looked liked death; the other like death's sister. Two cheating hearts sat in shadows in a corner. Other customers, young guys mostly, were parked at tables near the oak bar that had a stained-glass canopy over top and at lottery terminals around the perimeter of the room. Some of those not gambling were there to grind their nuts on the street girls who strayed in for a free drink and the chance of getting something more. Others came to drink and blow dope and let the numbing music and the blanket of coloured lights loosen their fears and inhibitions.

Peterson eased his way to the bar. He saw the young girl from the highway standing statue-like beside the dance floor. Then he saw the middle-aged woman from the coffee shop sitting alone and out of place at a table beneath a large print of *Custer's Last Stand*. She was trying not to be so obvious, not to look around, not to make eye contact, but she could not help sneaking peeks at the young couple dancing dirty on the two-by-twice dance floor. They writhed slowly, bathed in red and orange flares that pulsed from the terminals and the wall of monitors.

A waitress, early twenties, blue jeans and red plaid shirt, cruised among the tables with a tray of beer. She wore her long brown hair stuffed into a white cowboy hat and

71

disguised her pretty face with a frown. Hearing the music but not feeling it. She emptied her tray on a table of four milk-faced guys, one of whom craned his neck to look down her shirt.

A raw, raunchy guitar twang seemed to accompany the deliberate way the waitress turned from the table of four to face the middle-aged woman. They had an exchange of seemingly unpleasant words. Then the waitress stormed to the bar for another tray of beers. She was sobbing.

Peterson watched the middle-aged woman fuss with a square coaster, lining it up with the table edge. Disappointment had incised deep lines in her face. She stared straight ahead to avoid the glare of curious regulars at nearby tables.

The music swelled and the couple on the dance floor danced as one, their legs twined. The flashing lights were hellishly orange.

The girl from the highway weaved among the tables and stood in the flashing light at the centre of the dance floor. She looked in turn at the lottery terminals and the changing images on the monitors. Her face tightened. Her body trembled. She dropped her jean jacket on the floor. Then her eyes widened and her fists clenched and unclenched. Peterson noticed that her jeans were drenched in blood around the zipper.

One of the guys who had followed her in said something to the girl and did not wait for her to answer. He grabbed for her hand. She snapped it back and turned on him. Eyes stabbing. Lips curled and snarling. Spitting.

The guy laughed to his friend and reached for the girl's hand again. This time the girl stepped back and screamed.

A scream louder than the blaring music. She sidestepped the guy's effort to calm her, grabbed a bar stool, and started swinging it around her head.

The guy fell on the floor and scrambled to get clear of the girl. She strode across the dance floor, still brandishing the chair. The dancers fled, and customers sitting at nearby tables fell over themselves and over chairs and tables to get out of the way. The girl ran back and forth from one group to another. Threatening them with the chair. Shrieking. She chased the couple from the shadows and slammed the chair down on one of the lottery terminals, smashing the screen.

Peterson slid from his bar stool and along a wall to get behind the girl. He pulled his cell phone and called for an ambulance and police backup.

The middle-aged woman sat frozen with her back against the wall. Terrified.

A few customers had already cleared the place, and several more were not far behind, pushing past Peterson for the exit at the back of the bar.

The bartender bolted from behind the bar through a swirl of fiery lights. He looked for an opening to grab the girl, staying out of range. When she had her back to him, he lunged and threw his arms around her in a bear hug. Her scream was loud and piercing and full of fear. She went wild, broke free, then shoved the bartender with such force that he landed several feet away, between the barstools and the bar. He stayed there with his head down.

She grabbed a stool and swung it at the stained-glass canopy over the bar. The shattered glass rained on the bar and on the bartender, who flattened himself on the floor. He was shaking.

The girl flung herself against the video wall and punched and elbowed the screens, shouting at the flashing images, "Izi! Arigarizko! Izi. Izi."

Peterson had moved fast to get behind her but not fast enough to stop her from driving her fists through the screens and snatching at the electronics inside, as though trying to grab hold of the images that had been driving her crazy. Glass shards sliced her arms.

He grabbed her shoulders. She shook him off, ducked down, and came up with a long jagged piece of glass that cut viciously into the palm of her hand.

Peterson coiled down, ready to spring at her. Holding her stare, seeing her nerves on fire and hearing her snarl like a wild animal. Her black sweaty hair hanging below her shoulders. Her eyes unblinking, distant. Her blouse and jeans drenched in sweat and blood.

Blood ran freely from cuts on her hands and arms. One gash was a nasty zigzag the length of her forearm. It was spurting.

The two guys from outside had pressed themselves into a corner, one of them recording the action on his cell phone. He now stepped forward to get a better shot of the girl covered in blood.

The girl suddenly turned, shrieked, and threatened him with her glass knife. Then she swung to face Peterson, nostrils flared, holding up one hand like a bloody claw, the other cocked to stab him. Their eyes locked.

"Put it down," Peterson ordered, his voice lost in the blasting music. Drums like gunfire, the steel guitars whining.

The girl's face tightened with terror. She shouted something that was drowned by the music. Slowly she extended her arm toward Peterson, staring into his eyes, and just as slowly sliced deeply and diagonally along her forearm.

Peterson gasped. His senses were riven by the gushing blood and the girl crumpling like a rag doll at his feet. Time slowed to a moment that seemed to go on forever. Not a second to waste and yet all the time to see the guy with the cell phone stretched across a table, recording the bloody scene. Time enough to see the middle-aged woman peeking from behind an overturned table. Her face thin and long, with tears running from the corners of eyes that were dark and popping with fear.

Peterson dropped to the girl's side, kneeling in the blood that was spurting from the zigzag cuts in one arm and the severed artery in the other. So many cuts. So much blood. He pulled off his coat and pressed it against the cut that was spurting.

"Help! Help me! I can't stop it!" he shouted to the middle-aged woman who was shaking and crying and dragging her hands down her face. "Help!" he shouted to the guy still stretched across the table with his cell phone aimed at the girl bleeding to death in Peterson's arms.

Shock had gripped the middle-aged woman so tight that she could not move. She watched Peterson. Saw his desperation, his compassion. Saw the pain in his face, almost saintly in the coloured lights glittering off the broken glass. Saw something in him that made her tremble and roll to her knees. She hugged herself and closed her eyes. Her lips moved in prayer. Then she crawled forward, heedless of the broken glass.

"You'll be all right," Peterson said to the girl, leaning close so she would hear. Then to himself, "Jesus, God please!"

The girl's response was slow and laboured. Her words soft and rhythmic; more prayer than torment. "Albulla guberoa. Dead. Elbae dar albulla. Niandalaba nescato. Eba ska akelade."

Peterson heard the sirens. He continued to press her right arm as he gathered the girl into his arms. "Hang on. Please."

The girl reached her free hand for the woman's and guided it to draw something in the blood on the floor.

"Gone. Nothing. Elbae dar albulla," the girl said, her low voice slipping under the soft guitar chords of a slow song. "Elbae dar albulla. Niandalba nescato."

The girl slumped in Peterson's arms just as the paramedics came through the door. The woman's hand slipped from the girl's. She looked at the blood on her fingertips, at what the girl had drawn with her finger on the floor. The woman lifted her eyes and met Peterson's. He was crying.

CHAPTER
TEN

The hard light raked the emergency room revealing long and worn faces. Red and swollen faces. A few wrinkled and thin and smiling submissively. One ripe with bruises, another stupefied with pain. Most turned to follow the gurney as it was rushed past the admissions desk and curtained cubicles. Paramedics lifted the blood-covered girl from the gurney to a bed. A doctor called for a blood match. A nurse inserted an IV line into each leg and started saline drips, while another laid out an intubation tube. A doctor cut open the girl's blue blouse and pressed life paddles onto her chest.

A uniform cop guided the middle-aged, blood-covered woman through the waiting room, through air stubborn with the smell of illness and disinfectant. A triage nurse came out from her glassed-in booth. The cop explained something to her, and the nurse took the woman by the arm and led her to a cubicle where the curtains were pulled but not closed. She could see across to where the girl lay limp and rigged up to monitors and IVs.

Machines blipped the faint vital signs and then flattened, setting off an alarm that had the doctor and nurses thumping and pumping and checking the girl's eyes for life. The moment swelled with urgency as they tried to restart the girl's heart. Voices encouraged it. "Come on! Come on!" Calling her back. Demanding the return of something that had gone.

The woman gathered the curtain in her hands and pressed it against her face as though to hide from the brutality of dying. The nurse drew her away. The woman lowered the curtain, bewildered, grief trembling at the corners of her mouth. She looked into the cubicle at the girl's dead eyes. Filmy. Dry.

Danny barrelled through the emergency room and found Peterson standing near the triage booth, his clothes covered in blood, his hands bandaged. He was staring at the action in the emergency room and he was seeing nothing.

"I hear you had a rough night," Danny said.

Peterson blinked. He didn't answer.

CHAPTER
ELEVEN

A square of morning sunlight crept slowly over the few smashed dishes on the kitchen floor and over the table and the chairs lying on their sides and backs, unbroken. The fridge door had a big dent in it. A trail of family photos, some shredded, led from the kitchen into the dining room, where a blue porcelain lamp had been knocked from an oak side table and broken on the hardwood floor. In the living room a wall mirror had been smashed. There was glass in the carpet.

Peterson was slumped on a love seat, naked, staring into space, his eyes bloodshot, distant, his cheeks puffy and red, his hair matted with sweat. He looked like a man hanging on by his fingertips as the world spun to shake him off. He seemed small, his chest and arms sunken and weak. Tattooed over his left breast was a cupid with an empty quiver, and running diagonally across his stomach was a surgical scar. His cock and balls hung over the seat cushion. The soles of his feet were cut and bleeding. On the floor between his legs was a blue suitcase stuffed with his wife's dresses.

Bernie honked the horn and waited for Peterson in the driveway of his older two-storey in the north end. Two minutes later, Peterson was riding shotgun, wearing a grey windbreaker and carrying a plastic grocery bag.

"Lunch?" Bernie asked.

"Laundry," Peterson said. "Blood stains on my jacket."

"Danny said it was bad. He thought you needed a chauffeur."

Peterson made a face. "I've seen worse."

"That's nothing to brag about." She backed from the driveway and shifted into drive. "So you do have a home after all."

"You should become a detective."

"I'm working on it," she said, "but I'm having trouble mastering the pain in the ass part."

Peterson smiled. "Stop at the dry cleaners up ahead." They drove half a block, and Peterson said, "Rookie detective or not, you didn't have to pick me up. You have your own cases to worry about."

"Cold cases," Bernie said.

"They all have to be solved. Like what?" He'd welcome a diversion from his thoughts and feelings.

Bernie swung the car around a trash truck. "Convenience store hit two years ago. Closed-circuit video has a guy in a skull mask enter the store with a double-barrel twelve-gauge. Sawed off and fitted with a pistol grip."

"Heavy artillery for a stick-up."

"This was no stick-up," Bernie said, taking a corner. "Both barrels to the customer, an accountant with the city. Married. Two kids. The guy takes aim. No hot-dogging with shooting from the hip. All on video. Then he pockets the casing and chases down the wadding."

"A mercenary," Peterson said. "Knows forensics are useless for a shotgun without casing and wad. Connection to the victim?"

"None was ever established."

"Got to be," Peterson said. "No robbery, and it sure as hell wasn't random. Who had the case?"

"Andy Miles."

Peterson blew out a sigh. "You want the truth on that case, follow the dirt."

"I'm following it."

"You need help, you know where I sit."

"I was hoping you'd say that."

Peterson turned to look at the pink-coloured radio station they were passing. Before leaving the house, he had been listening to a female announcer on that station excitedly report an inaccurate account of what had happened at the Broken Promise. He had wanted to reach into the radio and wrench the drama from her voice.

Peterson followed Danny Little through the maze of open offices in Police Headquarters, past a waiting area, the lunchroom, and down a hallway that led to the Communications Unit in a new addition to the building.

"You left the channel open and Dispatch recorded everything," Danny explained. "Then the nerds in Communications pulled down the music and boosted her voice. They synced the audio off the dispatch tape with video off that kid's cell phone and the security camera in the bar. I don't know how the hell they do it."

From down the hall, they heard screams and loud grating music and then the girl's voice, her words thickly veiled behind guitar chords and a driving rhythm.

"Are you sure you want to look at this?" Danny asked.

Peterson nodded.

They entered a small video-editing room that was crowded with computers, monitors, and speakers, some mounted on the ceiling. The editor, Billy Bagnall, sat at a kidney-shaped table and played his fingers over a keyboard. He was in his midtwenties and had close-cropped black hair and a bullshit smile that tagged him as something of a hotshot within the Communications Unit.

"Is it ready?" Danny asked.

"Yeah!" Billy answered. "The cell phone video was all over the place, but cut against the wide shots from the security camera, I think you can tell what's going on. I tweaked the girl's voice too, made it clearer."

"It didn't sound like anything to me," Danny said to Peterson. "Her words are all screwed up."

Peterson positioned himself to watch the large monitor on a shelf above the editor's table. Billy started the video.

Peterson saw grainy, black-and-white video from the

security camera in the Broken Promise. He saw the entire barroom: the couple dancing dirty, the customers at tables, at lottery terminals, and at the bar. He saw the waitress stop at the woman's table. By their body language, he could see their discussion was intense, if not an argument. He saw the girl enter the bar and the two guys follow her in. He saw one of them confront the girl on the dance floor and the girl swinging the barstool. He heard his call for backup and an ambulance. Then the image cut to video from the cell phone camera with the girl flinging the bartender aside and smashing her fists and arms into the monitors, screaming.

He saw that horrifying night caught and captured in images that were unlike his memory of the young girl dying. He wondered what was true, what was real, what he could believe. Table legs and chairs. Flashing lights and noise. Broken glass and blood pooling around his knees. The flap of her flesh that he folded back to stop the bleeding. It seemed unrelated to this two-dimensional world squeezed into a narrow frame without regret, without shame, without the cringing pain that makes some days unbearable.

He watched the girl dying in his arms. Heard his voice begging for help. Saw the woman crawl over the broken glass to his side, fraught with helplessness and flooded with fear. He watched with such intensity that his legs went wobbly, and he grabbed the edge of the editing table.

"Her face bloody. Nothing inside," the girl was saying. Her voice coming through the ceiling speakers, electronically separated from the blasting music, sounded almost ethereal. "Dead. Albulla guberoa. Elbae dar albulla. Niandalba nescato. Eba ska akelade."

"Stop it there!" Peterson said.

Billy hit pause and caught the girl using the woman's hand to draw something in the blood on the floor.

"See that?" Peterson said. "Can you blow that up?"

The editor played the keyboard and the image grew to reveal what appeared to be a stylized cross.

The girl continued drawing with the woman's hand. This time the motion was a downward stroke that trailed off as her hand lost its grip.

"Her initials, maybe," Danny offered.

"Or a tag," Peterson said. "You never know." He leaned toward the monitor. He closed his eyes to listen.

"Gone," the girl said. "Nothing. Albulla guberoa. Elbae dar albulla. Niandalba nescato."

"What the hell is she saying?" Peterson asked. He looked at the monitor.

"It sounds Indian," Billy said.

There was a tap on the door and a female cop entered the editing room and caught Peterson's attention. "Anna Gray is here to see you."

"Who?"

"She said she was with you in the Broken Promise. She's in the coffee room."

Peterson hurried along the hallway to where the woman was sitting in a quiet corner of the room, cradling a coffee. Peterson sat beside her, struggling to hold himself together.

"I'm Detective Peterson," he said.

She kept her hands wrapped around the coffee cup. "My name is Anna. Anna Gray."

He played his eyes over hers and sensed miles of distance between them. "Are you all right?"

Anna shrugged off the question. The hard, flat overhead lighting accentuated the shadows under her eyes, the laugh lines, and the grief tightening her lips. Her hands were plain, unmanicured.

"I'm sorry about what happened last night," Peterson said. "You never should have seen that."

"Seen it?" Anna's voice cracked. Her mind seemed to go away for a moment and then came back.

Peterson could not take his eyes off her. He studied her face, her gestures. He saw her lips trembling, her fingers fidgeting over the coffee cup, her shoulders twitching, her eyes looking inward at images that frightened her, then searching the room for a comfortable place to settle.

"You're not all right are you?"

"No, I'm not all right," Anna said. She looked on the verge of collapse. "I want to cry but I can't. I want to scream but I can't. I want to let something out but I don't know how to do it."

She looked away sharply, as though she'd seen something fleeting from the corner of her eye. She turned back to Peterson. "All night I prayed and prayed not to remember. I didn't sleep. I just kept praying."

"You have to give it time," he said. "It will dull down, but it takes time."

Anna looked doubtful. He wondered about prayer, if it really helped or just covered over the loss the way dirt covers the dead.

"Were you praying for her?"

Anna looked past Peterson at the busy office, at a uniformed cop standing before a window that was bloomy with sunlight; at a thin young woman in too flimsy a dress for this time of year scrolling through photographs on a computer screen; at a large whiteboard hanging on a far wall, wiped clean and ready for inscription.

"She spoke to us," she said. "I don't know what she said, but she spoke to us as though she wanted us to know."

"She was dying," Peterson said, uncomfortable with what he was feeling. He too sensed there was something the girl had wanted him to know, and it disturbed him. "People say crazy things when they're dying."

"I just thought you would know what she said."

"I don't even know who she was."

"But the way she said it —"

He cut her off. "It was a different language. I have no idea what she said."

Anna closed her eyes, retreated into silence. Peterson waited. When she opened them, she seemed to see the busy office and him for the first time.

"I didn't know where to go. Peggy saw your name in the paper, and I came here but I don't know why. I keep praying to understand. I keep hearing her voice. Oh God, I keep hearing it."

"It takes time," Peterson said, his voice more caring. The practised voice he had learned as a uniform cop and used at front doors when he came bearing bad news. He reached for her hand but stopped short, sensing she might pull away.

"And I keep seeing her," Anna said. "I keep trying to feel who she is."

"Who do you feel she is?" Peterson asked.

"Someone lost. Confused. Someone desperate to make sense of what she's doing. Someone so hurt that she can't bear it."

Peterson noticed the different shading she gave these words. He wondered if she knew this girl. He asked.

Anna shook her head. "Not her. But so many like her. I see them every day. Just so lost. So desperately lost."

"I see them too. Their tougher side perhaps. Desperate, like you say. Willing to do anything. But I don't let it get to me. I do my job, and then I walk away."

Anna stiffened. She pushed the coffee aside and stood as if to go, but she kept her eyes on him, searching his face.

"I'm sorry," Peterson said. "What we saw the other night I see all the time."

Anna slowly shook her head. "Don't! Don't make yourself into something you're not. I saw what you did. I saw you hold her. I saw you cry. I heard what you said to her. Or am I talking about someone else?"

They stared at each other for the longest time, each so fragile before the other, each wanting to express something they could not put into words.

CHAPTER
TWELVE

Peterson stood in Carmichael's darkened office before the large unsigned painting of coloured boxes set against a dark, agitated sky.

Carmichael sat comfortably in one of the two armchairs, his legs stretched out, his left arm thrown casually over its back.

"This one comes too close to home," Carmichael said.

"Word spreads fast."

Carmichael smiled a disapproving smile. Peterson saw it. "I'm worried about the effect investigating this suicide will have on you."

"I need to work."

"You need a rest."

"I'm not a desk jockey."

"Your mental health is at stake."

Peterson muttered something and advanced toward the vacant armchair. He gripped its back with both hands as though to steady himself, to stop himself from lifting off the floor in a weightless moment of fear. Fear that he would say what needed saying and betray himself.

"Are you sleeping?" Carmichael asked.

Peterson shrugged.

"Nightmare or dream?" Carmichael asked.

"What would you call it?"

"You tell me."

"I wake up seeing her. Feeling the blood. Seeing her skin lose its shape. Her eyes on mine. And her voice . . . saying something I can't hear."

Carmichael drew in his legs and straightened in his chair. "Your wife, your daughter, or the girl in the Broken Promise?"

"I don't know. All of them at the same time. I can't tell which one." He looked off Carmichael and stared at nothing.

Carmichael inched forward in his chair, fixing Peterson closely, speaking softly. "Dream or nightmare?"

"Nightmare, for Christ's sake! I'm helpless. I can't do anything, for any of them. I try, but I can't."

"Because you weren't there?"

"Because I am there. Because I'm not there. Because she didn't want me there."

Peterson searched the dark corners of the office as though looking for something he had lost. Little feet padding across the kitchen floor. A beige afghan drawn over his wife's shoulders into a snuggle of warmth. Spilled wine dripping off the table and shattering into shapes and symbols that were shrieking, scolding, mocking.

Carmichael let the silence have its due. He studied Peterson's face and waited for his mind to slip back to the present, the way sunlight slips from behind a cloud and through a window without breaking it.

"Do you want to talk about your wife?"

Peterson avoided Carmichael's gaze. "Read the file."

"I've read it."

"Then you know."

"Know what?"

"I don't want to go there."

"Go where?"

"Where you want me to go."

"And where is that?"

"That's enough, all right? I'm done with dragging it up and hanging it out for all to see. There he is — Peterson. Fucked up Peterson, you know, the cop with the dead wife. Car crash. A blue Buick and a cement truck. I didn't have to read the report. I knew. I just knew!"

"What did you know?"

Carmichael watched Peterson's shoulders sag and his hands fidget. "Do you wish it had been you driving her car and not someone else?" Carmichael asked.

Peterson lifted his eyes from his bandaged hands to Carmichael. "What do you think?"

"I'm asking you."

"Sometimes."

"When?"

"I walked away from her grave and I got back on the job. I handled it."

"Did you?"

"Yes."

"A desk job?"

"Yeah, but I made something of it. Two months, and you know what, I dug out a ten-year-old cold case and cracked it."

"And during these two months, while you were at your desk, working hard, it was day and night from what I understand —"

"That's right!"

Peterson circled the armchair and eased into it, leaning forward, now face to face with the shrink. "Round the clock. I didn't let it go. Not like everybody else. I couldn't let it go. I needed to focus, concentrate, shift everything. I gave every waking moment to that case. And I stuck with it until I could punch holes in that son-of-a-bitch's alibi."

They were now so close their eyes filled with each other's stare.

"And during these two months after burying your wife," Carmichael said, "during all this time, while you were at your desk, day and night, working around the clock, cracking a cold case, punching holes in that son-of-a-bitch's alibi, where was your daughter?"

Peterson stared at Carmichael, stared at him the way one stares into the darkness of a theatre after the lights go out. Searching the dark for movement among the shadows. And waiting. Waiting for the slow fade-up of a follow spot to direct attention to the corner of the stage where a child is silently standing.

CHAPTER
THIRTEEN

For a few minutes, Peterson sat in the car outside Angela Harding's home with the photos on his lap. He couldn't bear to look at them. Yet he could not help looking at them, fixing their faces in his mind. Then he shoved them into his coat pocket and climbed from the car. He rang the bell and waited. This time the housekeeper answered.

"Who should I say is calling?"

"Detective Peterson." He flashed his badge. "Are you the one that goes to church with Mrs. Harding?"

The pudgy-faced woman was instantly defensive, as though Peterson had questioned her faith. "I just go with her. I sit in the back. I'm not Catholic."

"Did you ever notice that she often leaves her shawl behind?"

The housekeeper blushed and lowered her eyes. She

didn't answer. She didn't need to. She led him to the front room and to the same pink damask armchair. He didn't sit. This time he looked the room over, taking in the oil paintings and multimedia artwork on the walls, the intimate chair groupings with small side tables for drinks and finger food, the gas fireplace with its oak mantel. Brass lanterns sat at each end of the mantel, and in the centre was an antique clock stuck at 9:04. The room told him nothing about the Hardings other than that they were wealthy.

"More questions about my private life?" She caught him studying one of the paintings, an uninspiring scene of flowers set in a window overlooking a beach. Peterson thought still-life was an apt description.

"I just need to clear up something you said."

She gestured for him to sit in the armchair and lowered herself into the one opposite. She seemed to spread into it, at least her expensive blue warm-ups did. She was dressed for comfort, not exercise, confirmed by the reading glasses hanging around her neck.

He pulled a notebook from his green jacket, recently retrieved from the dry cleaners, and pretended to consult it. "You said you didn't know Father Boutilier. You said you didn't speak to one another and so you had no reason to like or dislike him."

"That's right."

"What about when you were younger? Did you know him then?"

For a second, Angela Harding lost her expression of gracious cooperation. "I don't know what you mean."

Peterson caught the facial stutter. "You said you grew up in this parish."

"I did."

"And you didn't know him?"

She weighed the question for a moment or two, as though waiting for Peterson to say more. He didn't bite. She scratched her right palm.

"I may have. I can't be sure."

"Mrs. Harding, this is a murder investigation. Here's how it works. I ask questions and you answer. When a suspect doesn't answer or doesn't tell the truth, that adds to my suspicion."

"Am I a suspect?"

"Top of the list."

She caught her breath. "Do I need a lawyer?"

"You can call a lawyer if you want, but that will take this little chat from the comfort and privacy of your home to an interrogation room at Police Headquarters. That usually has the press sniffing for a story, especially if it involves one of the city's prominent citizens. The choice is yours, Mrs. Harding. But one way or another, we are going to have this little chat."

He waited for that to sink in and for her to fathom the social consequences of being hauled into headquarters, lawyer or not. Then he got up. He'd taken one step toward the door when she responded.

"Please!"

He turned and saw her looking the way he had seen so many other rich socialites whose secrets were threatened — pale, chewing their lips, kneading their hands, staring into a past loaded with regret.

He tried making it easier. "What you say won't go beyond this room, not unless it bears directly on the investigation."

She nodded. He crossed the room and closed the door on the housekeeper's ears. He pulled the photos from his pocket and returned to sit opposite her. He let her break the silence.

"I knew him back then." Her eyes filled.

Peterson held out the photos. "We found these hidden in his dresser." He showed her the photos one at a time, studying her reaction. "Do you know these girls?"

She looked away and nodded.

"Is one of them you?"

She recoiled, as though to hide from the sordidness that Peterson held in his hands. Then she drew a deep breath and tried to compose herself. A girlish innocence replaced the silkiness in her voice.

"I trusted him," she said. "I thought I was special. I didn't know about the others. None of us did. Not until later."

Her voice broke, and it took a few moments for her to get her composure back. Peterson let her have the time.

"Can you believe I confessed what I did — to him? And he forgave me."

She fought back the tears.

"They sent him away. Susan Publicover told one of the nuns. At least that's what I found out later, years later. He was just gone. Another parish. A routine transfer the pastor called it. No scandal. God forbid that should happen to the Catholic Church."

She looked away through the window then dropped her eyes to the photos. Her voice was almost dreamy. "I knew. Not knew, but I sensed something about the others. I could tell just by looking at them."

Now she looked at the photos, hurrying from one face to another, from one past moment to another, her eyes widening with shock and closing with shame, irresistibly drawn to the deception of innocence.

"We were in our thirties when Agnes died. Breast cancer. That's when it all came out. Only four of us from the neighbourhood went to her funeral, the ones who had the most to forget. I still wasn't certain about the others, about Agnes, until Susan Publicover started on about him and what he'd done to her and Agnes. Then it was like a flood. It was the first time I ever talked about it. And I never did again until he came back."

Peterson took a chance and asked, "And when he came back, who did you tell?"

She met his gaze. "Some older women who were members of the Rosary Society when I was a girl. I knew he would find out. They're in a nursing home he visits."

"Did that even the score?"

"At first."

Peterson plowed a little deeper. "But that wasn't enough was it?"

She shook her head. "I went back to church. Sat in the same pew week after week. And I made sure he knew who I was."

"You said you had never talked with him?"

"I didn't. I dropped envelopes into the collection basket, pink ones with my maiden name on them."

"He never spoke to you?"

"No. He didn't even look my way, not directly. But he knew I was there, watching him."

Peterson waited.

"None of the others would come. Only two are still in

the city. It was too much for them to see him saying mass, being a priest, when we knew what he really was."

"Who were the others?"

She shook her head. "They've suffered enough."

"I'll find out anyway."

"You turn every stone."

"More than once." He handed her the notebook and pen he had been holding. "Write them down."

She put her glasses on. When she finished writing she closed the notebook and handed it and the pen to him. "Don't disrupt their lives. They don't deserve it."

"If they didn't kill Father Boutilier, they have nothing to worry about. Neither do you."

She considered this carefully. "I don't know what I felt toward him, but it wasn't something as vicious as hate. I just wanted him to see me sitting there, to torture him by just being there. That was enough. It was more than enough."

"More than enough for Father Ronny?"

"He had no idea. It's not something a woman talks about."

"What about your husband?"

"I told no one. All these years, and I kept it to myself."

There was a long silence. Then she straightened in her chair as though reclaiming her dignity.

"Isn't that enough?" she begged. "Please!"

Peterson nodded. "One more question. Why Father Ronny? Why another priest?"

Angela Harding stood to see him to the door. "I ask myself that every week."

CHAPTER
FOURTEEN

Reggie's Place was breakfast busy. Peterson arrived five minutes early and slid into a booth away from the hustle of the cash register and front counter where a counter girl was serving the hurry-up-crowd with quick and tasty. The waitress, a wide-hipped woman with swollen ankles, had his coffee on the table before he sat down.

Danny arrived at eight o'clock on the dot. The waitress brought him a coffee and topped up Peterson's. Danny ordered off a chalkboard behind the counter. Peterson stuck with coffee.

Danny doctored his coffee. "You only doing liquids now?"

"Is ice a liquid?"

Danny held up his hands in apology. "Only when it melts."

"Concern noted," Peterson said, placing two plastic evidence bags on the table. One held his notebook, the other his pen. "These should clear Angela Harding. My prints and hers."

"She has motive," Danny said.

Peterson straightened at a sharp stomach spasm. Then he tried squeezing the hangover from behind his eyes. He signalled the waitress to bring him number six on the chalkboard — cereal, hash browns, and buttered toast. He swung back to Danny. "All the women in those photos have motive. But I doubt any of their prints will match those in the sacristy."

"We're back to candles and blood."

Peterson nodded.

Danny watched the counter girl pouring coffee to go for two young women and a guy and the short order cook plating sausage and eggs and a side of toast and dinging the call bell for the waitress.

"That doesn't leave us much," Danny said. "Fisher's alibi holds. There are eight people who will swear he was with them until one o'clock."

"And the woman?"

"Alicia Wambolt. He was with her all night. She even bragged he got it up three times before they fell asleep."

"It's boiling down to an empty pot."

"We still have a street slug with a grudge," Danny said.

"Back to candles and blood."

"Fuck!" Danny said, loud enough that people at nearby tables lifted their heads.

"The dead ends are piling up," Peterson said. "The Airport Road, now this. And Bernie has one that'll go nowhere."

"She caught a break with the accountant," Danny said.

"A dirty accountant?"

"He had a little action on the side. Basement office where he kept two sets of books for the guy who owned a chain of convenience stores. He stashed the embezzled money in his wife's name."

Peterson allowed a smile.

The waitress brought their breakfasts. They ate in silence, Danny ravenously, Peterson with caution. Then Danny said, "If not Fisher, then maybe one of his members, or someone else playing voodoo. I'll interview Janis Low again. She might know more than she's telling."

Danny left his partner toying with his toast. Peterson's cell phone rang. He didn't check the caller. He didn't need to. He just answered and stared at the fleabag room that broke his heart. The shabby wall behind the unmade bed. The chair with a busted leg. The squalor that spread beyond what he could see. He heard a toilet flush, and then the screen went white.

FIFTEEN

That evening Peterson sat alone in the editing room in the Communications Unit reviewing the video images from the Broken Promise for the umpteenth time, advancing the video frame by frame, dragging out her death. Thirty frames in a second. Sixty fields in a frame. Imperceptible gestures. A shiver in her cheeks. Her eyelids closing. Her dry lips faintly whispering.

He reached to her wrist on the monitor the way he had reached for it in the Broken Promise, but he touched only pixels of coloured light. He saw his face stupefied with helplessness, his hands coated with her blood.

He now knew by heart the strange words she had said. He shaped them on his lips as the girl on the monitor shaped them with hers.

"Albulla guberoa. Elbae dar albulla. Niandalaba nescato."

Words thinned through an equalizer, then, for the sake of clarity, brightened to the point of sounding disembodied.

"What are you saying?" he said out loud to the close-up of the girl's blood-smeared face. "What do you want me to know?"

He leaned toward the monitor as if the girl could answer. Listening the way a child or true believer listens for a distant reply to a prayer. Lost in the listening. Abandoning time and space to hear her voice speak from outside the video's sounds and images.

His cell phone screeched, frightening him. He sprang out of the chair and pressed his back against the wall. He stared at the cell phone then lifted his eyes to see himself reflected in the monitor, ghosting over the girl's tortured face.

The cell phone stopped ringing. He reached for it and checked for messages. There were none.

He scrolled through caller ID and saw that the call had come from the Birthright Centre. He pressed dial.

After four rings a woman's recorded voice said, "You have reached the Birthright Centre, where all babies are special. This is Peggy Demming. Please leave your name and number and either I or Anna Gray will return your call within an hour. Thank you."

There was a short pause then a beep then silence.

He looked back to the monitor and to the girl still dying in his arms. He began to shake. He reached for the wall for support. Then he sensed someone behind him and turned quickly.

Danny was standing in the doorway.

"How long?" Peterson asked.

"Long enough."

Peterson dropped into the chair. Danny pulled up another.

"You need to get away from this," Danny said.

Peterson shook his head.

"You need a break. You need to go home."

Peterson rubbed his face. "There's nothing there."

"Then bunk at my place."

"I don't sleep. I think. I think too much. And then I drink so I can stop thinking. But I don't stop thinking. I can't." Peterson jabbed a finger at the monitor. "And now I have this to think about! Look at her! Who is she? I need to know who she is. I need to know why the hell she did that to herself."

Danny reached across Peterson and switched off the playback. He laid a file folder on the editing console.

"It gets worse," Danny said. "That's Crouse's preliminary. The girl was in her early teens. Crouse thinks she took something jagged to her vagina, like she was trying to hack away at something. She had a tattoo on her labia: the number nineteen."

CHAPTER
SIXTEEN

Danny played the video for Joe Christmas at Joe's place on the reserve. Peterson stood at the window and peeked through the blinds, pretending to watch two kids playing in a puddle.

Joe had been a Mi'kmaq band chief on and off for fourteen years. Now he was economic development officer for several reserves throughout the region. His house showed his success: upscale furniture, hardwood floors, Native American art on the walls, and an enormous high-definition television that made images so real they had Joe gulping coffee to avoid seeing the girl slice open her wrist. He grimaced at the spurting blood, and his gnarled hands fidgeted with the coffee mug as he strained to hear what the girl was saying.

"Albulla guberoa. Elbae dar albulla. Niandalaba nescato."

Danny watched Joe's reactions.

"That's enough," Joe said, reaching for the remote and switching off the video. "What the hell kind of a job you got?"

Peterson turned back from the window, and Joe pulled himself from the armchair to face him. "And you, after how many years you come to me with this! A girl talks different, and right away you think she's Mi'kmaq. Why's that? Because she's doped up and slices her arm like bologna?"

"That's not how it is."

"It's how it looks. You want me to tell you what you want to hear. You got some nerve, Peterson. You got some fucking nerve coming to me after what you did."

Peterson stepped away from the window. He had thought twice about bringing this case to Joe Christmas, and now he wished he had given in to his second thought and contacted a translator in the Justice Department instead. But a personal need and a hollowed out friendship had impelled him to slip Danny the band office's telephone number and Joe's name. There was something else, a need in his gut to come face to face with a man he hadn't seen or spoken to since . . . since when? He unwound a tangled memory of the night he brought Joe's daughter home from the hospital to this house, to this living room, to this sober, straight-laced sanctuary from the dope dealers and pimps on the Strip. Standing in this doorway with the beat cop's report in hand, trying to explain how a 911 call had brought the paramedics to that rabbit warren just off the Strip, where Joe's daughter was shaking uncontrollably from an armload of over the top. Folded double on a gurney, screaming through traffic lights, as the young paramedic sweat buckets that he'd get a flatline his first night on the job.

"You wanted her off the streets, Joe," Peterson insisted, calmly. "I did what I could."

Joe stared at the blank TV screen. "You sent her up."

"I got her help!"

"Help!" Joe turned sharply to face Peterson, advancing. "You call a woman's lockup help? You call her learning to be worse than she was help? You call that help? Three years, Peterson, you know where she is now?"

Peterson's face went stony. "I tried the teen refuge, but she bolted. Back on the street. Back with her pimp. What the hell was I supposed to do?"

"What you promised to do!"

"I spoke to the Crown on her behalf, but he wouldn't listen. Nobody would listen."

"Because she's Indian!" Joe exploded. "Because all our men are drunks and our women are whores. Because we're all shooting our veins or snorting gas. So what's one less fucking Indian?"

"That's not what I think!"

"Not now!" Joe turned slowly and bore a hole through Peterson that was big enough for all his guilt. "White girls blow their minds and run away too. It comes home to roost, doesn't it Peterson? It's not just Indian girls that fuck themselves up. It's white girls too."

Joe dropped into his armchair.

"You saying the girl in the Broken Promise wasn't talking Indian?" Danny said to break the tension.

"Peterson knows what I'm saying," Joe replied from behind closed eyes. "And this girl," he gestured at the blank screen, "she's not from around here. She's not speaking Mi'kmaq or Maliseet. It's not like anything I ever heard.

That's why Peterson brought all this to me. That, and because he wants to say he's sorry and doesn't know how, because he's worried like hell that what he's really looking for is someone who doesn't want to be found."

Joe pulled out the flash drive and handed it to Danny, looking past him to Peterson. "I don't know what she's talking. It's not my language."

CHAPTER
SEVENTEEN

Danny swung the car from the driveway and started off the reserve. They drove the unpaved road in silence. Then he said, "You want to tell me what that was all about?"

"You don't want to know," Peterson said and looked out the side window at the passing trees.

Danny's cell phone rang and he took the call.

Peterson stared straight ahead, unseeing, remembering, searching the back of his mind for a place to hide.

Danny ended the call as he turned right onto a secondary road, spinning the steering wheel and catching Peterson's brooding distraction. On the highway, heading back into the city, he spoke again. "We may have caught a break with the girl from the Broken Promise," he said. "Anonymous tip from a phone booth. Somebody doesn't want to get involved with a nutcase. Looks like the girl used to be a patient at Stoddard. A follow-up call to the hospital confirmed it."

↗

No tall iron fences or high stone walls surrounded the Stoddard Mental Health Centre, a bleak five-storey red-brick complex that sandblasting and repointing had not revived. There was just a low hedge and a stand of birch separating the building from a service road, a tree-shaded driveway, a flower garden with a pergola, and a grouping of several Adirondack chairs. Next to the building was a paved parking lot, one side for a dozen visitor spaces, and the other side, closer to the front door, with a dozen spaces reserved for staff. Five of the staff spaces were assigned to the hospital's administrator, staff psychiatrists, and communications officer.

The lobby was an enlarged hallway, more of a thoroughfare, between a small coffee shop at one end and elevators at the other. A security guard sat in a glassed-in booth dead centre. There was a bank of monitors along one wall of the security booth. Hospital surveillance.

From what Peterson saw, the cameras covered the parking lot, the main entranceway, the lobby, and the waiting area in front of the elevator doors on the patient floors.

Heather McBride, an athletic woman with auburn hair and long legs, met them in the lobby to take them to the boardroom on the fifth floor. She had an elevator key that unlocked access to the top floor. She gave them the ten-cent spiel about the hospital's dedication to relieving the anguish of the mentally ill and returning them to society as active, happy, and contributing members.

The boilerplate patter went in one ear and out the other, while Danny tried not to stare at the woman's legs and Peterson looked at their reflections in the stainless steel walls. The contrast amused him: Heather McBride neatly dressed in a beige skirt suit, and Danny and himself, two rumpled and mopey detectives who had abandoned the button-down look years ago. He tightened his stomach and remembered to smile.

The elevator doors opened to offices at the front of the building, and a small cafeteria, staff lounge, consult room, and executive boardroom at the back. The boardroom's wall-to-wall carpet, drapes, long oak table, and leather armchairs were various shades of brown. There were brief introductions. No handshakes, certainly none offered or accepted by Danny and Peterson.

Heather McBride sat down at the head of the table, flanked by Dr. Philip Hamlin and Dr. Karl Bettis. Richard Pratz, a member of the hospital's board of directors and the CEO of Blatch, Collins, and Werner Pharmaceuticals, sat behind the hospital administrators. Compared to the work-a-day appearance of Bettis and Hamlin, the silver-haired Pratz was well tanned, well attired, and well kept for a man Peterson figured was in his late sixties.

Heather McBride leaned forward to present Peterson and Danny with details about the girl. To Peterson's ear, Heather's voice had that stagy quality of delivering lines that were memorized. He hated the barebones of a prepared statement, the lack of dirt that often came with practice.

"Almost eleven months ago hunters found her under a blanket of pine boughs in the woods off the 104 Highway near Gowanus Corner. She was hungry but not starved, cold but not hypothermic. They called the RCMP. The RCMP reported her conversation as disjointed, hallucinatory. She either knew nothing or would say nothing about herself."

Peterson interrupted McBride by changing his seat for one closer to Dr. Bettis, a homey man in a wrinkled white coat and uncombed hair, yet grand in the way he held his shoulders back and kept his chin raised. He had hazel eyes, and his gaze flitted about the room like a butterfly. Nervous? Or just flighty?

Danny followed Peterson's lead and moved to a chair across from Peterson and beside Dr. Philip Hamlin.

"Did the Mounties try to ID the girl?" Peterson asked.

McBride answered with a little less confidence. "They said they checked her out against photos of runaways and missing persons."

"And they turned up nothing."

"That's correct."

"And you never asked the girl her name?"

"Of course we did. Every conversation." McBride looked to the others for support, as though she'd suddenly found herself on shaky ground.

Dr. Bettis responded, his voice as high-toned as his mannerisms. "No matter what ploy I used, she did not reveal her name. Within her own delusions, she may have had a very good reason not to. Or, and this is quite possible, she did not know herself. Could not remember it, or in her mind lost track of who she was."

Danny leaned forward. "How'd she end up here?"

McBride hesitated.

Dr. Hamlin suddenly straightened and leaned forward, lacing his fingers to keep his fidgety hands still. Peterson pegged him as a drinker: flushed cheeks, bags under his wandering eyes, lips dry and probably thirsting for a taste of something steady. Hamlin also spoke as though taking his cues from offstage. "The Mounties brought her here for a psychiatric evaluation. They had a court order."

Peterson made a note to check out the RCMP report.

Bettis picked up the thread, "When she first arrived she was wild and required restraint. With medication and psychiatric counselling she calmed down considerably."

Now it was McBride's turn. "She remained under our care, unrestrained. And there were no more violent outbursts."

"None?" Peterson was skeptical

"None at all."

"She was withdrawn," Bettis added, "at times moody. Her behaviour was no better and no worse than most other patients."

"Staff liked her," McBride insisted. "She seldom spoke, but she did what staff asked her to."

"And when she did speak," Peterson asked, "what did she talk about?"

"A lot was disjointed, unrelated to everyday experience," Bettis said, his voice loaded with authority. "You must appreciate she was undergoing psychiatric care and we hardly scratched the surface before she —"

"Escaped." Peterson said, his voice pointed with blame.

Bettis lifted his hands by way of consent.

"How did she get out?" Peterson asked.

Bettis looked to Hamlin for support, and then his eyes

shifted to Richard Pratz who so far had not reacted to what was being said. It was Heather McBride who answered.

"She was not confined, if that's what you mean," she said.

"She was delusional when found on the side of the road," Hamlin added, "but with proper medication, she behaved quite normally."

"Except that she didn't talk," Peterson said.

"She did talk," Bettis corrected. "But, as I said, a lot of her words were unintelligible."

"Otherwise she behaved in much the same way as other patients," Hamlin repeated. "Without restraint."

"So long as she remained within the building," McBride said.

"With supervision," Hamlin said.

Peterson recognized the cover-my-ass and protect-the-institution patter.

Danny did too, and he let them know. "With everyone supervising her, like your first-aid manual says, and with all those security cameras, how come no one saw her leave?"

Peterson saw Bettis sneak a nervous look at Pratz, and in the corner of his eye noticed a frown slip over Pratz's face.

"Not all security guards are conscientious about their responsibilities," Hamlin said.

"A snoozer," Danny said.

Hamlin nodded.

"What about the video tapes?" Peterson asked.

"We only record two of the cameras," Pratz offered, his voice squeaky like a thumb over a scrubbed bathtub, "the main entrance and parking lot. And they're recycled every two days. A budget cut. A small item, but who would ever think?"

"So the girl just up and walked away," Peterson said, "even though you knew she was crazy."

"We prefer to use terms that are more respectful of the individual," Bettis protested.

"Soften it all with words that mean nothing," Peterson muttered. Then, louder, "So tell me. What respectful terms should I use for a girl who staggers across six lanes of traffic, tears a bar apart, and slashes her wrist?"

Heather McBride blinked nervously. Bettis seemed undisturbed.

"It's nothing we haven't seen before, Detective," Bettis said. "Only we don't allow it to influence our response to those we have been professionally trained to serve. The mentally ill have the same human rights as you and I. We cannot confine and restrain everyone with a mental disorder just because they walk the streets talking to someone we can't see or act in a way we consider abnormal. We don't have the right to lock them away forever."

"Even if it's for their own good?"

"And who determines that?" Bettis snapped.

Peterson waved the argument away. "A team of shrinks for a start. But maybe I'm wrong. Maybe it's more respectful to pick the crazies up, dust them off, point them down the road, and tell them to take a hike."

"That's not fair!" McBride protested. "We don't have the budget for long-term care of the mentally ill. We do all that is possible within the time we have to do it."

"And then you show them the door and close it after they leave." They locked eyes. "So what was she?" He asked. "What clinical term describes her condition?"

"I think Dr. Bettis should answer that," McBride said.

Peterson rotated his chair to face Bettis squarely. "You were her doctor?"

"Yes."

"So?"

Dr. Bettis heaved a sigh. "There is not a lot to report for the short time she was here."

"How short?"

"Eighteen days. She was depressed and paranoid. Schizophrenic. Feared men in authority, but I had started to soften her defenses."

"Just men?" Danny asked.

"I believe so. She responded reasonably well to nurses and other female staff, and to me, of course. Though she spoke little, very little. Quite introverted. Closed inside her head. During the times she did talk there was little to no relationship to reality."

"She spoke English?" Peterson asked.

"When her mind was settled, yes, and with medication. Why?"

"We have a recording of her talking in the Broken Promise. It wasn't English."

Danny pulled out the flash drive with the video Billy had edited. "You have a way we can play this?"

McBride led Danny to a credenza that held A/V equipment. She flicked a switch and a wall panel opened to reveal a monitor. Danny inserted the drive into a USB port.

"This gets ugly," Danny said. He opened the video and cued it to the girl screaming wildly, played it, and stopped it at Peterson cradling the dying girl in his arms.

Everyone in the room was shocked. Peterson couldn't watch it again. He had turned from the monitor long before the video stopped.

McBride leaned toward him. "That was you," she said. "I'm sorry."

Peterson held her eyes, steeling himself against what he felt. Then he turned to Bettis. "It wasn't English, but it was like she was trying to tell us something."

"It was gibberish, and she probably was trying to tell you something." Bettis had turned to look out the window. "Under stress, agitation, or when her imagination was running wild, she often spoke in tongues. Hers was a divided mind. What she said may sound like a language, but I assure you it is gibberish."

"Gibberish?" Peterson repeated.

"Yes."

"Not a language?"

"No."

"You're positive?"

"This is not our first schizophrenic patient. You would be surprised how many we get. I video each patient when they first arrive. Study their behaviour. Listen to them. With some, their speech is unintelligible. I could get any one of a dozen videos from my office and show it to you."

This was not the answer Peterson had expected, or wanted. Words that are not words. A chattering of disconnected sounds. Syllables without meaning. Doodling out loud.

"So she runs away from here ten months ago and disappears," Danny said, "and then she —"

"We followed protocol," McBride said. "We contacted the police. How much they did, we have no idea."

"Apparently girls run away from home all the time," Bettis added. "At least that's the impression I got."

"They run away for a reason," Peterson said. "And they stay away for a reason. So what made this girl run?"

He looked from face to face. No one had an answer. Then Peterson asked, "Any idea why she suddenly flipped out and killed herself?"

Peterson's question hung in the air. The boardroom fell silent. McBride closed her eyes. Pratz and Bettis stared at their hands. Hamlin alone held Peterson's eyes.

"Something must have driven her into a deeper depression," he said, "deeper into her paranoia. My best guess is that it was something shocking. Not a physical shock, though it could be, but a shock to her mind."

CHAPTER
EIGHTEEN

Danny slid behind his desk opposite Peterson. He had bad mood written across his face. They both had been riding the side streets and back alleys, coaxing and strong-arming the wasted and unwanted to talk about the time they spent in St. Jude's church, warming up or sleeping one off during mass. Those who knew the dead priest had had nothing but good to say about him, and those that didn't couldn't have cared less that he was dead. Many had been more than willing to say just the opposite for a forty-ouncer of cheap wine. Some even had offered to point a finger if it meant lining their pockets with whatever the detectives had to offer.

Peterson's effort had been half-hearted, his attention span short. Two words from a street drunk or junkie and he would stop listening. His thoughts always sliding back to the Broken Promise.

"Two detectives and a half-dozen uniform cops nosing both sides of the Strip, and we turn up nothing," Danny said. "Zilch."

Peterson passed him a forensic report. "This will raise your spirit. The fingerprints of the women in the photos don't match those in the sacristy."

Danny rolled his eyes. "What about the one whose photo was still in the camera, the one crying when the priest snapped the shutter?"

"Her name's Wendy Levigne," Peterson said. "She has MS, lives up the Valley, and gets around in a motorized wheelchair."

"You talk to her?"

"Slurred speech. I caught every third word. Talk about the short end of the stick. She's been married eleven years and her husband packed his bag less than a year after she was diagnosed."

The landline rang and Danny answered. He covered the mouthpiece. "For you," he said. "A woman with a bedroom voice."

✧

Peggy Demming guided Peterson behind the reception desk and down the central hallway at the Birthright Centre, her spike heels clicking on the hardwood floor. Peterson tried not to stare, but he couldn't help it. Peggy Demming was an eye-catcher in a black knitted skirt.

"I could have called a priest," Peggy said over her shoulder, her voice husky from a day of tiresome meetings with municipal bureaucrats and financial donors, "but I didn't think a priest would understand."

She showed him into Anna's office, shrugging at the clutter and removing a stack of books from a folding chair for him to sit. "I suggested she take time off, but she wouldn't hear of it. She said work would help her forget. You don't know how many times I've caught her just sitting in here, staring at nothing. I thought she should talk to someone. I know she went to see you at the police station, and she said it helped. I thought you would know what to say. You were there."

Peterson remained standing. "I'm not sure what I can do. What she went through, it's not just shock. It stays with you. Talking to a shrink or priest might do her a lot more good."

"What about you?"

"I've been through it before."

The receptionist poked her head through the door and told Peggy she had a call from a mother-to-be. Peggy started from Anna's office and stopped.

"Anna's always been weird. Not weird, but different. It's worse now. Everything's happening all at once. Funding cuts. A chance we might have to close our doors. Now this. I just thought maybe you could help."

Peterson stood beside Anna's desk, taking in the photos of babies and a few mothers plastered on all four walls. He turned quickly to the sunny window, seeking glory in the bright leaves on the nearby maple. Finding none, he turned back to the framed photos on the walls.

"No one said it was going to be easy," he overheard Peggy say in her office across the hall, "but it is the right thing to do." There was a long pause then Peggy insisted. "You're not abandoning it! You're giving it life. You're giving it hope."

Peterson scowled, feeling daunted by all the babies that surrounded him. He found refuge in the framed reproduction of Bernini's sculpture of St. Teresa of Avila. He negotiated a file cabinet, a few stacks of books, and Anna's desk to get a closer look and to read the printed file card taped to the wooden frame.

"Beside me on the left appeared an angel in bodily form . . . He was not tall but short, and very beautiful; and his face was so aflame that he appeared to be one of the highest ranks of angels, who seem to be all on fire . . . In his hands I saw a great golden spear, and at the iron tip there appeared to be a point of fire. This he plunged into my heart several times so that it penetrated my entrails. When he pulled it out I felt that he took them with it, and left me utterly consumed by the great love of God. The pain was so severe that it made me utter several moans. The sweetness caused by this intense pain is so extreme that one cannot possibly wish it to cease, nor is one's soul content with anything but God. This is not a physical but a spiritual pain, though the body has some share in it — even a considerable share."
— St. Teresa of Avila

He was reading this when Anna entered the office. He turned to see her braced against the doorjamb, her arms wrapped around herself for strength or comfort or to hold in an anger that wanted to get out.

"I came by to see how you're doing," Peterson said.

"And what do you see?" Anna straightened up.

"It takes time," Peterson said. "Talking helps."

"Who would understand?"

"A psychologist. A priest. Me."

Anna stepped into her office and sank into the folding chair Peggy had cleared for Peterson. "And what about you? Who do you tell?"

"I get counselling."

"Do you talk about it?"

"Yes."

"Does it help?"

Peterson ducked behind a smile.

"Talking about it makes it real," Anna said, "as though it really happened."

"It did happen."

"I know, but I wish it hadn't. I wish it was all in my head."

"No, you don't want that. Fantasy you can't put behind you. Reality you can. Even the nightmares get less. It was real, Anna. What that girl did, what happened to us was real."

Anna's hands tightened into fists. "I didn't have to go there, but I was stubborn. I couldn't let her change her mind, not like that, not without talking about it."

"Her?"

"Sally Toomey, a waitress in that bar. She's pregnant. She was with us and changed her mind about having the baby, before it was too late. And I was there to . . . that's what makes it all so wrong. And then I failed that girl. I couldn't help. I couldn't stop all the blood."

He could have taken her into his arms just then, seal a bonding of sorts. Instead, he looked at the photos that covered the walls. Played for time to dissipate what he felt, and what Anna felt.

"A lot of babies," he said, without turning.

"A hundred and forty-seven throughout the building and some mothers, mostly the ones that kept their babies."

"No fathers?"

"Not many stay long enough to get their picture taken."

Peterson pointed to a photo of a man smoking and drinking coffee. Now he turned. Feelings in check. "This one stayed."

Anna smiled. "My father," she said.

"And I take it the woman is your mother?" Peterson said, and, off Anna's nod, continued. "And the beautiful novitiate in white is you?"

Anna looked away, embarrassed, off-put by the compliment. "I left the convent years ago," she explained.

Peterson knew she had been a nun. Danny had briefed him on her background check.

At age sixteen, she'd heeded a sudden calling from God to become a nun. Her Mother Superior had described her as "retiring." Her spiritual advisor, Sister Xavier, said she was, "deeply penitent and excessively devout." Left the convent when her parents separated. Attended St. Mary's University, BA in psychology. Entered a master's program. Dropped out after a year and enrolled in the Carmelite Order of Nuns. No talking, no visitors. Prayer and fasting. Left after four years to care for her sick mother. Worked in homeless shelters and food banks. After her mother entered a nursing home, Anna joined the Right to Life crusade. Founding member of the Birthright Centre.

Peterson moved back to the Bernini reproduction of St. Teresa. "This one baffled me until I read the caption. She looks like she's . . ." He looked to Anna for help.

"In ecstasy," Anna offered. "St. Teresa of Avila. She had visions of God and an absolute sense of His divine love."

"Is that what made her a saint?"

"The love of God, yes!"

"You can tell by the look," Peterson said, without taking his eyes off Anna. "The ecstasy. Do you want to be a saint?"

Anna's brow wrinkled as though she was puzzling over all sides of Peterson's question. Peterson watched her effort and wondered what was there to consider: you either wanted to be a saint or you didn't. Yet he waited, quietly, the way he waited for a suspect or witness to get around to saying what was on their mind.

"When I was a little girl," Anna said to her hands folded on her lap, "I went to church every day. I lit a candle and stared into the flame and prayed and prayed to St. Teresa until my eyes crossed. Then I would quickly look at the statue and it would appear to move. I believed the statue had come to life and had answered my prayers."

Anna lifted her head, her eyes glassy with tears. He extended his hand and Anna took it. He curled his fingers over hers.

"I don't know what's happening." She caught her voice before it broke. She squeezed Peterson's hand for support. "I keep seeing the girl. The blood. Her eyes reaching into me. She's saying something I don't understand. Her last words. I'm listening. I'm close to her lips and I'm listening, but I don't understand."

"It was gibberish," he confided.

"No!" Anna snatched back her hand.

"She was a patient at Stoddard Mental Health Centre," Peterson explained. "Paranoid schizophrenic."

"She said something she wanted us to know."

"The doctors said it was gibberish."

"Her last words. You heard her!"

"I don't know what I heard."

"It was in her eyes. You saw it. The way she looked when she said it."

"It wasn't any language. It was gibberish."

Anna was on her feet, shaking. Peterson reached to console her, but she pulled away, knocking over the folding chair and stumbling to the door. She grabbed the doorjamb to steady herself, then looked back at him.

"You're wrong. Listen to her. Listen to what she said."

CHAPTER
NINETEEN

Peterson sat in the same blue vinyl booth as he had the night he saw the girl crossing the six-lane. He felt as though a gash in his side had broken open. The cup shook in his hands and spilled coffee on his fingers. His eyes welled, and he was worrying his lower lip with his teeth. He had always been moody, sullen mostly, but in the past three days, after that night in the Broken Promise, his mood had been swinging uncontrollably from a deadened emptiness to a tumult of emotions. He had lost focus on his regular police work, so much so that Danny was handling the murder of Father Boutilier pretty much on his own, with nothing to show for it.

Last night, to avoid the loneliness of his house, he had driven to a dead-end street overlooking the harbour. He saw how the city lights made streaks on the water that shimmered with the tide. He heard music from a house on a nearby street, an acoustic guitar being gently strummed. Then all of a sudden his feelings erupted, choking his throat and threatening to leak from his eyes.

He had tried not to let the job get to him. But it had, a long time ago. The people too, every one of them, poking out their heads whenever his mind was still. Staring them down day and night. Faces of people he couldn't ever bring home to his wife and daughter.

Now Peterson was so lost inside himself that he didn't notice Danny pulling into a parking spot facing the window in which he sat. Nor did he notice Danny breeze through the door and slide into the booth.

"You don't stay home much," Danny said, snapping Peterson from his thoughts. "I called both numbers last night."

"I wasn't answering."

"Just me, or everyone?" Danny asked.

"She knows it bothers me when she calls." He faked a laugh. "But at least I know she's alive."

"You have other ways to know she's alive."

Peterson looked away. "A closed door would be harder to take than her calling and not talking."

"Yeah, well, I got a call from Joe Christmas. He had a name. A linguist named Piet Fromm."

"Joe doubting himself?"

"No. He thought this guy might be able to tell us what language it was."

"Then we should talk to him."

"I did. You weren't answering your phone last night, and you weren't behind your desk this morning."

"I had the Mountie from the Gowanus Road on stand-by."

"What did he say?"

"Tell me about Piet Fromm."

"Overly polite. Big words. University type — shaggy hair, a beard. He gave me a lecture about languages. Then he listened to the video and said the strange words the girl spoke weren't part of any language he was familiar with. He said it was gibberish."

"That's what Bettis said."

"But this guy said something else." Danny referred to his notes. "He said the few English words she spoke sounded like the West Country dialect in England, maybe even a combination of that and the dialect from southeast Ireland. He figured the girl was from Newfoundland, and if he was a betting man, he'd bet on the Western Peninsula."

Peterson signalled the waitress for more coffee. "Newfoundland?"

"That's what the man said."

Peterson thought for a moment. "She freaks out at home for whatever reason and runs away. Where to?"

"The ferry at Port aux Basques."

"Then she gets off the ferry and hitches a ride, or she hitches one while on the boat. Either way she's in a vehicle heading this way."

"Does she hustle the ride? Pay for it with herself?"

"Maybe," Peterson said. "And maybe a trucker picks her up and she won't put out."

"So he drops her off or dumps her on Gowanus Road."

"Hunters find her in the woods spaced out. She ends up in Stoddard and after eighteen days, she escapes."

"And stays in town. Then goes under wraps for almost ten months. Why?"

Peterson turned to the window and the traffic passing on the Strip. He pointed across the six lanes.

"She walked down from over there and crossed to the Broken Promise. Where was she coming from?"

"There's not much back there," Danny said. "A crack patch. A hobo jungle."

"She could have been holed up there."

"Not for months. She had to scrounge food from somewhere, and probably drugs. Beg the streets. Turn tricks. Squeegee. Some cop would have had a line on her one way or another."

Peterson toyed with his coffee spoon. "The Mountie thought she was a crackhead. He did what he could to ID her, but she was talking nonsense. So she ends up on a psycho ward and runs away."

The waitress stopped at their table to refill their mugs. After she left, Danny said, "So where does a teenage runaway end up?"

Peterson avoided looking Danny's way. He pulled a napkin from the dispenser and wiped up a coffee spill. "Same story, same ending," he said. "The street looks better than going home, and the pimp always wears a halo."

Danny knew where Peterson was coming from. "You and pimps don't mix real good. Not since your daughter left. If you want to talk to a pimp, you don't do it alone."

"You suddenly turn into a babysitter?"

"Guardian angel. You can't get your daughter out of your head, and a face-to-face with a pimp might just churn you up."

"That come from on high?"

Danny's grin hung off his earlobes. "You think they care about you? You're a fifty-year-old liability to anybody upstairs."

"Fifty-one."

"Yeah, well that makes you easier to pension off." He got up to leave. "I'll line something up for tonight if you promise to play nice."

Peterson almost laughed. "Only if he does."

Peterson sat there thinking. Then he followed a hunch to the downtown Sally Ann thrift store. A thirty-something brunette sized him up for a cop before he was ten seconds in the store. She knew all about the priest murder and why the cops had been combing doorways and side alleys, pestering those living on the street.

"I doubt the priest had anything the street wants," she said, after Peterson showed his badge and before he even asked a question. "Money maybe, but I heard he wasn't robbed. And I heard whoever killed him made a big deal of doing it, candles and shit and fucking up the altar. You're pulling the wrong end of the string."

Peterson agreed.

"Then why are you here?"

He showed her a morgue photo of the girl from the Broken Promise. "Have you seen her before?"

"You ran that in the newspaper. She looks familiar, but then again, between here and dishing out food at the Cottage, I see so many. They run away, and the street is no easy way to live."

The last bit had a heartfelt ring to it, as though she knew first hand what she was talking about.

"Most don't make it home," she continued. "They live hand to mouth for years. I get old women coming in here that turned tricks thirty, forty years ago. But you can't tell the young ones that. You can't tell them nothing." She looked at the photograph again. Shook her head. "I don't think so. No, I don't know her."

He made it to the station just as the day staff was leaving. He settled at his desk and checked his messages. One from Central Dispatch referred to a callback from 911.

Peterson entered the glass cubicle of Central Dispatch. The female dispatcher, a different woman from a few nights before, signalled for him to give her a minute. She finished doing what she was doing, then turned to Peterson and removed her headphones.

"Sarah left a note for me to contact you."

"Sarah?"

"The dispatcher from the other night. She had another 911 call. A screener thought it was the same voice that called before. Sarah left a time code number for me to bring it up. It's only a couple of seconds. You want to listen?"

Peterson nodded and the dispatcher handed him the headphones. She opened the recording and hit play.

"Nobody," the girl said, sounding more drunk than stoned to Peterson's ears, and maybe not drunk. Definitely out of it, but straining to hold it together. She muttered something and then shouted, "I can't have it! I can't!"

The girl whimpered and hung up.

Peterson asked the dispatcher to play it again. In the background he heard traffic noise and two male voices. The first one asked, "What number?" The second said, "Seven." There was a pause, and then the first voice said, "It should be here in a couple of minutes."

Peterson returned the headphones. "When did this come in?"

"Zero one thirty-seven," the dispatcher said.

"Last night?"

"Most don't turn around that fast."

"Then how long ago?"

"It could be three or four days."

Peterson scowled. "And I'm getting it now!"

The female dispatcher smiled faintly. "The number of bullshit calls to 911, you're lucky to get it at all."

The Investigation Unit had all but cleared out by the time he returned. Some clerical staffers were still tidying up their desks, and three robbery detectives were standing around a desk near the windows with their heads together. By the incident reports and mug shots spread over the desktop, Peterson figured they were wading through the details of the latest masked-man stick-up at a rural Credit Union. As Peterson neared, he realized they were talking about Bernie, sitting twelve desks away, their voices raised, unconcerned whether she heard. One comment stood out loud and clear, "I'd take her on just to break my back."

As Peterson passed the threesome, one of them, Archie

Allen, lifted his square head and pointed his nose Peterson's way.

"Bandana mask, short croppy hair, and big-ass belt buckle," Archie said. "Ring a bell?"

"Leigh McGovern," Peterson answered, without stopping. "Hit half a dozen Cineplex Theatres after showtime. Up for six, probably out in two."

"He's out."

Peterson stopped and turned.

"Same dress code," Archie added, "only prison must have taught him where the real money is. Credit Union heist."

Peterson took it in then said, "His grandfather had a cabin on a lake down the east shore. And he had a girlfriend that did a year for aiding and abetting. Brittany something or other."

"Burpee." Bernie chimed in, making no bones about having heard every word.

"All ears and legs that one," Archie said, nodding at Bernie.

"But a damn good cop," Peterson said. He leaned toward the three detectives as though he meant to whisper, but he spoke at the same volume. "Any idea how to find Brittany Burpee?" The threesome drew a blank at the suddenness of the question. Then over his shoulder to Bernie, he said, "Tell them!"

"Parole officer," Bernie said.

Peterson beamed at the three detectives. "It doesn't take much, does it?"

Bernie was standing beside his desk.

"Don't look so happy," Peterson said. "That wasn't for your benefit."

"That's not why I'm happy. I made a connection. Two hits, same shooter, at least that's what I think."

"I'm all ears."

"Another cold case," Bernie said. "Three years old. Jarvis Owens, a black kid, twenty-four, an art college grad, working at Astral Animation. He was moonlighting as a pizza delivery boy to pay off a student loan. Gunned down making a delivery in the Square. The woman at the door saw the shooter. Dark clothes and a skull mask."

"You're thinking same shooter as the accountant hit."

"Double-barrel shotgun," Bernie said. "Two in the chest. He picked up the casings and took his time to find the wads."

"No other witnesses?"

"None that will talk."

"Investigating officer?"

"Andy Miles," Bernie said.

"He worked both cases and never put it together?"

Bernie shook her head.

"You ask him about it?"

"He wouldn't talk about it."

Peterson smiled. "Connect the dots in these two cases and you'll be sitting at my desk." He held his arms open with pride, as though the dusty confusion of files, notebooks, and slips of paper was something to be sought after. He lost the smile. "Big question: who in this city hires a hit man?"

"The hire might not be from here. I found out the convenience-store owner is based in Moncton. And Moncton has strong ties to Montreal."

"You told Miles that?"

"I did."

"And?"

"And he wouldn't answer. But the coffee room crew said my digging has his shorts in a knot."

Peterson loved it. "Tie it to Montreal and the case goes to the Mounties."

"That's what I was afraid of."

"They have more staff and more resources. Besides, the pat on the back isn't why we do it."

"Auld Lang Syne" sounded from his jacket pocket. It was Danny.

"Don't book yourself a heavy date," Danny said. "My main man is home and sitting tight."

"Give me a couple of hours," Peterson said. "The Bone Man's sniffing out the Airport Road call, and I got to feed him something new."

Bernie hadn't moved. She had been studying his face while he was on the call. He looked distracted. His creases deeper, and his brown eyes more inward looking than out.

He pocketed the phone and caught Bernie looking. "What?"

"You want a coffee?"

Peterson waved it off. "Hot date."

Peterson tracked Bony Walker to a west-end house gutted for renovations. Peterson cross-beamed the empty house and excavated side yard until he spotted Bony with a shopping cart loaded with a three-foot-diameter coil of plastic tubing.

"Am I going to lose my badge for not reporting this?" Peterson asked.

Bony shook his head. "The contractor owes me big time. And I bring back what I don't use on a plumbing job I got."

"What do you know about plumbing?"

"What's there to know? No copper anymore. No soldering. With this plastic pipe, you don't need a big gut and ass crack to be a plumber. You just need this crimping tool." He pulled the tool from his back pocket. "Nowadays even a skinny shrimp like me can plumb a house."

"How far you going?" Peterson asked.

"Gainer's Pub."

"Throw it in the trunk and I'll give you a lift."

Bony canned the shopping cart behind a neighbour's tree and loaded in the plastic tubing.

"You got something for me?" Bony asked, as they headed north.

Peterson nodded and told Bony about the second 911 call and the background conversation between the two guys.

"That narrows the busy intersection to the number seven bus route," Bony said.

"My guess is she was walking the north end," Peterson said. "And ten to one the dead girl on Airport Road was another hooker. A friend. They may have worked these sidewalks together."

"She said a name in that first call," Bony said.

"I'm not sure it's a name, 'Tee fie' or something like that."

"This is close enough," Bony said, gesturing for Peterson to pull into the parking lot of an army–navy store about half a block from the pub. They unloaded the coil of plastic tubing from the trunk. "A few girls use Gainer's to wash up and get off their feet. I'll ask around. I'm in here for a couple of days."

"Careful!" Peterson warned and looped the coil over Bony's shoulder.

"Don't worry. I know whose ass is on the line."

CHAPTER
TWENTY

Both of them knew the way. This had been their beat, when they had prowled these scummy streets in uniform.

Peterson carried a flashlight that he used only when he needed to. Now he aimed it at a dark blue dumpster cornered against a brick wall. The light caught Little Bo-Peep, her mini-skirt hitched, her legs spread, and a startled middle-aged john grinding out his loins.

"Give it a rest, hotshot," Danny ordered.

The john fumbled with whatever he had left and pressed his back against the wall.

Danny went close and whispered so only Bo-Peep could hear, "Teabag's waiting on us."

She flicked her head toward a closed door, indicating Danny and Peterson should enter.

Danny leaned into Peterson. "She doubles as Teabag's

security. How's that for multitasking?" He grinned then turned to the john. "You're still paying full price."

They found the door and climbed the dimly lit stairs to the second floor and a suite of trashy rooms featuring smut for wall art and furniture from Walmart. Teabag, a twenty-something with a dome head and thick neck draped with more bling than a show horse, was waiting for them. He sat like King Tut, gleaming in an overstuffed red leather Moroccan armchair.

Teabag recoiled when Peterson filled the doorway and entered the room. He looked to Danny for an explanation.

"My partner," Danny said. "He's cool with the arrangement."

Teabag was not happy as the two of them pulled up wooden chairs and sat in positions that cornered the pimp on his throne.

Danny wasted no time. He flipped Teabag a morgue photo of the girl from the Broken Promise. "Was she a working girl?"

Teabag gave it a close look and flipped it back. "Can't be sure. You know what they say."

"Don't tell me," Danny said. "White girls all look the same."

Teabag's smile could just as easily have been a sneer. His voice was like grinding glass. "Pussy don't have a colour barrier."

"I heard that being said."

"Hearing ain't knowing."

Peterson interrupted, pointing to the photograph in Danny's hand. "Was someone running her?"

Teabag didn't answer. He waited for Danny to ask the

same question, and when Danny asked it, Teabag skated it by. "I'm leaving that out," he said.

Peterson leaned closer. "What are you leaving in?"

Teabag still wouldn't give Peterson a straight look. He kept his eyes on Danny. "It blows back and I get wasted."

"You buy insurance, you pay a premium," Danny prodded.

Teabag fiddled with a silver bracelet. "It's a business arrangement. Back and forth, here and out west."

"Where west?" Danny asked.

"Fucked if I know. I get out of town, and who knows which way is up."

"Fuck with me, Teabag," Danny said, "and I'll fuck with you."

Teabag stared back hard. "Long haul girls back and forth. Quebec. Ontario. That's what I know."

"Keep them moving?"

Teabag shrugged. "Like a franchise, man, like they get a piece of every transaction."

"Who's they?" Peterson questioned.

Teabag shook his head. His eyes pleaded with Danny for a break, but Danny wasn't giving one. "Pay the premium," Danny ordered.

Teabag made half a dozen different faces of anguish then he snorted and said, "Posse, man!"

"Wholesalers?" Danny asked.

"Fuck, yeah."

"You dipping their supply?"

"Sometimes I freshen up. Whores wear out."

An urge balled up from Peterson's guts and filled his mouth with a sour, stinking taste. It was all he could do to keep his fists still. He inched closer on his chair, reading the fear in Teabag's face. "Posse running girls at home?"

Teabag kept his eyes on Danny. He was telling Danny not Peterson. "You know what they say, supply and demand." He rubbed his fingers together. Money. "Baby snatch goes private. A driver makes deliveries."

"He have a name?" Danny asked.

"No name."

"Then give me a face."

Teabag squirmed. "I give him up, they'll know who," he said.

"We can tiptoe when we know where to walk," Peterson said.

Teabag considered the offer for a little longer than Danny appreciated.

"Otherwise," Danny threatened, "we'll be on you like a house on fire. Shut you down."

Teabag threw back his head and drew a deep breath. He talked to the ceiling. "You're looking for a skinhead with a face like bad news."

"That could be you," Peterson taunted.

Teabag lowered his head and stared hard at Danny to show his contempt for his partner.

Danny wasn't buying it. "I'm still not seeing this guy."

"Fuck," Teabag said. He was walking on thin ice now, and it showed in the way his eyes danced and his voice squeezed through his teeth. "A guy with a snake on each arm. Big ones, with flat heads."

"Cobras?" Danny asked.

"Yeah, that's what they are."

Peterson saw the sweat bead on Teabag's upper lip and knew Teabag's back was a river. Press too hard now and the pimp would clam up. Peterson chanced it. "The private deliveries come with names?"

Teabag shook his head.

Danny stood abruptly, circled his chair, and settled his hands on its back. "You ain't burning an IOU unless you have names."

"I don't have names," Teabag insisted. "We're talking suits, know what I mean? I hear but I don't ask. Posse lets me sell pussy, I don't care."

Peterson leaned so close he could have bitten Teabag's chin. "The suits wear ties?"

"Oh yeah," Teabag said, his eyes fixed on Danny. "They dressed."

CHAPTER
TWENTY-ONE

They sat on the patio outside Carmichael's office, psychiatrist and patient, uncomfortable in wooden lawn chairs. Beyond the patio was a lawn and flower garden with wooden benches, concrete ornaments, a huge sundial, and an abstract stone sculpture that looked to Peterson like a question mark. Colour blasted the men from all sides, challenging the dark probing of one and the moodiness of the other. A red oak shielded them from direct sunlight.

The casual setting and the iced tea were not lost on Peterson. He was on the defensive.

"I pressed a devil worshiper too hard," Peterson replied to Carmichael's question. "He griped, and his lawyer claimed police intimidation, threw in religious intolerance and whatever else he could scratch from his law books."

"Was it?" Carmichael sipped his iced tea, watching Peterson's reaction over the brim.

Peterson opened his hands in a gesture of remorse. Even his voice curried favour. "He's a suspect in a brutal murder."

"There are rules of engagement," Carmichael said.

"You finger a sore spot to get a patient talking. That's all I did."

"And it got you a reprimand for conduct unbecoming a police officer, and one very vocal member of the Police Commission calling for your head on a silver platter. He wants you riding a desk for the rest of your career."

"That's why I need a good word," Peterson said.

"I don't have a good reason to give you one."

Peterson took it on the chin and looked past Carmichael to the stone sculpture — a symbol of doubt and wonderment — and beyond to a bed of flowers, dark brown spots in bright yellow skirts.

"What are those called?" Peterson gestured toward the flowers.

"Black-eyed Susans."

Peterson heaved a deep breath and looked back at the shrink. "The job is who I am."

"And who is that?" Carmichael set his glass on the table and folded his hands. "You can start by being honest with yourself. You're all alone, Peterson. You've closed yourself off from what you love. Now you have to answer the question: Why?"

Peterson didn't answer.

"If the job is who and what you are," Carmichael continued, "then you're deeper in the woods than I suspected. You're more than just a cop, Peterson. You have wounds that won't heal. And you have a sensitivity you can't shrug off. So drop the baggage. Leave who you think you are behind. Lower your guard and start searching for the you that is hidden inside."

Peterson leaned his head on the back of the chair and stared through the tree branches at a single dark cloud drifting in a blue sky. "Anyone ever say you talk a lot of bullshit?"

Carmichael smiled. "More than once."

Peterson's cell phone rang. A scream. Then it stopped. Then it screamed again.

Carmichael watched Peterson go numb at the sound of the phone. Staring at it in the palm of his hand. "You're supposed to shut that off."

"I know."

"Then answer it," Carmichael said. "You know who it is."

Peterson checked the cell phone to see what he had seen so many times before: the fleabag room, the unmade bed, the peeling wallpaper. "Katy."

No response.

He turned off the cell phone. The fullness he had once felt so long ago had dissipated with the years. Carmichael was right; his life had shrivelled down to nothing.

"What are you afraid of?" Carmichael asked.

Peterson looked Carmichael full on. "To hear she is a corpse on a slab, with no one to claim her body."

Carmichael leaned forward to reach this man who had become little more than a shadow in a dark alley. "Then unmask the fear and face it. There is still time to become the father you wished you had been."

Peterson straightened and rose from the chair. "We must be into overtime by now."

"Or we could just start a new game."

"What game is that?"

"We start talking for real. We talk about the real you, about your wife and daughter. About what they meant to you, or didn't. We get inside the hurt you feel, and the guilt. We peel it back and see it for what it is. We drag up the past, all of it, back to when you were a kid. We face it. No more running away. We do what we have to do to help you mend your mind and your heart."

Peterson took a deep breath and stood. "Maybe we will, but not right now. I have something to do."

On his way out of the garden he stopped and turned. "Don't give up on me, not yet."

"My door is open."

CHAPTER
TWENTY-TWO

Searching the department's database for an ugly skinhead with snake tattoos was a snap for some, but not for Peterson. Opening files, searching folders, even patching in hard drives and scanners was one thing, but negotiating his way through a national database was like mapping out a driving tour around the world. He needed help, but asking for it was tricky. He had to keep the search on the Q.T. In a police department that was all ears, someone trying to keep details of an investigation under wraps was the first thing everyone talked about, especially Miles and his cronies. And one thing Peterson was sure about was that any organization making big money under the table had someone in the cop shop who would tell them the news before it hit a briefing session in the squad room. The Posse would be no different.

His dilemma resolved itself later that night. He was

sitting in the empty Investigation Unit, in his customary pose — flask in hand, feet propped on a file box, staring into the overhead light — when he heard Bernie call his name from across the room. Then a sandwich sailed through his line of sight and landed square in his lap. He snapped forward and reached for the floor in time to stop himself from toppling out of the chair. "What the —?"

"Food," Bernie said, towering over him. "We eat and talk. No argument." She dropped into Danny's chair with a sandwich of her own.

Peterson righted his chair, looked at the smoked meat sandwich and then at Bernie. She was dead serious.

"Eat, for Christ's sake," she said, "and if there's any left in that flask, you're sharing."

Peterson unscrewed the top and gave her the flask. She took a big sip and passed it back.

"I thought you had a son to go home to," Peterson said.

"Don't be a smart ass," Bernie snapped. "Jarvis Owens, the kid delivering pizza, the hit on him was a mistake. That night he was covering a shift for Leon Allen, who delivered pizza and juggled crack. Allen had been cutting a bigger slice for himself, and someone intended to make him an example. The connection between the hit on Allen and on the accountant was pure coincidence. Two different hires, same shooter."

"How'd you find that out?"

Bernie grinned. "I squeezed someone on a parole violation."

"That's not playing fair."

"I faked nothing. The guy was smoking up outside a known crack house."

"And you just happened to be there."

"I got a phone call from a friend of a friend. No rules broken."

"And he told you about Jarvis Owens?"

"No, about Leon Allen. He said Allen pissed someone off, someone up the line."

"Montreal?"

"Looks that way."

Peterson nodded and toasted her with the flask, took a sip, and passed it over. "You tell anyone?"

"Fultz. He said there's enough to pass it to the Mounties."

"You pleased with that?"

Bernie glanced across the empty room to its reflection in the dark windows. "Like you said, we don't do it for the pat on the back. So what the hell, right?"

"Yeah, what the hell," Peterson said, feeling envy and admiration. They each had another sip. Then Peterson said, "Before you pull out another cold case, I could use some help."

Bernie had ID'd the skinhead before Peterson had eaten half the sandwich and drained the flask. She passed him a six-page printout that painted Terry Sylvester as a home-grown hard ass with previous convictions for assault, sexual assault, driving under the influence, breaking and entering, armed robbery, and violating probation. He lived in a trailer park fifteen clicks out of town.

Peterson and Danny knew the trailer park for what it was: a dump for three-time losers. A previous generation of cops had nicknamed the trailer park "Calcutta" after the notorious city in India. It still lived up to its reputation, even under the cover of darkness.

They coasted up to Sylvester's trailer with their car engine and headlights off and closed the doors without making a sound. The front yard was dirt and littered with a junk car, car parts, a ten-foot tripod for hoisting out engines, scrap wood, rubbish, a hot water tank cut in half for an empty flower box, and a rusted half-ton truck. They climbed the rickety porch to the front door, and that had the rubbernecks across the lane at their window.

From inside Sylvester's trailer a man's voice hollered, "Get the fuck out!" Then a woman's voice screamed something back that was too high-pitched to make out but sounded crude. Within moments, the man and woman started going at it, yelling and smashing dishes.

Danny and Peterson found themselves in the middle of a domestic battle. They entered without knocking.

The inside looked like stink. Dirty dishes and glasses. Beer bottles left wherever they ran empty. On the kitchen side was a chrome table and chairs with the vinyl backs and seats torn and the stuffing coming out. The living-room side was crowded with a metal case for knick-knacks, a big TV, and a shabby yellow couch and even shabbier vinyl recliner that had a board propping up the back.

The man had his shirt off and he was sloppy fat. He was also bleary eyed and drunk. His face, thrust forward in defiance, was snarly looking behind a few days' growth and under a shaved head. The snake tattoos on his arms were the give-away.

He wore jeans. So did she, standing ten feet away, a wiry little thing with her face on fire under a mop of dirty blonde hair. Her eyes were popping and her mouth was going a mile a minute. She was cutting the man to shreds, a harpy with a sharp tongue that sounded like car wheels spinning on ice. She called him a no-fuck fucker who was no goddamn good like most of the shitty-assed men she had ever met.

They went back and forth with "fuck you" and "screw you" and how neither was any good and never would be. There was no sense to what they were saying, no root to the argument, and no way to take sides, except to line up hard against the woman's stabbing screech.

Peterson sensed right off that if they didn't get those two apart, the fight would get a lot uglier than it already was. And that's what Danny tried to do, stepping between them, pointing at one, then the other, telling her to shut up and for him to step outside.

Danny had no sooner said it when the woman spit at the man and sprayed Danny in the face. Danny's eyes sharpened to razors, and he bellowed again for the woman to shut up.

But she didn't. She coiled against the table and never let up. She called Danny every foul word there was. And Danny blew steam right back, going at her face to face and calling her whatever name came into his head.

The skinhead was at Danny's back with his fists balled and ready to pounce when Peterson grabbed him by the shoulders and dragged him outside, nearly taking the door-jamb with them. He stuffed the man into the back of the car and climbed in beside him, still holding his shoulders. Now he twisted him around in the seat, grabbed his arm and cocked it up behind his back. That brought a deep belly groan and then silence.

Danny slammed the trailer door then slid behind the wheel and started the car. He drove to the back of the trailer park, where the residents dumped their trash. There was a mountain of it, and it stank as bad as it was high. Danny negotiated around the trash heap and down a grown-over logging road about a hundred metres and stopped. He climbed from the car, nodded to Peterson, then stepped from the skinhead's view, staying close enough to hear what was being said.

Sylvester reeked of booze, but Peterson could still smell the sickening sourdough odour of OxyContin seeping from his pores.

"I'm quiet, all right," Sylvester slurred. "Calming down. I'm calming down."

"Your name Terry Sylvester?" Peterson asked.

"Yeah."

"I got you down for a hit and run."

"What the fuck?"

"The license number and truck description matches the one parked in front of your trailer, and the registration is in your name."

Sylvester denied hitting anyone and kept denying it until Peterson wrenched his arm to shut him up.

"I scraped threads from a yellow dress off the dent in the right front end."

That had the skinhead blowing more steam, cursing everything and everyone. Another arm-wrench silenced him.

"There was a girl on the sidewalk," Peterson continued. "She saw the whole thing and picked you out of a mug shot file. She gave a description: a skinhead with a face only a mother could love."

With his free hand Peterson twisted Sylvester's head so he could see the skinhead's face. "Yeah, you're him."

Again Sylvester denied it, claiming he'd been drunk and doped up for three days.

"Yeah, but we got an eyewitness," Peterson insisted. He pulled a photograph from his jacket pocket, a photograph of the girl in the Broken Promise. He showed it to the skinhead.

"Ever seen her before?"

Sylvester studied the photo. "What the fuck? That bitch is Looney Tunes."

"You know her?"

"Fucking right I know her! She's one crazy whore bitch."

"How do you know her?"

"I drove her around."

"Drove her where?"

"Appointments."

"Appointments with who?"

The light suddenly went on behind Sylvester's bleary eyes. He started sobering up in a hurry.

"What is this? What the fuck you pulling?"

"I'm pulling nothing," Peterson said. "I got a hit and run and —"

"There's no hit and run! I want a lawyer and I want him now!"

"You're probably going to need one, because the old woman you hit is dead."

"Nah, Nah! There was no hit and run."

"I got a hit and run, negligent homicide," Peterson said. "I got to pin it somewhere, and your name came up."

"Fuck you talking about? My name come up? How did my name come up?"

"A guy told us to throw the book at you."

"Who?"

"You tell me!"

"I don't know what the fuck you're talking . . ." Sylvester turned his head to look at Peterson. "You're jerking me around. There's no fucking hit and run. You're juicing me, motherfucker!"

"Tell me about the girl." Peterson again held up the photograph for Sylvester to see. This time the skinhead didn't look at it.

Peterson wrenched Sylvester's arm again and made him squeal. "Try again," Peterson said.

"No way!"

"Yeah, way!" Peterson lifted the arm higher. "Another inch and it breaks."

Through clenched teeth Sylvester said, "They'll waste my ass for doing this!"

"They'll only get bones if you don't."

"You're a fucking cop!"

"Yeah, but not the good kind like you see on television. Tell me about the girl!"

Sylvester looked scared. His voice sounded it. "A dancer. On her back. On her knees."

"Where?"

"Where do you think? But not on stage. Strictly private. I taxied her after hours. Private party."

"Where?"

"Where they like them young and fucked-up."

Peterson raised the arm, and Sylvester squealed.

"Try again! Where?"

"I drop her on a corner and drive off."

"What corner?"

"Different corners. Different nights."

"How often?"

"How often does a guy get horny?"

Sylvester's face emptied. His eyes went glassy. Peterson could feel him shaking.

"What about the last time you dropped her off?"

Sylvester didn't answer.

"What corner?" Peterson insisted.

"At that fire station."

"What fire station?"

"Where the hospitals are."

That caught Peterson by surprise. "The hospital district?"

The skinhead nodded.

"Which way did she walk?"

"She doesn't move until I drive off."

"Careful," Peterson said.

"Oh yeah. Very."

"You pick her up?"

"Yeah. I get a call. Same corner."

"And she doesn't run away?"

"Fuck no. Drugged up. Scared. I wouldn't run, not from them."

"The Posse?"

Sylvester didn't answer.

"But she finally ran," Peterson said.

Sylvester shrugged. "Ran. Let her go. She was squirrelly

155

as hell. Fucked up, more fucked up than the others. They're all fucked up. I heard that's what these johns like. The crazy ones are the money-makers. Knock on any hole and they let you in. But what the fuck do I know?"

"Her name?"

"None of them have names."

Peterson remembered the tattoo on the girl's labia. "What about a number?"

"Yeah, they had numbers. I don't know hers. Didn't need to."

Peterson thought for a moment. "Tell me about the johns."

Peterson loosened his grip as much as to say, This is it. Give me this and we're done. But Sylvester had nothing to give. He had never gotten close enough to see anyone.

"But they got to be somebody," he said. "Very special. Very private. They got to be somebody to get room service like that."

CHAPTER
TWENTY-THREE

It was a rainy Sunday morning, and she invited him into the front hall of her two-storey house in the west end of the city. A dark-stained Douglas fir staircase, gleaming with polish and reflected in an ornate mirror, dominated the narrow space.

"Anna visits her mother at the nursing home on Sunday mornings," Peggy Demming told Peterson. She was still in her pyjamas and housecoat, no makeup but still attractive in the way she set her back against the newel post and smiled. "She takes the bus out there. And after, she sits in St. Joseph's church around the corner and listens to a group of musicians practise. Classical stuff."

She had an easy way of smiling and a confident way of angling her body so her daily workouts would show.

The time he saw her at the Birthright Centre she had been wearing heavy makeup. He now saw it had betrayed her natural features. Eye shadow and liner had dulled the sparkle in her hazel eyes. And her full lips needed nothing to make them more kissable.

"Not my kind of music," Peterson said.

"What kind do you like?"

Peterson hedged. "I don't listen to much of it."

"No time?"

"Not much interest."

"What does interest you?"

There was a lot of suggestion in that last question, especially with the sneaky smile that went with it and the quiet shift of weight that caught his eyes.

"Work interests me," Peterson said. "I work a lot."

"Maybe too much."

"Maybe."

He thanked her for telling him about Anna and reluctantly turned to go.

Peggy forced a smile that suggested she gave a man only one chance to high jump the crossbar. Peterson had missed the jump.

He found the church easily enough, and as he entered he thought about the fact that he had been in a church more times in the last two weeks than he had in the last thirty years.

A dozen or so people were scattered throughout the nave. An older woman was lighting a vigil candle to the patron saint whose statue stood beneath a stained-glass window. At the transept, musicians were sitting in a pool of sunlight. A white-haired man was conducting.

Peterson spotted Anna sitting on the right side of the centre aisle, midway from the altar. In a pause in the music, he went over, surprising her.

"I don't often say I'm sorry," he said.

She lifted her head a bit, then scooted over to make room for him to sit.

"Some things just don't come easy," he added.

The music started again, and she put a finger to her lips.

The organ peeled back the silence and slowly drew sadness from the shadows with a melody that was terribly beautiful, gloriously penitent. Peterson looked at the crucifix behind the altar and at the stained-glass window of the Holy Family above it. The strings took up the theme, giving voice to a great loneliness that ached to be filled.

Peterson saw that Anna had given herself over to the music. He could almost see the wheel of her mind turn slower and slower until it was entirely thoughtless and ready for inscription. He closed his eyes to follow her.

To him, the music seemed to trudge a mountain road. Stony and slow with sad men and even sadder women bent and burdened, their clothes in scraps, moving with heavy feet. A rumble of carts with broken wheels and hungry children too tired to cry. Music imitating life. Note by note, moment by moment. There was a circling of sounds and images. The strings were unashamed of their tears. The organ sobbed.

Then for a moment, all was still.

"Albinoni," Anna whispered, and Peterson opened his eyes. "His Adagio. It's beautiful isn't it?"

"It makes you think," Peterson said.

"And feel."

Peterson nodded. He was feeling something more than his usual stress and discontent. He was feeling lighter.

"Music like this in a church makes me feel something more than just myself," Anna said.

Peterson followed her gaze through the slants of sunlight and into the rafters, but he was unable to doubt his own senses the way Anna could, unable to slip outside his own religious disbelief to experience something pure and full of awe. He suddenly wondered if his daughter had ever experienced something so beautiful that she drifted outside of herself. Did she ever suspend her sulk and anger long enough to walk through a park alone or watch the waves splash ashore? He wished she would call right then so he could ask her, even though he knew he'd get no response, just a strained silence.

Then he thought about the girl in the Broken Promise and whether her life had been nothing more than a scab of discontent and disillusion. And that had him wondering all over again who the girl was.

Anna must have seen his face tighten, because she took his hand. Her slender fingers curled over his. He felt her heart beating in her fingertips.

"The music is searching, isn't it?" Anna said. "Deeper and deeper. Like an onion: You peel away layer after layer until all that's left in your hand is a tiny bulb, and even that peels away to nothing. An invisible truth."

She took back her hand.

"You can't base your life on nothing," he said. "Nothing equals nothing, and nothing is not worth a lifetime of onion peeling."

Anna searched his eyes. "Did you ever just know something was true without knowing why?"

Peterson returned her look without responding.

"Something beautiful," she said, "and terrifying. Something that leaves you full and empty at the same time. Something you can't explain but you just know is true."

Peterson wished that he could lose himself in thoughts of something other than the ugliness of the streets and the hardened doubt in his mind. His gaze drifted to the stained-glass window above the statue of St. Joseph. The musicians were packing away their instruments.

"An expert, a linguistics professor, thinks the girl may have come from Newfoundland," he said.

Anna stared straight ahead, composed, her jaw set.

"I have someone working on it," he added. "With a little luck, I think we'll have a name soon."

"What else aren't you telling me?" she asked.

"Not here."

The rain had stopped. They strolled along a gravel tree-lined pathway that circled the church. Anna carried a yellow slicker over an arm, careful around the puddles so as not to muddy her white sneakers.

"We think the girl was a runaway, picked up on the streets and forced into a life she didn't want to live."

"You don't have to walk on eggshells, Peterson," Anna said. "I see runaways all the time. Most of them get forced into miserable lives by pimps and by circumstances. She wasn't pregnant was she?"

Peterson shook his head. "Not according to the medical examiner."

They walked a short ways in silence then Anna said, "We get outside the church and it all gets ugly and sad. I suppose I go there for the quiet and the little bit of peace it offers."

"Peggy said you take the bus out here every Sunday."

"After visiting my mother in the nursing home. I need the comfort."

He took a chance reaching down for her hand. She took a bigger one by letting him hold it. They circled the church again, this time without saying a word, each enjoying something they had not enjoyed in years. Then Anna broke the spell by saying that after the rehearsal she had intended to visit a mother-to-be, the girl named Sally Toomey, the girl she had gone to the Broken Promise to talk to about her pregnancy. Peterson offered to drive her there.

Peterson sat in the car and watched Anna enter the run-down apartment building in a seedy part of the city across the harbour. He waited less than a minute then followed her into the building and up two flights of a garbage-strewn stairwell. He heard her voice from an open door, glanced in, then hung outside the door and listened.

At the end of a narrow hall was a small kitchen where Anna was standing and a young woman was sitting. He recognized the young woman as the waitress from the Broken Promise.

"Why make it harder than it is?" Sally said.

"It doesn't have to be," Anna replied.

"I wasn't clean, you understand. I'm fucking around and I'm not clean. Who wants a baby like that?"

"There are good people who would take the baby no matter —"

"I wouldn't give it up!" Sally cut her off. "Once it was born, I wouldn't give it up. Would you?"

The question seemed to tear a strip off whatever resolve Anna had possessed when she had entered. Now her voice was hesitant, almost unsure. "What's growing inside you is life —"

"What about my life!" Sally shouted. "I'm a party girl and not some baby's mother."

"Sally."

"You know what your problem is? You don't know what it's like to be a woman. You skipped that part. Sure I'd keep it. I couldn't help but keep it. But I don't want it. I don't want a kid getting in the way of what I do. I fuck and I like fucking. Now get out! Take your holy goddamn self and get out!"

Peterson caught Anna in his arms as she cleared the door. He held her close and felt her tears on the side of his face. Not a word was said. Then he guided her back along the hallway and down the stairs. Still not a word, not until they were back in the car.

"She's right," Anna said.

Peterson listened.

"I have no idea what she's feeling. I hid myself until it was too late."

He wanted to pull her close, but he didn't dare.

"I go to bed feeling cracked down the middle," she said. "Humpty Dumpy. Half of me desperate to hold on to who I am, the other half prying my fingers loose."

"And you're afraid to fall."

Anna locked her hands together on her lap. "I'm trying to untie a knot with no ends. There's nothing to grab. Would you take me home?"

He drove her to her flat in Peggy Demming's house and walked her to the door.

"I'd like to see you again," he said.

Anna found a smile to give him. "Thank you for being there. For listening."

She turned to go inside, but Peterson just couldn't let her go, not just then.

"I don't have any friends," he whispered.

Anna left the door open for him to follow her in. She offered tea and he accepted. Neither said a word while the kettle came to the boil. Peterson sat at the kitchen table, playing his hands along the edge. As she was pouring she said, "We're not very alike, you know. I doubt we have much in common."

"I know."

She passed him a cup and let him touch her hand as he took it. "I keep busy," she said. "I try not to think about that night."

Peterson lifted the cup and watched her through the steam. "I have a runaway daughter in Vancouver. My wife died in a car accident. She was with another man. That was two years ago, and I'm still carrying it around. I lied when I said I don't have any friends. I have one, and maybe another. I'm moody, and there isn't any part of this job that doesn't eat the hell out of me. But I love doing it. And like you, I think about that girl day and night. I think about who she was. I can't help it. And I worry about her parents, about them not knowing what happened to their daughter. About her mother worrying."

Anna suddenly straightened, struck by a thought. "That's who should get it."

"Get what?"

"Her jacket. It was in the bar, on the floor. I picked it up."

Peterson was surprised. "You should have said something. You should have told me."

"I know." Anna looked nervous. "It was hers, and I wanted it. I just wanted . . . I needed it. I needed something to hold on to."

CHAPTER
TWENTY-FOUR

The elevator opened. All of a sudden the air filled with the smell of ammonia and formaldehyde. Stencilled red letters on a concrete wall pointed the way to the morgue.

Janet Crouse was sprawled in a chair at a cream-coloured metal desk, eating take-out, too tired to care how she looked. The autopsy of an elderly man bludgeoned in a suburban housing development had made for a long Sunday.

"This better be good, Peterson," she warned.

"You don't like surprises?"

"Not when I should be home with my family."

Peterson held up a white plastic bag. "This belonged to the girl from the Broken Promise, her jacket."

"Too small was it?"

Peterson let that one sail by. "The woman who was

helping me in the Broken Promise picked it up and took it home."

"She did what?"

"There's something in the pocket. Where can I dump it?"

"Here." Crouse wiped her hands on her green scrubs, pulled on latex gloves, and grabbed the plastic bag from Peterson. She pushed through double doors that bore an amateurish sign in a devilish script: The Cutting Room. Peterson followed her in and saw an uncovered body on a stainless steel table. Old, naked, scrubbed clean, bony. The room smelled of chemicals and something else. Something sickening.

He nodded at the body. "Who has that one?"

"Jamie Gould. He already has a suspect in custody, a twenty-two-year-old, second time around. Left his prints all over the two-by-four."

Crouse emptied the bag onto an empty metal table across from the one with the body. The jacket tumbled out in a tight ball. From one pocket, she pulled a pointed object.

"You playing games?" she asked.

Peterson shook his head. Crouse held up the find.

"A crucifix," she said.

Peterson shook his head. "Not quite. That's what Father Ronny called a Chi-Rho."

Crouse laid it on the metal table and pulled something else out of the same pocket.

"What's that?" Peterson asked.

"A flash drive," Crouse said, holding it up. "It's covered in blood." She dropped it into an evidence bag.

"Maybe the dead do talk," Peterson said.

"They talk to me all the time, only not with words. You

167

can have the drive after I do a blood analysis and take the prints. But I think we already know the results."

Peterson picked up the bag with the flash drive and took it into the outer office where he sat at Crouse's desk. He laid the bag down and stared at it. His fingers played a soft tattoo on the desktop.

Crouse tidied up the cutting room, stored the old man's body, and joined him.

"You looking a gift horse in the mouth?" she asked.

Peterson nodded. "It came unwrapped with no ribbon. Not quite the perfect gift."

Crouse turned toward the dressing room to change from her scrubs. "Murder never is."

Peterson raised his head. "Why the ritual? Why the rag doll? Why the candles? And the cloth letter on the floor of the church? The letter was in a pool of blood and circled with candles. What the hell was she doing?"

He took a deep breath and steepled his fingers under his chin.

"I know she was at Stoddard," he continued. "I know she was crazy and that crazy people do crazy things. But usually there's an explanation for why they're crazy and for the crazy things they do."

"Why was she at Stoddard?"

"Paranoid schizophrenia."

Crouse went back into the cutting room. She returned with the Chi-Rho in a plastic evidence bag.

"I think she used this on herself," she said. "A ragged incision, mid-pelvis and deep into her uterus." She shuddered. "She was cutting herself for some reason. Cutting herself up.

Or cutting something out." She thought for a moment then said, "Maybe she was cutting out what wasn't there."

Peterson cringed and closed his eyes. He remembered the girl's bloodstained jeans when she stood facing him in the Broken Promise. He remembered the way she drew the piece of glass across her wrist and opened an artery.

Crouse pulled a medical volume from a bookshelf — *Taber's Cyclopedic Medical Dictionary*. She thumbed through the pages until she found what she was looking for.

"Pseudocyesis," she read. "Phantom pregnancy. A condition in which a patient has nearly all of the signs and symptoms of pregnancy such as enlargement of breasts, weight gain, cessation of menses, morning sickness, but is not pregnant. Usually seen in women who are either very desirous of having children or desperate to avoid pregnancy. Treatment is usually psychiatric."

CHAPTER
TWENTY-FIVE

Monday morning, Danny and Peterson were sitting across from each other at the same small table in the same small undecorated meeting room. The space wasn't much wider than the arm span of a seven-footer, but it was longer than a coffin. It was close like a coffin too, stale and humming with the feisty smell of a late night with a bottle.

Peterson was irritable. Danny couldn't figure him out.

"You cracked a murder case, for Christ's sake," he said.

"Backed into it."

"You got lucky, so what? We don't step in it and half of them go unsolved. So what else is eating you?"

"She bolts from a john and ends up in church. Why? None of what the skinhead told us explains that. The black face on the statue, the candles, the rag doll, it doesn't explain any of that."

Danny frowned. "She wasn't playing with a full deck."

"That still explains nothing."

"Are you thinking whores at a private party in a hotshot neighbourhood end up dancing in church?"

"I don't know what I think. A loose end bothers me."

"We don't have time to tie bows," Danny said. "We've got another drug hit and an old man dead with somebody playing sniper." He tapped the Father Boutilier murder file on the desk. "And this one's out of our hands. We know who did it. We just don't know her name. And that makes it a problem for Missing Persons. You want the worst of it?"

"I heard already. The grapevine is a sieve."

"You know how happy that makes me," Danny said. "I could be working these cases on my own."

"You got that from Fultz?"

"No. I got it from the same source as you, only I listen better. You give Fultz a case of the ass, and your shrink just handed him another reason to stand you in the corner."

"The shrink told on me?"

"Looks that way," Danny said. "And that means they might not let us play together any more. I'll be working the drug hit and sniper shooting, and you'll be home in pyjamas, tying up loose ends all by yourself."

Peterson caught what Danny was driving at. "If it comes to that, we keep the link between the girl and the Posse to ourselves. And that goes for Teabag and Sylvester."

Danny arched his eyebrows. "I ain't talking. Are you talking?"

Peterson cracked a sleazy smile.

Danny grinned. "But the skinhead might."

Peterson shook his head. "He blows the whistle for

police brutality and the Posse will figure it out. He won't risk that."

"His girlfriend?"

Peterson shook his head again. "He'll stretch out the hit and run as far as it will go. She'll buy it."

"Then there's always the small matter of time," Danny said. "You're strung out to breaking, and I now have a drug hit in the Square and the Cove Road sniper."

Bernie knocked and walked in. "I have what you asked for," she said to Peterson.

Crouse blew through the door close behind. Danny made room for Bernie to sit, and Peterson slid over for Crouse.

"Who's first?" Peterson asked.

Crouse pulled rank. "It's just' what we had suspected yesterday. The girl's fingerprints match those on the flagstaff, the Chi-Rho, the ciborium, and a dozen more we found in the church. My educated guess is . . ." She beat a drum roll on the tabletop. "The girl, in the sacristy, with the flagstaff."

"Blood match?" Peterson asked.

"In a couple of days."

Danny pointed at Peterson. "Sourpuss wants to know why the ritual."

Crouse laced her fingers under her chin and flashed an angelic smile. "Thankfully, I skipped Criminal Behaviour 101."

Bernie slid the flash drive to the centre of the table.

"Eight minutes and twenty-seven seconds of bad video of five naked girls." She looked at Peterson. "Your girl from the Broken Promise was one of them. It's been heavily edited to shots of the girls stripping down to nothing, fondling themselves, and masturbating."

Peterson squeaked back his chair. "No other people? No johns?"

"That's what Billy thinks was edited out. And from the background, it looks like it all took place in the same location."

Crouse gathered her files and stood to go. "You three can look at dirty pictures. I have a hospital death to tend to."

Peterson watched the video of all five girls with his teeth clenched and fingers chiselling fibres from the editing console. Bernie sat on one side of him, her chin in her hands, and Billy sat on the other, playing the keyboard and mouse to stop and play, reverse and fast forward. Danny stood behind the others with his back against the wall, watching Peterson as much as the images. Each girl came on the screen and did her thing. They all looked the same: underage, awkward, stoned. Faking it for the camera. Posing the pouty way the models do in the wall murals in Victoria's Secret.

Peterson studied the face of the girl from the Broken Promise. He got Billy to freeze-frame her more often than the others. Robotic. Going through the motions. Doing what she was told.

"Let's print photos of all of them," Peterson said. "If we can ID any of them, maybe we can get them home."

The next time through, they studied the background. The camera revealed little more than the plum-coloured armchair that all five girls sat in to masturbate. It was in a corner of a room. One wall was painted a dark red, the other midnight blue. Part of a painting showed on one wall, out of focus.

"Not much to go on," Billy said. "They shot it so tight, we can't see a lot."

"Little things," Peterson said. "That right there!"

Billy hit pause on a shot of the painting. The camera had drifted off the girl to reveal more of it.

"Abstract art," Peterson said. "Geometric shapes. Bright colours."

"I like paintings that you know what it is," Billy said. "They paint this shit to screw up your mind trying to figure it out. Who has that kind of time?"

"You like simple," Bernie said.

"My mind's messed up enough working here. I go home, I have blank walls painted that tan colour. Nothing complicated. A calendar on the fridge. One chair, my laptop, and a TV."

"Don't get married," Danny said. "You wake up one day and wonder how the hell a department store got inside your house."

"Like you know," Bernie said.

"I dream about it," Danny said. "Nightmares!"

Peterson was studying the monitor, only half listening.

"These guys like it kinky weird," he said. "Surround themselves with it. The girls they choose. The place they take them to."

"Liking weird doesn't make them weird," Danny said. "Regular Joes and important people sometimes like it kinky too."

"You making a confession?" Peterson said.

Danny smiled. "Twenty-something on the job, five in

Vice. Weirdos don't have a monopoly on kink. Concentrate on weird and we could miss most of the potential suspects."

Peterson nodded. "What was it Sylvester said? Something about private parties and room service for important people."

Danny pointed at the monitor. "Abstract art has upscale written all over it."

"Provincial capital, university town, medical centre," Peterson said. "How many rich art-collecting mucky mucks you think there are?"

"How many of them like kinky sex?" Danny countered. "Problem is, not many in *Who's Who* make the pervert list."

"Maybe I should make the rounds," Peterson said. "Stir the pot and see what scum rises to the top."

Danny smiled his approval. "You won't get yourself any deeper than you already are."

The door opened and the deputy chief's secretary poked in her head. "You've been summoned," she said to Peterson.

CHAPTER
TWENTY-SIX

Fultz's office. Peterson was getting used to it. He stood, hands behind his back, trying for contrite but coming up with obstinate.

Fultz tossed aside the file he was reading. "If you were starving, you'd screw up a free meal. Your shrink thinks so too. He didn't say it like that, of course."

He reopened the file and thumbed for a document. "He thinks you need a rest. 'A relaxation from duty,' he called it. His report says you are, and I quote, 'unwilling to explore the pivotal problem and circumstances for your anger and psychological instability.'"

Fultz put away the document and addressed Peterson with as much frustration as disappointment. "You're chasing ghosts, Peterson. But from now on, you're chasing them on your own time. Suspension with pay. No time limit. And you either keep seeing Carmichael, or you're out on your ass. Your call."

Peterson stopped at his desk to grab his personal items. Case files covered the desktop. He opened the top drawer. Inside was an unopened package of notebooks, a micro-cassette recorder that his wife had given him and he had never used, a photograph of his wife and daughter in a silver frame. There was also the usual assortment of pens, pencils, paperclips, and the bits that accumulate over the years. He made a face and closed the drawer.

Danny met him as he turned to go. "And?" Danny asked.

"I'm a basket case," Peterson said.

"You needed Fultz to tell you that?"

"I needed myself to tell me that. Fultz just said indefinite suspension."

"We figured it was coming," Danny said.

Peterson looked over the large room buzzing with people. "That doesn't make it any easier."

Danny smiled sympathetically. "You might have the brass up your ass, but there's a few in this building who have your back."

Peterson shifted his eyes back to Danny. "I left my badge and gun on his desk," he said as he reached into his jacket pocket, pulling out the badge, "but I copped it when he took a phone call."

Danny wagged his finger. "That's not playing nice."

"You know what they say about nice?"

"Yeah," Danny said. "Bottom line is not getting caught. Let's hope we get away with getting you everything else."

"What's everything else?"

"Billy's running dubs of all the videos and Bernie's scanning files." Danny looked over to Fultz's office and saw the deputy chief locked in a phone conversation. "But there is something you should see before you get escorted from the building."

Peterson followed Danny into the editing room. He could tell by the greetings he received on the way that word of his suspension was travelling fast.

Billy looked up as they came in. "We got a flash frame," he said. "I was jogging the video back and forth when Bernie picked it up."

"What the hell's a flash frame?" Peterson asked.

"I'll show you."

Billy moved the cursor backward on the timeline and hit play. Peterson watched intently. Nothing.

"What the hell am I supposed to see?" Peterson said.

Billy moved the cursor again, this time farther back. Then he double-clicked the mouse and advanced the video in slow motion.

The girl they were watching was empty-eyed. Expressionless. Her mouth slowly opened and closed as though whispering something to herself. Then Peterson saw it. A flicker from a sudden change of scene.

"Flash frame," Billy said. He took the video back one frame at a time, so slow the girl's facial movements were almost imperceptible.

"There!" Billy said. "Whoever edited this left in one frame of video they wanted to cut."

"Explain." Peterson said.

"They have a master recording, and from that they edit out scenes or parts of scenes they don't want. In this case the edit isn't precise enough, and a single frame from a scene they cut stayed in."

"That's what I'm looking at?"

"A single frame, like a photograph."

"And you're saying there's more that's not on this flash drive?" Peterson asked.

"Yeah," Billy said. "This was cut from a hard drive with the master recording. Just looking at all the edits, you know, five girls, multiple sessions with the same girl, different times of day . . ."

"You can tell that?"

"Sure! Some shots with the same girls have daylight mixed in with the lights they used. Other shots don't. They were at it with these girls day and night. So we're talking a sizable file, probably stored on an external drive."

Peterson went back to the freeze frame, the image of a man with his back to camera humping one of the young girls from behind.

"She's grimacing, isn't she?" asked Peterson. The young girl had her head turned to camera and a pained look on her face.

"It's a wider shot than the others," Billy said. "We can see more of the room. The painting is soft focus, but you can make it out."

"There's a glass case with figurines," Bernie said, pointing.

"And check this out," Billy said. He isolated the section of the screen that showed the man's left shoulder. Then he played the keyboard to enlarge the image.

"A tattoo," Peterson said.

"Yeah," Billy said. "An animal."

"Look at the curved horns." Bernie traced what was clearly the head of an animal with thick rounded horns. "It's a ram. Look at the horns. Here's a guy that's full of himself."

Peterson took a closer look at the monitor then leaned back and swivelled his chair to face Danny. "You know who the girl is?"

Danny flattened his hands against the back wall. "Yeah."

Bernie and Billy now focused on the young girl's face. They recognized her too: the girl from the Broken Promise.

CHAPTER
TWENTY-SEVEN

Peterson drove to the home of a former cop on the drug squad who had been dismissed for working undercover with his hand open. His name was Jesse Overton. He lived outside the city in a bedroom community where bungalows crowded up against bungalows in a maze of courts, circles, drives, and cul-de-sacs, a tract development that the Canadian Housing Design Council once identified as the national example of how not to develop a community.

Overton's house was an L-shaped bungalow with blue vinyl siding, surrounded by a manicured front lawn and a stone wall that was losing the battle against the heaving of winter frost. He was in the backyard stringing up a clothesline.

Overton looked up and saw Peterson and went right on looping the clothesline around a metal pulley. He had a thin, stern face. Late thirties. A jogger's body. Wearing greasy, grey coveralls with a heavy beige sweater underneath.

"You slumming it," he said, without giving Peterson the benefit of eye contact.

"Checking out life on the outside," Peterson said and lifted the clothesline to make it easier for Overton to string the pulley.

"Yeah, I heard you fell off a tightrope."

"Word travels fast."

"Not so fast that I don't hear it."

"What else you hearing?"

Overton stopped with the clothesline and gave Peterson a tight look. "Depends. Some I hear real good, and some I go stone deaf. What are you after?"

Peterson crowded him a little. "A gang called the Posse. Involved in local and long-distance whoring."

Overton pointed at two lawn chairs under a spindly birch struggling to survive in this mostly treeless neighbourhood. The chairs were out of earshot of the neighbouring houses. Overton sat hunched over, his elbows on his knees. Peterson leaned back and stretched his legs.

"What's in it for me?" Overton asked without looking Peterson's way.

"Civic duty," Peterson said.

Overton sucked through his teeth. "I'll tell you what. I've been set adrift for a year and a half. No excuses. I know what I did. Nothing more than a lot of others and what goes up the chain of command, but what the fuck, right? I mean, take a look around. Modest house in a low-rent neighbourhood. I wasn't skimming off the top like some I know. But I'm the one that gets tagged with persona non grata."

Overton swept his eyes over the backyard, slyly looking for someone listening in. A habit from his days on the street.

"I saw you park," he said, "walk up the driveway, and I thought, here it comes, the all for one and one for all bullshit. I've been expecting it. I figured sooner or later someone downtown would want to know what I know. Surprised it took so long. Then again, not too surprised."

Overton stood up, his shoulders braced and his jaw set and determined. He laced and unlaced his fingers.

"I'll tell you what I want," he said. "I want the monkey off my back when it comes to looking for work. I want the chart smudged up a bit. You don't have to clean it so I come off like some fucking choir boy, but enough so I can get a job, doing what I know how to do. I'm not a thief, Peterson. I took sweetener like everybody else sniffing for coffee grounds. I want to work security. That's not too much to ask is it?"

Peterson shook his head. "I can promise everything you want, but I can't keep it. I got Fultz so far up my ass I'm going blind. I'm suspended until I get my head together. How far do you think that's going to go?"

Peterson stood and offered Overton his hand. "I can't pay, and you can't deliver. No hard feelings."

Overton shook his hand. "Does this have to do with your daughter?"

Peterson didn't answer, letting his silence play the angle. He turned to go.

"Sit down," Overton ordered. "I'll tell you what I know."

They sat as before, Overton talking to the ground at his feet and Peterson leaning back and listening.

"The Posse is a loose arrangement. Small groups,

independent. And tied in with bikers in Ontario and Quebec. Down here, one man calls the shots."

"Name?"

"Tooka. He's smart. A college boy but street talks when he needs to. Cool and fucking ruthless. Hot temper that doesn't show. He gets even fast. Does nothing himself. He's careful that nothing directly ties back to him. We went for him a couple of times and came up empty. He has firewalls between himself and what happens on the street. And he dresses like a bank exec. Same morals, too. Has a dress code for his soldiers: no baggy pants hanging off their asses and no hoodies. Everything under the radar. And no drugs. That's the key. That's what keeps them flying low."

"Tooka have a last name?"

"Like he needs one. You want a beer?"

Peterson nodded, and Overton went into the house and came back with two Keith's. He picked up where he left off.

"Drugs are big money and big risk. We make a drug bust and the drugs are evidence, easy to produce at a trial. Trafficking women is safer. Nobody really fucking cares. Most of the big shots go to peeler bars and lap dances, here, Ottawa, Toronto, and that includes judges, lawyers, and our sainted elected officials. That's why nothing gets done about running girls or busting johns. The movers and shakers like what they see shedding their clothes on stage, and they like the young ass they get off the corner or in the backroom of a strip joint."

Overton took a big swallow and then a big breath. Peterson hadn't touched his beer.

"We can't convict a pimp even if a girl turns on him," Overton said. "No evidence. It's a year before the case goes to court and by that time the girl is missing in action or no longer willing to testify."

He took another big swallow. This time Peterson followed suit. Overton continued.

"That's why Tooka turned the Posse off drugs. They net the girls here, break them in, and ship them to the strip clubs and whorehouses in Montreal, southern Ontario, and out west. The older ones they trade off to local pimps. They use long haul trailers to take them back and forth. A rotation. Nobody gets bored. And they're close with the biker boys up there. Protection and a distribution network to the clubs and whorehouses. Simple and safe as total fucking abstinence."

Peterson let it sink in before saying anything. He took a few sips of beer then said, "They have a favourite club in town?"

"The Posse used to deal dope out of the Rendezvous. That's what got me looking in the first place. Now it's just girls. Tooka has a stake. My guess is the partners are just paperboys. He works out of the Flame, a late-night bar off the Strip. Like I said, he's careful. Plays nothing close to home."

"What about private dances? Top secret? Men that like them just out of the cradle?"

Overton drained his beer. He waited a long time before answering, rolling the bottle between his hands all the while. "Very private. Big shots."

"They above the law?"

"From what I heard, they make the law." Overton glanced around his backyard again. "A few like them young and unused. We're talking kids. Tooka supplies."

"You have details?"

"Nothing definite. Taxi squad. Home delivery. Loosey goosey so nothing feeds back. Drugs and sex. The drugs are what caught it on the radar. Not the johns, they're home clean and stay clean. It's the girls they keep high, so they can use them any way they want. Raunchy. Cruel. I never got close enough to know more. Didn't care. Whores doing drugs wasn't what I was after. You know the story in this business — whores don't count. One gets out of line, she gets buried somewhere between here and Manitoba. No body. Half-assed investigation. Just another whore the boys in blue can't find."

"Names?"

"Never asked. Like I said, I didn't care. I'm talking way more than I wanted."

"Did you report on this?" Peterson stood to go.

Overton almost laughed. "Turn over little stones, and nobody gives a shit. Look under big ones, and you start looking over your shoulder. I had enough worries without creating new ones."

Overton walked Peterson back to his car. Peterson climbed in and Overton leaned through the open window.

"Don't poke the Posse without a halo," he said.

"They overlooked that when they suspended me."

"A badge isn't body armour. It may get you in, but you'll have a fuck of a time getting out."

Peterson offered his hand and Overton took it.

"Thanks," Peterson said.

Overton stayed beside the car. "After forty-eight hours the girls won't shit without Tooka saying so. Get one early, and you have a chance. I hear anything, I'll let you know."

"Thanks again."

"Thank my nine-year-old daughter. I worry like hell because I know more than I should. But I'll tell you this — and I'm not telling you what to do — anyone ever gets their hooks into her, and I'm loading up a scoped Springfield 30-06 and picking them off one at a time."

Overton nodded sharply, turned, and went back to stringing the clothesline. Peterson watched him for a moment or two before he drove off. He'd travelled a few blocks when he noticed a dark sedan following him. He recognized it as department issue and pulled over to let the car draw alongside.

Tommy Amiro was at the wheel; Andy Miles was riding shotgun. The passenger-side window went down and Miles leaned out. Peterson lowered his.

Outside the station, Miles had a habit of spitting through his teeth and he did so now, spraying the back tire of Peterson's Jetta.

"Hey, Peterson, funny thing finding you out here holding hands with a scumbag," Miles said. There was no warmth in his smile.

"You tailing me?"

Miles feigned innocence. "Why would I be doing that?"

"I don't know," Peterson said. "You're the one who can't juggle more than one ball at a time, so I figure you have nothing to do."

"At least I'm doing nothing on the company's clock and not ragging my ass playing at private eye."

"Who says I'm doing that?"

"Rumour."

"The thing about Mr. Rumour," Peterson said, "is he

gets it wrong ninety percent of the time. But then again, that's pretty much how you do police work."

Miles faked a laugh then leaned farther out the window and patted Peterson's arm. His voice fell so what he said was between him and Peterson. "Why don't you just sit on your hands for a while, collect your check, and tell your shrink how you wet the bed? Better yet, go somewhere. Sort things out and let the world go by."

Peterson slowly removed Miles's hand from his arm. "I'll think about it."

"I'm telling you for your own good," Miles said and raised his window.

Tommy Amiro shifted into gear and drove off. Peterson watched them go.

CHAPTER
TWENTY-EIGHT

Bony set the time and place: two that afternoon at the Drop Zone. He had information and something for Peterson to see. He had sounded jumpy, insisting he would get across the harbour and along the waterfront to the condemned dockside warehouse on his own.

He was peeking between the broken boards that covered the doorway when Peterson arrived. Peterson was ten minutes late and Bony was itchy from having to wait.

"I stopped for refreshments," Peterson said and offered Bony a pint. Bony took a deep swallow then held the bottle up to the light and saw none but the heel was left.

"Hitting it hard," Bony said.

Peterson faced it off. "It files down the edge."

"Right now, mine needs filing." Bony drained the pint and tossed it among the rubble. Peterson raised his eyes.

"I scratched on something that don't like being scratched." Bony said. He waved Peterson to follow him.

Daylight through the smashed windows eased the stress of Peterson's last nighttime visit. They passed the body-shaped pile of burlap and the graffiti-covered brick wall. Peterson couldn't help looking for and finding his daughter's angry scribble.

"I talked to a hooker all strung out," Bony said as they stepped over damp mattresses and broken boards. "Bouncing off the walls at Gainer's, doing one line after another and backing them up with a needle. We're talking four o'clock in the afternoon, and she's going on the street for the hurry-ups on their way home. A kid for fuck's sake." He turned to face Peterson. "You know what I'm talking about."

Peterson winced and let it go.

"So I followed her to see if I could help. She thinks I'm a john and cuts up an alley to this junked out Chevy in some backyard."

They walked through the brick archway where the heavy sliding door had slipped its rollers and lay on the floor.

"She's pissing her pants, Peterson. Leaning against the Chevy and pissing her pants. She can't be twenty years old and stoned so bad, so fucked up."

They entered the long hallway with the sagging boards underfoot. Daylight streamed through the open door at the far end. Bony trod carefully, and Peterson did the same.

"I stayed with her an hour at least. Sat her in the car. Dreamland conversation. Making no sense. Then she said something that made me listen. She said, 'Tee fie,' and then a lot of other shit I didn't understand, until she blurted some craziness about the Drop Zone. She was talking blood, Peterson, and about another girl seeing it and telling her about it."

Bony stopped at the open door, the one Peterson had shouldered open several nights before. "I should've stuck to listening," Bony said, "but I didn't. I pressed her. And now someone knows I asked one question too many."

He led Peterson into the massive room with the collapsed back wall that opened up a ragged view of the harbour mouth. The daylight was intense. They rounded the pile of mortar Peterson had sat on in the dark, then around a mound of rubble.

Bony pointed to an inside wall where Peterson saw large yellow spray-painted letters: T-Fi.

Peterson stared at the words. "It wasn't here that night," he insisted. He thought for a moment. "Or I was too drunk to see it."

"Or too caught up with your own memories about this place."

Peterson gave the truth a side-glance then looked back at the letters. "The girl, what was her name?"

"Asking names is your job."

"I should talk to her."

"Yeah," Bony said, "like the working girls all stand in line to bleed their hearts out to you. You know better than that. You'll get nothing, and you'll get someone hurt. And that someone could be me. Especially if someone saw me talking to her. Take what I gave you and be happy." He pointed at the yellow letters. "Besides, you got what the caller wanted you to get."

Peterson rubbed his face and head. It took him a few minutes to accept Bony's silence on who the girl was. It went with their arrangement. Then he said, "What about you?"

"Uncomfortable feeling," Bony said. "Not much more than that, but it has me thinking about slipping away for a little bit."

"How long?"

"Long enough."

Peterson leaned back and covered his ears as though that would keep the cell phone from vibrating through every nerve in his body. He was sitting in his car in an underground parking lot. Windows up, car running. Eyes wide but unfocused.

"I'm not answering," he said to the empty car. "Katy stop! Please stop!"

The phone kept ringing. Then it stopped. A moment later it started ringing again. Peterson lowered his hands from his ears and reached down between his feet to retrieve the phone from where he had dropped it. "Katy," he said. No response. He refused to click open the Skype image.

Then he heard the disconnect and breathed out slowly. It was over.

Not long afterward, Danny pulled into the parking lot and parked in an empty space nearby. He sat for a moment then climbed from his car and into Peterson's.

"Bernie ran T-Fi through Missing Persons and drew a blank," Danny said. "If the girl ran away and holed up in the Drop Zone, nobody reported it and she never caught enough attention to get pinched."

"Hard to believe."

"Nothing's hard to believe," Danny scoffed. He popped open the glove box and pulled out a pint of Johnnie Walker. He held it up. "Case in point."

"Don't start."

"You know what you're doing to yourself?"

"I bought it yesterday," Peterson said.

Danny checked the seal then pursed his lower lip and nodded. "I'm impressed. But not that impressed. Keep it sealed for six months and then you can brag." He returned the pint to the glove box.

Peterson shrugged. "You check on Miles?"

Danny nodded. "From what I heard, he wasn't tailing you. Overton gets a close watch now and again, usually before a drug bust is going down, and you just happened to drive into the radar. Surveillance ran your licence, made a call, and Miles responded. He says he was just busting your chops."

"You believe it?"

"Not for a New York second." Danny said. "I don't know what it is, but something's not right."

CHAPTER
TWENTY-NINE

"Auld Lang Syne" woke Peterson from a drunken sleep. He rolled off his couch to the floor to find it, his arm knocking aside the now-empty pint from the glove box and half a dozen cans of beer. No caller ID. He checked his watch: 5 a.m. He answered anyway. It was Overton.

"I think I got what you're looking for," Overton said. "You do breakfast?"

"Where?"

"I got a job interview downtown."

"Reggie's?'

"In an hour."

Overton was waiting in a booth toward the rear of Reggie's Place. Six o'clock and the diner was packed with young lawyers and business execs getting a head start to impress.

Peterson waved to the counter girl on his way by. A thirty-something he had once fixed a ticket for. He slid into the booth. The waitress with a pot of coffee was not far behind. Overton ordered eggs and bacon. Peterson asked for toast.

"Your partner lined this up for me," Overton said. "I gather on your say-so."

Peterson sipped the coffee. "The job works out, everybody's happy."

Overton spread his elbows on the table. "A twenty-year-old at the Rendezvous wants out. One of the Posse's. Dancing one night. Turning tricks at the Port City Motor Inn the next. Three months in the game, and she's pregnant. She wants to keep the baby."

"Catholic?"

"Love. She knows the father, or thinks she does. A lover boy, the only one she lets ride bareback. They're making plans."

"Testify?"

"Who knows? But she's a source. String her out for as long as you can, at least until her belly shows. But talking won't be easy. Dribs and drabs. Five minutes at a time with her on your lap. Unless you want a half-hour at the Motor Inn, but that gets real chancy. Her dance name is Honey. I don't think even her boyfriend knows her real one."

Breakfast arrived. Overton dug in. Peterson nibbled.

"It's none of my business," Overton said, pointing his fork at Peterson's order of toast, "but I know the signs."

Peterson looked over his coffee. "It helps me sleep."

"And then you wake up and wish you hadn't," Overton said.

"I haven't reached that yet."

"Keep pounding the bottle and you will."

Overton wiped egg yolk with his toast. Peterson held down what he had eaten.

"Take a few days or a week to become a regular," Overton said. "Don't stand out, but don't avoid people. Make a move when you feel it's right."

CHAPTER
THIRTY

The Rendezvous was a knot of shadow splayed around a stage dripping in coloured lights. A stand-up bar lined the back wall, and behind it was a blonde bartender who might as well have gone topless for all she wore. She mixed drinks with an eye to the house, never a full shot, not even for the regulars, and she knew the trick of floating a drop of booze on top for the drunks so liquored-up the smell of alcohol was enough to fool them.

The servers were all skimpily dressed women, some middle-aged and past caring who touched what and where. Others were barely drinking age, unloved, unschooled, and locked into service by hard times or a habit they couldn't shake.

The bouncer at the door was a bruiser with a Captain

Hook moustache and smile, and the two thugs guarding the stage wore their rap sheets on their slung-jawed faces.

Peterson squeezed his big frame past a dozen tables to sit in the anonymous middle. He wore a dark blue suit, light blue shirt, and no tie, like many of the other out-of-towners here to get their nuts off without bringing something home to mama. Three of these men had brought dates. Peterson figured they must be girlfriends or wives, tag-alongs on a business trip. From the way they were egging their men to drop forty bucks on a lap dance in the backroom, they were probably hoping to horny up their men for a good time back at the Holiday Inn.

This was Peterson's fifth night in a row at the Rendezvous. He could nod to the regulars, the beer-nursers hardening under the tables, watching one dancer after another without changing the intensity of their gaze. They came in sport shirts and golf shirts, and all seemed to wear their hair gelled and uncombed.

On the first night, Peterson had tried to pick out Lover Boy, the guy who had gotten Honey pregnant, and narrowed the choice to three: a twenty-something with spiky hair and a hangdog face sitting alone near the stage; another of the same age with curly blond hair standing at the back and holding up the bar; and a third in his thirties, a wimpy-looking guy who wore a tortured face whenever Honey took to the stage to strip.

One of them didn't show on the second night, the night Honey was over at the Port City Motor Inn turning tricks. But he was back the third night, curly blond hair and standing at the bar.

Curly Hair was at the bar now, and Peterson was about to relocate from the anonymous middle to stand beside him for a chat when he overheard one of the three men with dates say something about a local hockey star. Peterson sensed an opening that would cover off his first visit to the lap-dance room, in case anyone was giving him even the slightest bit of attention. And that had him making a move, leaning in with his own two cents on the local hockey star. He and the guy went back and forth about hockey and then the guy, seeing Peterson was alone, invited him to join their party. Peterson did. Introducing themselves, first names only. Tom, Dick, and Harry for all Peterson cared. And he cared just as little about the names of the women. He called himself Fred and said he had just moved down from Chatham, Ontario. Divorced.

The conversation turned to the dancer on stage, and Peterson let them talk, their voices rising above the heavy beat from a stack of woofers. He told the group he was waiting for a particular dancer, a petite brunette with thick ankles and no sense of rhythm. She was young, awkward, and almost embarrassed at stripping in front of a house full of men.

When she finally walked on stage, Peterson got antsy, saying out loud that this one turned his crank. The group immediately got on his case about liking them young, and then two of the women, one with big earrings and the other with a big mouth, goaded him into taking the young dancer to the backroom for a lap dance. Peterson protested for a while and then gave in, as though happy to be forced into doing what he really wanted to do.

When the young dancer dropped her thong with a

half-hearted wiggle, he turned off his cell phone and, like a teen on his first date, went to the Jezebel cashier beside the bar and laid down two twenties for a five-minute lap dance with Honey.

The rules were simple: arms straight down at his sides, no touching, and no kissing.

Peterson entered the tiny backroom and swept his eyes through the deep shadows for cameras. No camera, but that had him figuring someone had an ear to the door. A lava lamp on a small table was the only light, and this bubbled a red glow over the kitchen chair placed dead centre. He pulled a photo from his pocket, then sat and waited for Honey to appear.

Music with a pulsing beat started from two tinny-sounding ceiling speakers. Then Honey came through the door with a lopsided smile. She straddled his lap and stared at him. Glassy eyes. Brain geared down. Hips that revved without pleasure. Arms held above her head and waving. The skid lines in her arms were easy for him to see. Her gaze drifted off his face and into the shadows that played along the back wall.

He hardened against his will. Shamed himself.

"It's not why I'm here," he whispered. "I want to talk."

"Talk?"

Honey kept grinding, her rhythm set on automatic.

He raised the photo of the girl from the Broken Promise into her line of sight. She stopped mid-grind. Her eyes went to the door.

"You know her, don't you?" he whispered.

Honey just stared at the door. Swallowed hard. Didn't answer. He could see cracks in the heavy makeup on her face.

He had planned how he would play his cards, and now he played what he thought was an ace.

"I can help you. I can get you out of here. Contact your parents if you want me to."

Fear clipped a breath and started her eyes darting.

Peterson realized he had moved too fast and set off the alarm bells the pimps had drilled into her head. "It's all right. Believe me, it's all right."

She slowly looked back at the photo. Nodded. She knew the girl.

He sensed the clock ticking down the time he had left. He took a chance. "Tell me about her. Please."

"Who are you?" Honey's voice was strained. Her body trembled.

"Someone that cares about her."

"Her father?"

Peterson nodded, and the gesture tore a strip off his heart. His eyes welled, and Honey saw it.

"She didn't dance. She was too young, and they wouldn't risk it," she said.

"What did they do with her?" He returned the photo to his jacket pocket.

Honey didn't answer. She looked again at the closed door and her face tightened. Then she gave Peterson a nervous nod. "I knew her name. We weren't supposed to tell. Just numbers, that's what we are. She talked crazy sometimes, but we all do."

Peterson nodded as though he too knew the girl's name. "Her mother named her," he said. That was another ace he hoped would make a difference. It did.

"Molly was different, but I liked her. She was so young,

and they whored her out with a few other young ones." She suddenly realized what she was saying, and her head swivelled back to the door. "Oh my god, they'll hurt me!"

She started off his lap and Peterson pulled her back. "You have to sit right here!"

She settled back on his lap, trembling. Looked at him. He smiled warmly, and she tried for one but failed.

"I can help you," he said, pressing a piece of paper into her hand. It had his personal cell number and nothing else. "I can get you out of here. I'll be back. I promise."

Honey shook her head, her eyes wide in fear. The lava lamp bubbled its grim red glow over her face. The shadows stirred, tightening the space around them.

"It's all right," he whispered. "It's all right. Just tell me what happened to Molly."

Honey covered her mouth. Then she lowered her hand to her chin. "Her friend didn't come, and she went nuts. Climbing the walls."

Peterson was about to ask what friend, when his cop sense warned him to get it done. "Grind on me!" he ordered.

Honey also sensed the time. She looked at the door again.

"She never came back," she said and rotated her hips slowly, pressing herself onto him. As the Jezebel opened the door, she leaned forward and whispered, "My name's Debbie Wilson, Mississauga."

✦

Peterson returned to his seat in the anonymous middle, forcing a smile for the sake of the couples, who were grinning at the pleasure they thought he was feeling. He ordered a beer from a server who had the wild look of having just done a line. The woman on his right, the one with the big mouth, gripped his bicep and asked in a voice even the bouncer could hear, "Still hard?"

He nursed the beer, waiting until Honey was back on stage. Then he leaned forward in his chair as though he knew more about her dance routine than anyone else in the place. When she left the stage, he excused himself from the group and split.

The following night Peterson staked out a corner in the hospital district. By one o'clock Sylvester was a no-show. He then swung over to the Port City Motor Inn and took up a vantage point across the street in the parking lot of a strip mall. It took him less than a couple of hours to read the operation the Posse had going at the motel: three rooms, two girls to a room, taking turns, a half-hour in the sack and a half-hour to wash up, needle up, or smoke a joint. Steady traffic. Each room turning over a hundred, maybe two hundred bucks an hour.

He used binoculars to ID the johns and pegged the boyfriend as the guy Honey saw out the door and kissed goodbye. Same guy as in the bar: Curly Hair. Slouchy in checked shirt and jeans, he crossed the parking lot to a black Ford pickup. Peterson got the licence number as it drove off.

He saw something else: A dark blue SUV with two dudes in front and one in back fired up and followed the Ford out of the motel parking lot. Less than an hour later Curly Hair returned, but not for a second helping. This time he drove behind the motel and nosed the pickup out from the far side, just enough for him to watch the three doors to the sugar shack. The SUV slipped back into the same parking space near the front office and killed the engine. The three-some remained in the SUV.

Peterson hung in there for another hour and a half, then went home, where he sat outdoors in a lawn chair, staring at the stars, not wanting to go inside.

The following night, Peterson looked for Curly Hair at the Rendezvous. He was standing at the bar. This time Peterson had a name to go with the hair: Darryl Palmer, son of an eastern shore fisherman. He had two arrests: drunk driving and a bar fight that caught him a charge of aggravated assault.

Peterson watched Palmer look around the room, peeking into the shadows as though he was looking for someone. Peterson figured Honey had told Palmer about the man who had refused the lap dance and had promised to get her out of this business, and Palmer was now searching the Rendezvous for him.

Honey came on stage and Palmer turned his attention to her. She was wobbly as she danced, or tried, holding the pole for support and grinding on it as part of her routine. Her eyes were empty and her face bleak. She slid down the pole to her knees and struggled to get up. Stoned out of her mind. Awkwardly peeling off what little she had on.

She would be twenty years old in two weeks, according to the background check Danny had run on her. Stripping and screwing and getting high, and now she was pregnant by a john she loved and desperate to get out. How? She was already in too deep to do anything on her own.

Peterson watched her, wondering why he still wanted to help her. He doubted she could tell him more about Molly than she already had. So why did he feel he had to stick around and chance blowing his cover and wind up no closer to the Posse than before he had started? Why throw a rope to someone who may already be drowned?

He knew why. He had silent cell phone calls to remind him.

He knew how he could do it. He just had to flash his badge in here or at Port City Motor Inn and take her into custody. That would be the easy part. The hard part would be what to do with her once he had her out. Bring her home to her parents in Mississauga, and the Posse would find her. Help her run off with her boyfriend, if he really wanted her, and the Posse would track her down, not to bring her back but to shut her mouth.

Peterson looked up from toying with a coaster to see her naked now and just standing on stage, staring into the coloured lights, unblinking, and making no attempt to dance. Her mind lost between a morning's promise and no tomorrow. A little girl on a backyard swing, Debbie Wilson, the girl someone had flensed of innocence and turned into a whore. It cracked his spirit to think of it.

Honey backed off stage as another girl danced into the pulsating lights and to a different beat, one that groaned with a sleazy horniness that she intensified with flashy moves across the stage and up the pole. She hung there for a moment then slid down.

Then someone was at Peterson's shoulder, talking in his

ear. "She won't be lap dancing tonight. Too much gas in the tank."

Peterson turned to a forty-something server leaning over, giving him a free show down her blouse.

"Might as well horny up on someone else," she said.

"You have someone in mind?"

She winked at him.

Peterson cracked a smile. "I don't do much more than look, and I already got an eyeful." He got up to leave. "Besides, I'm a one-woman man."

"You must be the one and only," she replied, lifting her tray of beer and turning to serve a nearby table.

Peterson navigated through a full house to the exit, scanning the place. Darryl Palmer was not at the bar.

CHAPTER
THIRTY-ONE

Palmer stood beside the black F-150 and came on hard as Peterson exited the Rendezvous. His hands hung at his sides, fingers opening and closing, shoulders hunched.

Peterson sized him up in a second — a village punk on the muscle, the kind of guy that gets his balls from a bottle. Ten feet from Peterson's Jetta, the punk had words.

"You hustling my girl?" The question came out like a challenge.

Peterson reached his car and turned. He shifted his weight to his back foot. "Who's asking?"

A dumb look filled Palmer's face, as though the question had introduced a new idea into a head that only had room for one. Peterson took it back. "Don't answer. I know who you are. Darryl Palmer, a half-ass from the eastern shore. Can't fish, can't cut bait. So what lie you stringing her?"

Palmer stopped three feet away and raised his fists. This question had him perplexed and his brain in overdrive.

Peterson smiled, egging him on. "It must get crowded in that little brain of yours."

Palmer lunged forward, off balance just long enough for Peterson to pivot out of the way and brace his hands against Palmer's shoulder and the small of his back. Then Peterson drove his weight forward and slammed Palmer into the Jetta and held him there. He kicked Palmer's legs wide apart.

"You good at anything?" Peterson asked, angling his head so Palmer could see the smile on his face. "If you're done fighting, we can talk."

Palmer ground his teeth.

"Or I could rabbit you in the kidneys," Peterson said, "and leave you for the bouncer to find. It's up to you, kid. One way or the other, I'm home before bedtime."

Palmer struggled a bit more then settled down.

"We talking yet?" Peterson asked.

Palmer nodded.

"Good. Talking's always the better part of valour."

Peterson guided Palmer to the black pickup and they both climbed in.

"I'll answer your questions," Peterson said. "No hustle. Not on my part. How about you?"

Palmer didn't answer.

Peterson shrugged. "All right, let's try this on. You park out of sight at the Port City Motor Inn and count johns through the swinging door. Adding up the take. A hundred bills an hour. Six to eight hours a night. Beats the hell out of fishing. Price of fish falls, her value goes up. And what's your cost? Sweet nothings and a belly full of little Daryll. Am I getting some of it right?"

Palmer stared through the windshield. "That's not how it is."

"Then tell me what I'm not seeing."

Palmer turned to Peterson. "Why should I tell you anything? Who the hell are you?"

"Think of me as pain relief," Peterson said. "I'm the guy that keeps you from getting her ass in a sling and your chops on the floor."

"You a cop?"

"No."

"She thought you were a cop."

"I'm a do-gooder. Sir Lancelot to damsels in distress. Now what are you playing at?"

"I'm playing at nothing."

"You got her pregnant."

Palmer frowned, and Peterson read it as a favourable sign. Most would be off like a shot before the girl's finished telling them, leaving mother and child in their dust.

"I thought we could go away together," Palmer said. "Not far. But far enough." He glanced over the parking lot, searching for the right words. "I know what she is, but . . . She won't go anyhow."

"Scared?"

He nodded.

"Smart girl."

Palmer looked straight at Peterson. "I can take care of her!"

"Like you took care of me?"

Palmer looked away.

"You're in over your head," Peterson said. "You run with her and it's non-stop hide and seek. And they'll find you. You can bet your ass they'll find you."

"I got a camp they won't find!"

"And you go there with your friends who wouldn't say a word even if someone was breaking their legs."

Palmer frowned.

"That's the problem," Peterson said. "So leave it alone."

"Then what?" Palmer thrust out his chin indignantly. "A few days, a week, and she won't be here anymore."

"She tell you that?"

Palmer nodded.

Peterson remembered Overton telling him the Posse kept the girls on the move.

"I won't see her," Palmer said. "She won't be back. She said once she gets big, they'll mess her up."

Worse than that, Peterson thought. They'll force an abortion whether she's past term or not. Risk her life. But what do they care?

"So you're making plans," Peterson said.

"She told me to see if the cop would do what he said. She fucking believed you would help."

"But you're the jealous type. Mugging me in a parking lot was your way of asking. Then you'd go back and tell her I was nothing but bullshit and make-believe."

Palmer gripped the steering wheel with both hands. "You know how many guys —?"

"Yeah, I know how many guys. But there's no love if you keep count. Eats you from the inside out."

"It's eating me now!"

210

"It'll get worse." Peterson opened the passenger door. "There's no half way. Forgive everything or forgive nothing. And the guy that can forgive everything is a better man than me. Are you ready for that?"

Palmer said nothing.

"Take heart, kid," Peterson said. "None of us are. My advice? Walk away. Get on your father's boat and go fishing."

Peterson climbed from the pickup and walked to his car.

Palmer rolled down the window. "I'm asking," he said. "How can you help?"

Peterson walked back to the pickup. "You know her real name?"

"Debbie."

Peterson pulled a pad and pencil from his jacket pocket and wrote a number. "Keep an eye on Debbie, day and night. You get a hint they're moving out, call me. Otherwise, do nothing else. Leave it with me."

CHAPTER
THIRTY-TWO

Peterson sat in his parked car a half-block away from the corner in the hospital district that Sylvester had identified. For the umpteenth time, he tried to think of a place he could tuck Debbie and Darryl away for safe keeping. So far he had nothing, which was also what his stakeout had come up with. He had been warming his ass in the car for the past two nights, waiting for Sylvester or someone else to drop a girl off.

Between eight and eleven, the traffic had been the usual comings and goings in the hospital complex and university campus. Most pedestrians were hospital staff and visitors, and after eleven they were university students stumbling back to residence after doing the bar scene downtown.

He had long ago forgotten the boredom and back stiffening discomfort of a stakeout, drinking oily coffee and feasting on takeout. He left the pint untouched in the glove compartment. He completed half of the daily crossword before giving up on a three-letter word for mouth, starting with G. Then he read the newspaper for the second time and relieved himself in an empty coffee cup.

Shortly after midnight, a brown sedan stopped at the intersection. A teenage girl got out, dressed in skintight jeans and a jean jacket, much like what Molly had been wearing. This girl offered no goodbye to the driver, not even a backward glance. She walked toward the university campus.

Peterson waited for the driver to drive off, and in the harsh white of an LED streetlight got a good look at him. It was Sylvester, his skinhead hidden under a ball cap worn backward. Peterson looked for anyone else watching the girl. Seeing no one, he hopped from his car and followed her, sticking to the opposite side of the street.

She turned left at the first side street and walked under tall maple and beech trees, past two- and three-storey flats rented to students. She turned left again and then made a quick right onto another side street, this one lined with upscale homes belonging to university faculty and the descendents of the city's founding families. This was the elegant, understated section of the wealthy south end, where old money only whispered extravagance, unlike the loud opulence of the homes farther south. She stopped under a streetlight to check something written on a piece of paper — an address, Peterson surmised. In the glow, he could see the girl was fourteen, maybe fifteen, and that no attempt had been made to age her jailbait look.

She shoved the paper in her coat pocket, looked at the

address on the house beside her, and continued along the street. She reached the next corner and turned right.

That move didn't add up. Wrong address? Wrong street? Too stoned to know where the hell she was going or where she was? It was too hit-and-miss, too ragged an operation from what Overton had said about Tooka. No. Something was up.

Peterson stopped to listen for footsteps coming up behind or on the other side of the street. He dialed in a distant siren and the groan and bang of rail cars being shunted across the harbour. He stretched his senses to reach beyond the noise of night for someone he couldn't hear or see. There was nothing but an uncomfortable stillness.

He walked on. At the corner he hugged the houses to keep out of the glow of streetlights. He picked her up half a block away, slipping in and out of shadows that seemed darker beneath the thick canopy of trees. She walked slower now. Then she jaywalked to his side of the street and started toward him. Twenty metres away she stopped and stared at him. He stopped and stared back. Then he sensed someone behind him.

The first blow caught him across his shoulder blades. It sent him to his hands and knees. Stunned. The second one slammed into his ribs, and the third into the small of his back straight through to his kidneys. That one flattened him on the sidewalk. His stomach sickened and he coughed up a clot that caught in his throat and gagged him. The next blow landed across the back of his skull. His head went hollow, and his gaping mouth filled with concrete.

Hours passed before his mind rolled over. He smelled jack pitch and diesel and heard an engine droning, the clink and grind of chains, and the lap of water against a pier. He fought for consciousness, losing his grip and falling into a dark gulf, falling, then fighting back to see a canopy of bright lights, and beyond that a bad luck moon. Its horned rim draped in gossamer. He remembered the brown sedan and Sylvester behind the wheel and following the girl up one side street and down another. He heard a voice, or thought he did, a voice garbled and croaky as if talking through crusty lips. Only now it wasn't croaky, it was scared. It was Molly's voice in the Broken Promise and Honey's in the Rendezvous. And it was Katy's voice too, all blended together in his mind. Then the canopy of lights snapped off, and Peterson drifted into a confusion of words and symbols scrawled on a warehouse wall, and then into darkness.

✦

He woke to a heavy hammering in his head and to sunlight scratching at his closed eyelids. He rolled to his side and the hammer pounded unmercifully. He remembered the side street and the girl jaywalking toward him and stopping and staring at him. A set up. Then the sudden shriek of pain across his shoulders and his ribs. He coiled at the memory, groaned loudly, and flung open his arms.

He jerked his head away from the sharp light reflecting off the water and felt his head explode and his mind go dizzy. He closed his eyes and lay still for a time. He wondered where he was. A wharf. But where? And how had he gotten here?

He lay there breathing in short gasps. Then his breathing quieted. He slowly opened his eyes and held them open despite the pain like a rasp across his eyeballs. He rolled away from the water and saw he was just outside the chain-link fence that surrounded the container terminal, lying on a jetty that poked into the harbour. After a while, he heard voices coming closer. And then a man and a woman were crouched beside him, the woman asking if he was all right, and the man calling 911.

His pockets were turned out, and the woman was gathering up his things when she came to his badge. She told the man he was a policeman, and that seemed to make everything more hurried and even more confusing.

They kept him most of that day in the emergency room, testing him for signs of concussion, and that's when he made a vague, noncommittal statement to the young cop who had responded to the 911. Later, a nurse explained that the hospital would not discharge him until he had someone to take him home. And for some reason, he did not reach for his phone to call Danny. Instead, he asked the nurse to find him the number of the Birthright Centre, and he called Anna.

CHAPTER
THIRTY-THREE

Peterson woke up with no idea where he was. The room was small, white, and, except for a framed woodcut of an old man with a pointed beard hanging on the wall beside the narrow single bed, it was undecorated. Monkish. A hermitage, he thought. There was a nightstand with a radio and a flexible desk lamp with a black metal shade. A small dresser stood in the corner near the door, and on it were a hairbrush and a hand mirror, along with his wallet, badge, change, and cell phone. Sunlight through a birch outside the window dappled the patchwork quilt on the bed and brightened this otherwise dull room.

His brain was groggy from a drugged sleep, and somewhere between thought and memory, a distant ache reminded him of last night's mugging. The shooting pain in his rib cage when he threw back the quilt and tried swinging his legs from the bed, and the stiffness and ache in his shoulders and back when he lifted himself to a sitting position, confirmed that someone experienced in taking a big man down had done a serious number on him. Then he remembered it wasn't just one person that had pounded him, put his face into the sidewalk, and kicked in his ribs. There had been two of them: one sounding as croaky as a frog, the other with a hitch in his voice like a skip in a vinyl record.

In a mirror hanging on the back of the door, he saw himself standing in his boxer shorts with bruises like oil stains over his ribs. There were also deep purple bruises across his shoulders and back. He stepped closer and saw his left cheek and jaw puffed and dark red. That was from his face hitting the sidewalk.

Then it all started coming back, and he remembered Anna helping him into a taxi outside the emergency room and giving the driver her home address.

His shirt and pants hung on a wooden chair in a corner. He gingerly pulled them on and combed his hair with his hands.

Anna sat at the kitchen table, nursing a coffee. She was dressed in a tweed skirt and blue blouse, and on the back of her chair hung a matching jacket.

"Coffee?" she asked.

Peterson nodded and slowly lowered himself into the chair opposite her.

Anna brought the coffee pot and a mug to the table. "There's cereal and toast for breakfast. I could boil you an egg if you want."

"Toast is good," he said, "but not yet."

She sat and cradled her cup in both hands, an expectant but anxious look on her face.

"You were confusing last night," she said. "Doped up I suppose. What happened?"

Peterson told her. He tried to lighten it, but he couldn't. The girls, all of them, the one in the Broken Promise, the dancer in the Rendezvous who was pregnant and wanted to keep the baby, and the fourteen-year-old he had followed along side streets just dug into him too deep.

When he finished, Anna went to the sink to rinse her mug, standing with her back to him. "You said she called her Molly?"

"Molly, yeah," he said. "The dancer called her Molly."

Anna turned to face him, wide-eyed as though something shocking had just occurred to her.

"It's not worth finding out about her," Anna said, "not to risk your life. Not to me. Not any more. They could have killed you."

"I think they meant to. They searched me and found the badge. Killing a cop brings down a whole lot of thunder."

"And if they hadn't found the badge?" she asked.

Peterson made light of it with a shrug, but the strained look on his face said something different. They both fell silent for a moment, then Peterson said, "Thanks for bringing me here."

Anna shook it off. "I take in stray cats too."

"They stay long?"

"Never more than one night. You ready for toast?"

He nodded, and she pulled a loaf of bread from the breadbox and popped two slices into the toaster. Then she sat back down across from him.

"What are you going to do now?" she asked.

"I'm not sure. The girl in the Rendezvous told me her name, Debbie Wilson, and where she was from. A few more minutes with her — you never know — but she was scared. Maybe too scared. Maybe I should have left her alone. And now they know who I am. Tricky to go back, to help her. To find out about Molly's friend."

"Her friend?"

"Debbie said Molly panicked when her friend didn't come. That's why she ran away."

Anna reached for his hand and clicked her tongue at his innocence. "It's girl talk, Peterson. Her friend didn't come. She missed her period. I thought you said she wasn't pregnant."

Peterson suddenly realized what Anna was saying. "She wasn't. But she believed she was. Desperate about it." His brain hurt to think, to remember what Crouse had said about the girl cutting out what wasn't there.

"That's why the rag doll," he said, more to himself than to Anna. He pressed his hands to his pounding head. Then he lowered his hands and looked at her. "I have to go back to the Rendezvous, don't I? I have to get Debbie out of there. I told her I would. I promised her. I told her boyfriend to leave it with me. She's pregnant, and I have to go back and get her out now."

Anna spread her arms and gripped the sides of the table. "We had a woman at the Birthright Centre two years ago, a woman who was sleeping around, doing drugs, working the street. Old looking. Haggard. She was Roman Catholic and didn't want an abortion. I was on duty the night her pimp broke through the locked door and dragged her down the stairs by the hair. He threatened to cut my face if I said a word. I didn't. I was so scared . . . I was so scared I couldn't move. You have no idea what it's like to be a woman and to be that scared. To be so vulnerable. These girls don't have a choice, Peterson. They don't."

"And you want me to give them one?"

"I don't know if you can. It's a vicious circle these girls go through. They work the streets. They get pregnant. Some get abortions, some have the child, and then they're back working the street. No one cares. No one really cares."

She wrung her hands, then got up and pulled her jacket from the chair back. "I don't know what I'm saying. There's nothing I can do. Nothing you can do, and you're a cop."

She stared out the small window above the sink. "There's nowhere for her to go, is there?"

"Not where they wouldn't find her."

"So what are you looking for?"

Peterson hesitated.

"You're not thinking of here?"

Peterson saw it frightened her just to say it. He shook his head. "They'd find her here. They know I'm a cop. She runs, they'll think she's running to me, and they'll button-hole anyone close to me. They'll kill her for that. Her boy-friend too. And if they find her here, they'll kill you."

Anna blanched. Her arms hung stiffly at her sides.

"Even if she turned Crown witness against them, I can't protect her," Peterson said. "I can hide her, but for how long? Then what?" He stared into his coffee mug. "Real life. It's ugly and it's hopeless."

Anna started for the door.

"Anna!"

"I'm going to mass," Anna said, "and then the nursing home. Right now, I need to pray. I need something to believe in, something more than the ugliness of your life."

Painkillers didn't help much. It hurt to sit, to stand, and to walk. It even hurt to breathe. Peterson winced and groaned his way out to Danny's car and had to hold his torso stiff and straight as he got in.

Danny watched all this with great amusement, his tough friend mewling like a cat. "Tell me the other guy looks worse than you."

"Two other guys," Peterson corrected, "and I never laid a glove."

"A week off the job, and you get sloppy and don't call for backup?"

"I didn't think I needed it."

Danny reached into the back seat for the morning paper. He handed it to Peterson. "You'll need it now. Front page, bottom left."

Peterson read the headline out loud. "Body found in city park." He skimmed the item then lowered the paper. "No details?"

"I'm holding back for a couple of days."

"How ugly is it?"

"Ugly enough to keep seeing it."

That caught Peterson off guard: cast-iron Danny going white just talking about it.

"Did you ID the body?"

"Oh yeah. A friend of ours. Terry Sylvester. They strung

him up between two trees and gutted him like a deer. His insides spread all over the ground like sausage. No gunshot wounds. No head contusions. Just a deep slit from his balls to his throat. Crouse thinks he was alive when they cut him."

Peterson stared out the windshield. Message sent; message received. He imagined a box filled with bad things, and he had flipped open the lid.

"That's problem number one," Danny said. "Problem number two is Sylvester's girlfriend. She's downtown boiling over about cops muscling him for information. That could go upstairs. But that one, we can skate around. Number three is a little more complicated. The street knows about Sylvester, and that has Teabag so scared his face is all eyes. He's holed up in that abandoned military housing complex and he wants to talk. He wants to spill what he knows to get the protection I promised. Only I had no authorization to make such a promise."

Peterson tried to draw a deep breath but cut it short with the pain. He waited for it to pass before speaking. His voice was cold. "Then we should hear what Teabag has to say, while he can still say it."

"I doubt a prosecutor will accept him as a key witness," Danny said.

"Not on his own. But if we have someone else."

"The dancer?" Off Peterson's nod, Danny added. "We wouldn't get a nickel from the department to protect one of them let alone two. Collar a gang of big-time drug dealers, maybe, but we're talking pimps and whores. Only johns spend money on whores."

Peterson showed his frustration. "Then we go for information, stockpile evidence, and build a case from there."

"Teabag will negotiate."

"So we make more promises."

"And we pay them off with what?"

"How many promises do you think he's ever kept?"

Danny started the car, and they drove across one of the harbour bridges to an area of tenements that had once housed married military personnel. It was now a wasteland of broken windows and sun-bleached paint. Treeless and dry, with empty laneways and alleys of cracked asphalt. A forsaken community of ghosts, dense and curdled behind a chain-link fence topped with razor wire.

Danny grabbed a flashlight from the back seat and gestured for Peterson to take the smaller one from the glove box.

The gate was open and the padlock lay on the ground, still attached to the heavy-duty chain that was cut in two.

"Someone didn't have a key," Peterson said.

Danny unsnapped his holster and laid his palm on the pistol butt.

They walked around empty oil drums and entered the first of the three-storey tenements, its door off its hinges. They could hear rats' feet running on broken glass. Almost on cue, they both reached for their cell phones to turn them off. Peterson found that his was already off, and he realized it must have been that way since the other night, when he started following the girl.

"Déjà vu," Danny whispered.

Peterson didn't answer. He knew what Danny meant: storage warehouses on the waterfront thirteen years ago. They were beat cops following up a call that a gut-shot drug dealer was holed up in one of them and was dying. They went in just like this. Frightened.

Now they were careful as they made their way under sagging ceilings and around piles of rubble. There was broken plaster and damp-smelling dust throughout the labyrinth of small apartments and narrow hallways. They picked their way through the debris, down one lifeless corridor after another.

Peterson sidestepped a fallen beam. His rib cage shot with pain. He winced and held it down, along with the fear of what was behind the closed door at the end of the long hall.

"Where?" he whispered.

"Inside," Danny said. "It's a big meeting room. I set him up, far right corner. Mattress. Camp stove."

"You worried?"

Danny forced a smile. "Shitting bricks."

They waited outside the door, their backs pressed against the wall, listening. Then Danny called out, "Teabag! It's me. Be cool, all right? I'm coming in."

Without moving position, Danny reached for the doorknob, swung the door inward, and flashed his light into the dark room. Peterson slipped in and crouched at one side of the door, catching the pain before it leaked out. Danny dodged around the open door to the other side. They played their flashlights over the room till Danny's landed on Teabag. He was propped against the back wall with a bullet hole between his eyes. Peterson's light fell on another body in much the same position.

His stomach was in his mouth before he knew it. No

holding back. He bent double and cried with the guilt he could not stand to feel.

Debbie Wilson, Mississauga. Honey from the Rendezvous. Her eyes popping. Pistol in her mouth, and the back of her head blasted open. There was a cell phone beside her body, and not far away a piece of paper with Peterson's phone number.

CHAPTER
THIRTY-FOUR

Peterson was shuffled to the sidelines and out of the picture. A cop under suspension. His version didn't make even a sidebar in the local press.

Carmichael called, deeply concerned about Peterson's mental state. He had set aside all the time Peterson needed, but Peterson didn't go. Wouldn't go. Wouldn't give anyone associated with the department the time of day. Fuck 'em all, he told a reporter, who didn't report it. Then he ripped out the land line. Left his cell phone off. Waddled around inside his head for three weeks, behind the walls of the house he had always avoided coming home to.

Danny entered without knocking. It took him one look around the downstairs to know his former partner had lost what little grip he had. The stack of dirty dishes just showed a man living alone, but the pots and pans scattered on the floor among the pieces of broken glass, the dents in the refrigerator, the holes punched in the walls, and a stove element burning bright red told him something else.

The living room confirmed it. Danny couldn't walk in it without stepping on broken glass. He saw why. The glass-topped coffee table was shattered, wall mirrors smashed, and two porcelain table lamps demolished. It looked like a frat house on Sunday morning. Smelled like one, too, of stale beer and the cloying stink of a meat sandwich rotting somewhere.

Peterson came from another room and stopped short at seeing Danny.

"You having guests any time soon?" Danny said.

Peterson ignored it. "It took you long enough."

"I wanted to give you time," Danny said, his voice quieted by a touch of guilt. The brass had ordered him to stay away until they closed the disciplinary hearing. Their subtext was plain: keep clear of bad rubbish.

"Yeah," Peterson said. "I ran out of things to bust up."

Danny saw the stringy look in Peterson's face. "You all right?"

"You tell me!"

"Doesn't look it."

Peterson shrugged.

Danny negotiated the obstacles in the kitchen and turned off the burner.

"Is this a social call or am I still under investigation?" Peterson asked.

"You were never under —"

"Two cops parked outside for two straight weeks, what do you call that?"

Danny didn't answer.

"The department said it was observation," Peterson said, "so I gave them something to observe. I walked across the street and punched one of them out. Then they called it just cause for dismissal."

Danny knew the story. It had been coffee-shop talk for days.

"The union argued PTSD," Peterson said, "and Carmichael confirmed it. I get two-thirds pension and a disability top-up. You want a beer?"

Danny nodded. Peterson made his situation sound better than it was. The condition of the house proved it.

Peterson led the way into a dark wood-panelled den that was tidy compared to the disaster zone they had just passed through. The den served as television room and computer station. He pulled two beers from a bar fridge, handed one to Danny, and settled on a leather love seat, gesturing for Danny to take the recliner.

"How did you make out?" Peterson asked.

"I still have my job," Danny said, not meeting Peterson's eyes.

Peterson took a big slug of beer. "How much you pay to keep it?"

"Cut the shit," Danny scowled. "I didn't like looking the other way any more than you."

"I didn't look the other way!"

Danny leaned over the arm of the chair to look into the smashed-up living room. "And where did that get you?"

"Not much farther," Peterson said, "but far enough that I can still use a mirror to shave myself." He emphasized the point with another long slug.

"Yeah, sure. Nothing eating at you."

Peterson ignored the put down. "Crouse go along too?"

"It was Crouse's call from the start. You know that. There was nothing to go on. The girl's prints and only her prints on the gun. Bang, bang, close range for both of them. The girl killed Teabag and then herself. That's how Crouse read the evidence, that's how two investigators read it, and that's how it made the press: whore kills pimp."

Peterson balled his fists and pounded the arms of his chair. "No! It wasn't like that. I know it and so do you."

"How do we know?"

Peterson was shaking. "Because we know." He glared at Danny. "Who investigated?"

"You know who investigated."

"And you don't think Miles and partner cleaned it up?"

"We can't prove it," Danny said. "We can't prove shit. So what the fuck, huh? What the fuck was I supposed to do?"

Peterson let it go. He drained his beer and got up to get two more. When he sat down and passed Danny another beer, he saw that his friend had tears in his eyes.

They sat in silence, trying to find a way around what had come between them. Then Peterson reached for his cell phone and scrolled to a text message. He showed it to Danny.

"She sent that text the night before they killed her. I had my phone turned off."

Danny read the text: Please!!!!!

Danny jumped up and walked out of the room. His eyes

jumped from one broken object to another. He came back and sat.

"You can't wear it like that." Danny said. "And you can't wear it for the both of us."

"She called me!" Peterson shouted.

"And I kept my mouth shut!"

Danny was back on his feet, walking into the living room and back again. There was something else pestering him and now he brought it out. "It's going the same way with the Sylvester murder."

Peterson studied his friend. "That's why you came."

Danny ignored it. He sat again. "City maintenance found the knife in a nearby sewer. Sylvester's blood up the blade and then some. There were fingerprints."

"Let me guess. A two-time loser."

"Another Stoddard runaway. Stephen Emery. Paranoid schizophrenic. Hears voices like goddamn Joan of Arc."

"Funny how two and two always make four."

"We're the only ones who think so," Danny said

"Miles and partner again?"

Danny let his silence answer for him.

Peterson leaned forward, his voice soft and cajoling. "You're nosing after something."

Danny was back on his feet, walking through his thoughts. Still standing, he drained what was left of his first beer and started on the second. "They're getting away with it."

"I've been thinking that for weeks and taking it out on the walls and furniture."

"Word came down to clean it up fast," Danny said. "Gruesome murder. Put the public's mind to rest. Some shit like that. Then all of a sudden the knife turns up. I know it happens, but this was just too . . . I mean how many times does city maintenance check the sewer lines, and what's the chances of them going down that one, you understand?"

"You said something?"

"Yeah I said something, loud and clear." Then off Peterson's quizzical look, he added, "Fultz said we work with evidence. We don't speculate on circumstances. I mean what the fuck is that, huh? We question everything. Everything. That's our job."

"And everyone went along?"

"Like we're goddamn civil servants," Danny said. "Go along to get along. We called it according to how it looked, how Miles wrote it up. No questions."

Peterson sipped his beer slowly, his thoughts racing. Danny couldn't sit still. He was pacing again, into the living room and back, three or four times, then he said, "And there's nothing we can do."

Peterson smiled.

Danny saw it and stopped moving. He dropped into the recliner, his eyes on Peterson. "You're working on something, aren't you?"

Peterson sipped his beer.

"You going to tell me?"

Peterson said nothing.

Danny's face flushed. "We backed up each other for how many years?"

"I have nothing to lose if things go sideways," Peterson said.

"Now who's being a guardian angel?"

"There's no place for coincidence in a murder investigation," Peterson said. "There's a link between Stoddard Hospital and the Posse." He laced his fingers together. "I just have to ruffle some feathers and find out what."

Danny took his time. He took a long slug of beer. Then another. Then he leaned toward Peterson. "What do you need?"

CHAPTER
THIRTY-FIVE

Peterson parked outside Three Oaks Nursing Home and waited for her bus to arrive. He had cleaned up his act before coming: a haircut the day before, and a new plaid shirt and chinos. He still wore the same beat up pair of Rockport walkers. He even lost the beard stubble, but not the gloominess that seemed to follow him always.

The bus arrived and Anna stepped down, and after it drove off, she started across the street and stopped dead when she saw him climbing from his car. He gave her the Queen's wave, and that seemed to have been the right thing to do, because she smiled, finished crossing the street, and took his hand.

They walked over to the nursing home and through the empty lobby to the elevators. His walkers and her white sneakers, squeaking across the polished grey tile floor, made a syncopated rhythm, accentuated by the steady purl of their voices.

"I needed time to get my head together," he said.

"I know. And I needed time to figure out who I am and what I want."

"How far did you get."

"I thought it through."

He waited in the hallway as she entered her mother's room, a room made forever sad, despite the bright paint, by its institutional furniture and the hospital corners on the bedcover. Photographs and knick-knacks covered the top of the dresser (no nails in the walls), and a yellow and brown afghan on the recliner attempted cheeriness. He watched her straighten what did not need straightening, tidy what did not need tidying, and fuss the way you fuss over someone you love.

Then she led him down the hall, past the nurses station, toward the sing-song coming from the Great Room. Her mother sat off by herself, unwilling to join the dozen or so seniors around the piano. The old woman with an apple-doll face stared into the blur of the window glass, singing to herself. "When the Red, Red Robin goes bob, bob, bobbing along . . ."

She looked up at Anna as they approached and asked, "Is it Sunday already?"

"Yes," Anna said, laying her white sweater over the back of a nearby chair.

"You went to mass? Took Communion?"

"You know I did."

The same questions. The same conversation. The same way of holding on to a moment of clarity.

Anna leaned down and gave her a kiss. "You're not with the others."

"I enjoy being alone."

"You always did."

Peterson backed out of the Great Room, leaving mother and daughter to have their time together. He grabbed a magazine from a side table in the lobby, settled in a wingback chair, and waited. An hour later, Anna appeared beside him.

"Let's walk," she suggested.

"No music in the church?"

"That would be too convenient," she said and took his hand and led him from the nursing home.

They hadn't gone far when she said, "This is my life. The Birthright Centre and a nursing home. There isn't much else in it, except for my willingness to believe in something more than what you once called real life. I also have books and music, and that's about it."

Peterson said nothing. He held her hand and was well aware of its softness and the shape of her fingers.

"I caught myself feeling for you," she continued. "There's a goodness in you that you keep so well hidden. And I understand why. I would too if I had to live your life. But I can't live it. I won't let myself be part of it. Do you understand?"

Peterson nodded and let go of her hand. "I can't live it either," he said, "but I have to."

CHAPTER
THIRTY-SIX

Tatiana Emerson ran her Irish Setter along one of the bridal paths that crossed the mixed stand of hardwood and soft-wood trees in the 190-acre park in the south end of the city. She was a black-haired, dark-eyed beauty in a cranberry duffle coat and brown slacks. When she reached the parking lot at the lower end of the park, she leashed her dog.

Peterson was waiting beside her silver Mazda. He'd got her name from Danny and her whereabouts from her live-in boyfriend. Peterson greeted her with his friendly face and a good-old-boy voice.

"Tatiana, I'm Detective Peterson," he said. Not entirely a lie. An equivocation perhaps. He ruffled the dog's fur then flashed a badge he had dug from a bottom drawer in the den, the one he had kept against regulations, a memento of his days in uniform before the four municipalities were amalgamated into one sprawling city. "I'm investigating the girl who killed herself in the Broken Promise," he said. "She used to be a patient at Stoddard."

"Yes?" Tatiana said. She had a soft voice with a hint of an accent from overseas somewhere.

"Mind if I ask you a couple of questions about the night she went missing?"

"Right here?"

"It will only take a minute or two."

"That's about all I have. My son gets out of daycare at three."

"No more than that."

"Let me get Ginger in the car." She opened the hatch on the Mazda and ordered the dog to jump in.

"You were working that evening?" Peterson asked.

"Yes. But I don't remember much. You must know what it's like. By the end of a shift your mind's a mess."

"Tell me about it."

The dog barked and Tatiana tapped on the window to shush her.

"I reported her missing," Tatiana said.

"Do you remember what time?" Peterson asked.

"Around nine. One of the other patients had a visitor and they were playing Scrabble and she threw something, a pillow I think, and it hit the board, and she just blew up."

"That was before nine o'clock?"

"It was after supper. So it could have been anytime between six and nine."

"And after that, she just walked away from Stoddard?" Peterson said.

"It happens."

"But there's a locked door on the teen ward with a security guard," Peterson said.

"I know," she said, "but they still get out. They are teenagers and they'll find a way. Especially with the pass system."

"How does that work?" Peterson asked.

"Dr. Bettis uses security passes to coax his teen patients out of their shells. To smoke outside, walk the courtyard, go to the coffee shop on the ground floor. Passes for consultations on the fifth floor. Staff never liked them. The whole thing gets confusing. Who has what pass and for how long. And then they double up on one pass or sell a pass for cigarettes."

"Security doesn't stop them?"

She frowned. "They try, but a pass is a pass to them. They complain. We complain. But . . ." She raised her hands in surrender.

"Remember who the security guard was that night?" Peterson asked.

"No idea. They change a lot. And we're so busy, by the end of shift I can't remember the staff I was working with."

Peterson opened the car door for her to climb in. "What about this last patient to run away, Stephen Emery?"

Tatiana was half in the car when she stopped. "Oh my God, I don't even want to think about that."

"I understand. Do you remember who had security on the teen ward the night Emery took off?"

Tatiana settled behind the steering wheel. "I thought you interviewed Bill Gibson already," she said.

"I'm just following up," Peterson said. He pulled an old card from his wallet. "If you think of anything else about that night when the girl went missing, give me a call." He scratched out the printed phone numbers to the police

239

station and wrote his cell number on the back. Then he handed it to Tatiana. "This number is more direct. Thanks for your help."

Peterson caught up to Bill Gibson coming off his shift that evening. He told it much as Peterson had read it in Miles's report. Emery had a smoking pass. He signed out, went for a smoke, and never came back.

"You'd think they wouldn't let a lunatic out of the building," Gibson added. "I shake my head, you know what I mean? Half of them should be in straitjackets. But what do I care? Six months and the province pays me to stay home."

Danny had Bernie track down the name of the security guard who worked the teen floor the night Molly ran for it. She came up with Jackson Parks, midthirties, rough around the edges, a cop-wannabe, a guy who loved wearing a blue uniform, eager to talk cop to cop, so to speak. He now worked the gate at a local brewery.

The gatehouse was at the entrance for the tractor-trailers, a grey box with windows all around. There was a bank of closed-circuit monitors set into a console where the guard sat on a raised platform, which provided him a clear view of the loading docks, the street, and the main entrance to the administration building.

"You want my opinion?" Parks said, intending to give

it whether Peterson wanted it or not. "The staff there are crazier than the patients, and they're crazy enough."

"You got a candidate in mind?"

"Bettis was off the wall," Parks said, "and a couple of nurses. I think they were taking the pills the patients didn't swallow."

Peterson laughed to keep him talking. Then he said, "I heard patients could come and go as they pleased."

"Not on my watch," Parks said. "I had a lock on those going in and out." He tapped the table with an index finger. "Log book."

"You remember the girl that killed herself in the Broken Promise?"

"Oh yeah," Parks said. "The papers made a big deal once they got hold that she'd been at Stoddard."

"You remember when she was there?"

"I have a good memory."

"You were working security on the teen ward the night she went missing. We checked the staffing."

Parks suddenly got defensive. "She had a pass. She didn't leave that floor without a pass. You check the log book."

"You remember that?"

"Yeah. Admin questioned me about it after she took off, like I let her out. She had a pass for upstairs like a lot of the teens. It was only good for the elevator between the teen floor and the doctors' offices. They could go up to meet their doctor. But not when they wanted. They had to have a pass. Or have a doctor come down and get them."

"Much of that?"

"Doctors coming down for them?"

"Yeah."

"Some. Bettis mostly."

"The pass to the doctor's offices didn't get them to the ground floor?"

"No," Parks said. "Just that one elevator and it only went to the offices and stopped at the teen floor coming down."

"What would stop a teen patient from taking another elevator?"

"Me!"

"So to get to the ground floor from upstairs, they have to get off on the teen floor and change elevators?"

"What are you getting at?" Parks asked, back on the defensive. "Are you coming down on me for something?"

Peterson let it go. "I'm just trying to find out what happened that night."

Parks shrugged it off. "If she got to the ground floor from upstairs, then she was with someone that maybe took her down, a doctor or a nurse."

"You're saying they don't have to change elevators?"

"No. Doctors and some administrative staff have a bypass key."

"So a patient could get to the ground floor?"

"So long as they're with someone with a bypass key."

"And once on the ground floor they can walk out the front door?" Peterson asked.

Parks shrugged indifferently. "Who would notice?"

"Not security on the front desk?" Peterson asked.

"I worked there a month," Parks said. "Who's a visitor? Who's a patient? Unless you're checking wrist bands, you can't tell."

"And there's no way of reviewing who comes and goes?"

"You mean the video tapes," Parks said. "I thought erasing them was a bad idea from the get-go. But who the hell am I?"

Peterson thought about the girl not being missed in the ward until nine o'clock that evening.

"What shift were you working ten months ago?"

"Back then? Nights."

"You remember that?"

"Yeah. I had a day job as a floorwalker in Walmart. I would have clocked in at Stoddard at seven. She would have gone up sometime after that."

"With a pass or with her doctor?"

"All I can tell you is that they don't get off that floor without either one. Not on my watch."

"Patients often meet the shrinks at night?"

"Sure." Parks said. "Night was when most of them went screwy. You know, the boogieman. They need to talk. Bettis was in a lot at night. Hamlin too. But Hamlin mostly had the older patients in the other wards. Bettis had the crazy teens. How's that for a fucked-up job?"

CHAPTER
THIRTY-SEVEN

Morning saw Peterson sitting on a wrought-iron bench across from his wife's grave. His shoulders rolled forward, arms slung over his knees, holding his smart phone in both hands. Wishing it to ring. Sending his thoughts across a few thousand kilometres to urge her to call. He had activated his own phone camera and thought he could turn the tables. Hold it up to the headstone and let his daughter read the epitaph: *In Loving Memory*.

The police report was on the bench beside him. Bernie had pulled it, and Danny had passed it over. The report was three weeks old, but somehow it had landed on Bernie's desk at the bottom of a stack of paperwork from forensics. It had taken her that long to get to it. The name of the victim had caught Bernie's attention: Darryl Palmer.

A woman walking her dog had found him sprawled

across a little-used trail in the city's wilderness park. She had thought he was dead. Whoever had busted him up had thought so too. Now Darryl Palmer was in the rehab unit in the hospital re-learning how to walk.

Peterson straightened up and set the cell phone on top of the police report. He wasn't one to talk to dead people. He had seen enough of them to know they were way past listening. What marked their departure were just silent stones.

He walked back to where he'd parked his car. Andy Miles was leaning on the Jetta, waiting for him. Tommy Amiro sat in the dark sedan across the street.

"You should drop a deposit on the one next to your wife," Miles said with a self-indulgent smile.

"You suggesting I'll need an early one?" Peterson said. No smile, just business.

"And if I am?"

"You know better."

"You're not a cop anymore," Miles warned.

"No, but I'm a certified screwball who'll bust your knee cap if you don't get off my ass." He glanced across the street. "And I wouldn't bet on Tommy Amiro taking sides. Unless you're dropping change his way. And the frown says you're not."

Miles glared. "You don't listen too well."

"My mother always said the same thing. Deaf when I want to be. It makes choice easy."

"This time you chose wrong," Miles said.

"Like Terry Sylvester and Teabag and Debbie Wilson?"

"It could come down to that."

"Now that does sound like a threat," Peterson said. "Let me check my pulse to see if I'm scared."

Tommy Amiro blew the horn to get going. Miles raised his arms in a mockingly submissive way and crossed over to the sedan.

Peterson watched him get into the car and waited until they cleared the corner. Then he blew out a deep breath. His hands trembled and his legs felt weak.

Darryl Palmer shuffled straight-legged along a hallway, wearing two yellow Johnny shirts, one worn back to front and the other front to back, to cover his beat-up body. Braces on both legs and a foam collar around his neck held him upright as he pushed a walker a few inches ahead of himself then tried to catch up. A female physiotherapist walked beside him. When Darryl reached the end of the hallway and turned to walk back, Peterson saw that someone had also rearranged Darryl's face.

They were ten feet apart when Darryl saw Peterson and coughed out the anger that had been choking him for weeks. His body shook and the therapist took his arm and coaxed him to a nearby armchair on wheels.

She turned to Peterson, showing concern at her patient's sudden outburst, but before she could say a word, Peterson held up his badge and smiled. "He's just happy to see me."

Darryl turned to Peterson. Winced when he saw the badge. "You said you weren't a cop." He squeezed out the words through a wired jaw.

"I was undercover," Peterson said, stretching it for convenience sake.

Darryl shifted his weight in the chair, and it was obvious it pained him to do so.

Peterson gave the therapist the eye and she wheeled Darryl to a small lounge with a wide-screen television and tables for playing games. She positioned Darryl's chair near a window where the light was flat.

It took several minutes for Darryl to settle, then the therapist left the lounge. Darryl tried not to look at Peterson. Then he did. The anger was still in his eyes.

Peterson stood by the window, looking beyond the flat roof of the emergency department to the large empty lot where a high school had once stood.

"She called you," Darryl said. "I called you." He spoke from the back of his throat, his voice a low growl.

Peterson peeled his eyes off the skyline and looked at Darryl.

"There was no answer," Darryl said. "I left it with you like you said. Look what happened."

Peterson flinched. He made no apology, no admission that he had let them down; nothing he could say would make it better. He looked back out the window. "The police report said you couldn't ID the guys that tried to kill you."

"No." Palmer's eyes filled just to think of it.

"The RCMP found your truck burned out on a woods road, but you didn't drive it there. You said you left it at the Rendezvous."

"She called," Palmer said, "begging for help. I went, but . . . they were waiting for me."

"Was she there?"

"No."

Palmer fell silent and Peterson let it last, not knowing what else to say, what to ask, but uncomfortable at the thought of just leaving.

"I know what they did to her," Palmer said.

"Yeah," Peterson said. "I found her."

They stared at one another for most of a minute. Then Peterson realized someone was standing in the doorway to the lounge, watching them: a guy in his early fifties, high forehead, thick arms, and a stance that said he knew how to handle himself. When Peterson lifted his head, the guy walked over. He offered his hand.

"I'm Darryl's father, Dickie Palmer."

Peterson shook Palmer's hand. "Peterson."

"You're a cop."

Peterson smiled to suggest he was.

"You know who did this to my son?"

"Not yet," Peterson said, "but I'm sorry about it. I'm sorry for him and his girlfriend."

"I'm just worried about my son. When you find out, I want to know who did it."

Darryl had shrunk in his chair, as if there was no love lost between him and his father. Peterson figured it had to do with the girl. A whore and a stripper, hardly the match his father would want.

"You find out, then what?" Peterson asked. "The guys who did this to your son and the girl, you don't want to tangle with them."

"That sounds like you know who they are."

"I know the kind of scum they are. They didn't leave your son to be found. And the girl and the pimp? It wasn't murder–suicide. Those guys blew out the backs of their heads."

Darryl groaned and Dickie Palmer stepped closer and set a hand on his son's shoulder. "Maybe I won't be alone," he said to Peterson. "Maybe there's a small army to do what needs doing."

"You shouldn't say that," Peterson warned. "Let the law handle it."

"Like the law handled it for my son and that girl?"

Peterson fumed but held it tight.

"My son has family," Palmer said, "and his family has friends. We won't just let it go."

Peterson had been feeling it too: civilized outrage. A deep desire to connive in an act of revenge. And he knew something else. Yeah, the cops would break out the shovels, but they wouldn't break a sweat. They'd hardly dig. Scratch the surface, maybe, and if nothing turned up, so what. Another news day carries the public's attention elsewhere.

"I better go," Peterson said and turned away.

Dickie Palmer's voice followed him to the door. "We may be fishermen, Peterson, but we're not stupid. We're asking around. We don't need the same proof as you. When we find out, they'll get worse than my son got, and we won't leave them anywhere to be found."

Peterson came back at him, going face to face. "You can't say stuff like that," he said, hissing the words through his teeth. "Feel it all you want, but don't say it."

CHAPTER
THIRTY-EIGHT

Peterson had Heather McBride's daily routine down pat: a Starbucks coffee before driving herself to Stoddard Mental Health Centre, lunch in the hospital cafeteria, eight hours on the job. On the drive home, she stopped at a gourmet food store to pick up supper for two, something she could pop in the oven or heat in the microwave. Then a second stop at the same Starbucks for a latte or an herbal tea, depending on the day. She sat in the coffee shop until her boyfriend showed, usually a half-hour later, sometimes more.

On the third day, after making sure Miles was not following, Peterson was inside waiting for her, playing with a teaspoon, playing a hunch, and watching for her red Ford Focus through the plate-glass window. Once she was inside, he moved behind her in line, his eyes fixed on where a lock of her brown hair flipped over the collar of her suede coat.

"I heard the staff at Stoddard are crazier than the patients," Peterson said to the back of Heather McBride's head. "Any truth to that?"

McBride snapped her head around. "That's not funny!"

"That's what a security guard said." He flashed a smile and let it fade. "Has me worried, because a nurse told me your pass system doesn't work, that patients come and go at will."

"Latte or tea?" asked the counter girl, bug-eyed behind big glasses, knowing Heather McBride as a regular.

McBride turned to answer. "Latte, thanks." She swung back to Peterson, bristling. "I spoke to your cop pals weeks ago."

"I know. But another nut getting loose and committing a crime rings of coincidence, and coincidence never sits well with a cop."

The girl brought the latte and McBride used her iPhone to pay the bill. Peterson didn't order and followed her to a side bar where she doctored the latte with a packet of sugar.

"Was there something you wanted to say?" he asked.

"About what?"

"Why don't we take that corner table, and I'll tell you?"

"I'm expecting someone."

"He won't show for half an hour."

He guided her to the corner table, the one with no view from the window and out of earshot of most everyone in the coffee shop.

"Hand in your resignation yet?" he asked.

"Why should I?"

"You dusted it off the last time we talked."

She looked surprised.

"I'm paid to find things out."

"About me?" She sounded nervous. He liked that.

"About the people you work for and the easy way patients seem to slip out of Stoddard."

"I had nothing —"

"I didn't say you did."

"Then what are you suggesting?"

"That you might know who opened the door."

"This is crazy!" She stood to change tables, but he barked at her to sit down. The colour drained from her cheeks. She sat.

"Let's not make a scene," he said. "We don't want to talk about this in my office, do we? It gets cramped in there."

She shook her head. Her hands gripped her mug.

"Let me play this by you," he said. "Restricted patient has a pass to go upstairs for a consult. The doctor uses his bypass key for the elevator to take her to the ground floor and out the front door."

"I don't think so."

"Why not?"

"They are doctors! Why would they help a patient breach security when they could just as easily discharge them?"

"Because one of the patients I'm thinking of hadn't said a sensible word the entire time she was at Stoddard. Hardly the right material for a discharge. And the other one could have been discharged, but it played better to the cops and press if he just up and walked out on his own."

McBride shook her head, her confidence back, her voice derisive, almost impudent. "You're talking about the girl that killed herself. She didn't need help getting out. The nurse you talked to was right. The pass system has problems. Not as bad as patients walking out at will, but there have been incidents."

"She used a pass to go upstairs," Peterson said. "The security guard remembers it. She went up in the restricted elevator and never came back to the teen floor. She would have been difficult to discharge. She wouldn't tell anyone her name."

"Why would a doctor do that?"

Peterson let her ponder that herself. He changed direction. "Tell me about this last one to take a hike on his own. He was violent, wasn't he?"

"I don't know. I don't work the floors."

"And he just walked away?"

"He had smoking privileges, and there's no smoking in the building."

"Violent schizophrenic has a pass to go outdoors?"

"I don't know how violent he was," she said. "And maybe he didn't have a pass. Maybe he just . . ."

"But you knew he had smoking privileges."

She didn't answer. Clearly troubled by the contradiction.

Again Peterson shifted direction. "Whose idea was it to clean the video tapes?"

McBride had to think about it. Then she said, "Mr. Pratz wanted budget cuts."

"That's not what I asked."

"We had staff meetings. Lots of suggestions. I don't know who suggested it. I was new. Not even a month. But Gloria Melanson kept minutes of all staff meetings. She might know."

"Does she work the teen floor?"

"Gloria? Yes. Well, no, not anymore. She retired months ago. She'd worked there forever. A nursing supervisor."

"You have her home number?"

"Home?"

"I want to keep this out of the hospital for now, out of the press." The last part came to him out of the blue and he liked the effect it had on her. She was, after all, the hospital's communications officer. She reached for her shoulder bag hanging off the back of the chair and took out a cell phone. While she called up her contacts list, Peterson kept digging.

"Stoddard gets lots of young patients."

McBride looked up from the cell. "Teens and young adults seem to be the most disturbed. We have a separate floor for teens. Here it is!"

She gave him Gloria Melanson's address and phone number.

"Do all the doctors work with the young patients?" he asked.

"Mostly Dr. Bettis. It's his specialty."

"What about Hamlin?"

"Dr. Hamlin is the administrator. He has patients, but not many, and they're adults."

"Is Pratz in the building a lot?"

"He's on the board," she said, sipping the latte and getting foam on her upper lip, licking it off. "No, I don't think so," she said. "Not a lot. Once a week."

"Does he patrol the halls or just stick to certain wards?" Peterson asked.

"I don't understand . . ."

"What does he do?"

She had to think about this. "I see him around. I don't know what he does. He consults a lot with Dr. Bettis and Dr. Hamlin."

"Consult with you?"

"At times."

"About what?"

"Upcoming events. Staff and government reports."

"Is Bettis really off the wall?"

"What?"

"That's what I heard," Peterson said. "The security guard said it."

"He's quirky," McBride said.

"How quirky?"

"I don't know. Funky might be a better word. His office certainly is, and one of the rooms in his house."

Peterson held down his surprise. "You were at his house?"

She nodded. "A Christmas party for administration." She smiled. The smile grew wider as she thought of it. "It was weird."

"How weird?"

"I don't know, psychiatrist weird. One room had these sculptures. Primitives, I guess you'd call them. Figurines of a woman with huge boobs and . . . my god, it had the two of us laughing."

"What did?"

"The Earth Mother, he called it. A fertility goddess, a replica, I think he said, of something really old."

"What was funny about it?" Peterson pressed.

"It didn't look like anything. Not at first. Then we

255

realized, me and Dr. Hamlin's assistant, that it was a pregnant woman with these enormous boobs, and —" McBride looked away as she said it "— a vagina that wasn't even close to normal size."

"Not something you expected to see there?" Peterson said.

"I don't know if I expected it or not. He's a psychiatrist."

Peterson smiled as though he knew exactly what she meant. Then he played a hunch. "Bettis lives in the south end, right, near the hospitals?"

"A couple of blocks away," McBride said.

Peterson pushed himself back from the table. "When are you getting out of there?"

McBride saw he was genuinely concerned. "As soon as I find something else."

Peterson got up to leave.

"We're done?" she asked.

He nodded. "Yeah, we're done."

CHAPTER
THIRTY-NINE

Gloria Melanson was silent for a long time before agreeing that he could stop by. She lived alone in a green split-level across the harbour. Never married. Early sixties. Pudgy face behind thick glasses. A big, matronly woman who waddled when she walked.

She led Peterson through the house, which was nothing special. A hit-and-miss décor with shelves of knick-knacks from many North American tourist traps. She was having a white-wine cooler on the stone patio and offered him one. He declined, said he was on duty.

They sat at a teak table with a closed umbrella in the middle. The evening sun, a comfort for mid-fall, played peek-a-boo through a stand of white birch and splayed shadows over two kidney-shaped flower beds abloom with hydrangeas and marigolds.

Peterson broke the ice with questions about her job and responsibilities at Stoddard. Her responses pulsed with pride; her voice was firm and matter of fact. She was a nurse with nearly forty years under her belt, a by-the-book RN who could comfort and scold in the same sentence. She understood better than many of the younger nurses what it meant to be a professional. Then he asked about the girl who had run away ten months ago, the one who had killed herself in the Broken Promise. Gloria lost the matronly demeanour.

"She never did settle down," Gloria said. "I don't remember what it was, three weeks she was at Stoddard, the whole time her eyes and body never settled. I'm not talking out of turn. It's all in the nursing reports."

Peterson liked the way she said it, practically telling him where he could find what she wasn't at liberty to say.

"Bettis was her doctor?"

"Yes he was," she said, barbing each word.

"You didn't care for him, did you?"

Gloria folded her ample arms. "Not everyone gets along in a high-stress job. There is always tension, less with some, more with others."

"More with Dr. Bettis, I take it?"

"Oil and water for three and a half years."

Peterson held out his hands. "I assumed Bettis was there a lot longer."

"It seemed that way to me too."

Peterson salted his tone to make it sound as though he was in the know. "And that's when the difficulties began, with the young girls?"

"Not long after."

He sneaked that one through. Now he waded into

deeper, purely speculative waters. "Why do you think Dr. Hamlin didn't do anything? I'm talking about after you brought it to his attention."

She took her time with that one. Too much time, Peterson feared. Then she said, "Philip Hamlin is a kind man and a caring doctor. But he is not a good administrator. Bullies on staff take advantage of him."

Again Peterson nodded to suggest he knew exactly what she meant. Then he shifted direction.

"I talked to another nurse and to Heather McBride," he said. "Both of them suggested the pass system didn't work that well, and that it was easy for patients to make the great escape."

"Male patients mostly," Gloria said. "Some females. But that wasn't the problem. Not from what I saw. The real problem was premature discharges. We had plenty of those in the last three and a half years."

She was talking about Bettis. He knew it. And she looked at him until she was sure he did.

"You want to tell me about them?"

"Maybe there's too much to tell. Closed doors. Private consultations."

"Elevator pass upstairs? After dark?"

Gloria didn't answer. Her eyes wandered over the garden, and her hands worried in her lap. Peterson let the silence tie a knot between them. Then it hit him. The hesitation, the suspicion, the bitterness he sensed in this woman. He lowered his voice to a whisper, picking his words to gently slip the knot.

"The call that tipped us to the girl in the Broken Promise being from Stoddard was anonymous. That was you, wasn't it?"

Gloria nodded and took her first sip of the wine cooler. "Why?"

"I knew certain ones would try to keep it quiet," she said. The barb had crept back into her voice.

Peterson thought he knew why. "You didn't retire on your own, did you?"

Gloria stared at the stand of birch. "I should have known better than to ask so many questions, to challenge his methods. But my duty is to the patients."

"We're back to his private consultations, aren't we?"

Gloria shifted in her chair as though her thoughts and feelings were making her feel physically uncomfortable. "Betty Martin brought it to my attention. She was ready to go to senior staff. So I investigated her complaint on my own."

"And they forced retirement?"

"Not they!"

"Bettis?"

"He questioned my nursing skills. Took his concerns to the director of nursing."

Peterson leaned forward to suggest his question and her answer would be a confidence between them. "Are you saying Dr. Bettis was inappropriate with the female patients?"

She removed her glasses, placed them on the table, considered the question carefully. And just as carefully she phrased her answer. "If you are suggesting that his behaviour made Betty Martin and me uncomfortable, the answer is yes."

"You could have gone to senior management," he said.

"I raised questions with them."

"That's not the same as an official complaint."

"Not in the medical field." She paused to think through what else she wanted to say and how to say it. She lifted her glasses, fingered them, and set them back down. "Mental illness is a matter of control. Counselling and medication help. A change in environment, a change in circumstances can reduce the struggle. We try our best to stabilize anxiety, reduce stress. But at the end of the day, these young girls are still at risk, still vulnerable. To discharge them before they're ready, before they're prepared to go back to the street is just so wrong!"

She held his eyes, allowing hers to reveal much more than what she had said. But he couldn't leave it at that. He had to settle it. "Is that what Bettis did?"

She sipped her wine cooler, a clear indication she was going to let that stand for her answer.

"You took notes at staff meetings," Peterson said.

"Yes."

"Do you remember who suggested erasing the security video tapes?"

Gloria clicked her tongue derisively. "It was hardly a big item in the operating budget, but Pratz insisted, and Bettis agreed."

Peterson pulled out the photos of the girls printed from the flash drive. He reached them to Gloria. "Ever seen these girls before?"

Gloria looked at the photos, inhaled sharply, and seemed to sink into the chair.

"His patients?" Peterson asked.

Her face was filled with sadness. "They all didn't kill themselves, did they?"

"Just the girl in the Broken Promise," he said. "Her name was Molly. The photos are from video recordings. They're not pleasant."

She returned the photos. "They were his patients," she said. "I remember three of them very well. Hospital records will have all their names, but I can give you three right now — Tiffany Banks, Ella Hargrove, and Mickey MacKinnon. Mickey's for Michelle, she called herself Mickey Mac. And staff used Tiffy for Tiffany Banks, but she always called herself T-Fi."

The unexpected seldom surprised him. But this time it did. His head snapped up at what she had said, and his hand shook as he flipped open his pad and wrote down the names.

"Tell me about Tiffany Banks," he said.

"She was a sweet child. I call her a child because she acted like a child, had the mind of a child. The others called her a baby doll, though she was twenty or twenty-one and belonged in the adult wing. But Bettis kept her with the teens because of her behaviour."

"One of his patients?"

"One of his first, along with Mickey Mac."

"Early discharge?"

"Again one of the first."

"And you disagreed?"

"We don't have much say in that regard." Gloria said. "Even at staff meetings, we have to hold our professional opinions in check."

"What about her background?"

"Oh, I don't know. Lived on the street, I suppose." Gloria paused to reflect, then she added, "I almost think she came in on her own. Most don't."

Peterson shifted gears, keeping his voice quiet. "Did you know the patient who recently escaped from Stoddard?"

"Stephen Emery."

"You knew him?"

"He was hospitalized many times when I was there. This was just the latest."

"You know what he did?"

"I know what the newspapers said he did." Her voice trembled with an overtone of anger. "He was terribly disturbed, confused, but he was not violent! He was agitated, but he never needed restraints. Stephen was not the animal you and the press have made him out to be."

"You don't think he did it?"

"I would be very surprised if he did."

Solar garden lights brightened where the shadows had deepened. Peterson stood to go.

"Would you tell a court or a journalist what you just told me?" he asked.

Gloria thought about it for a moment then slowly pulled herself to her feet to see him out. "I owe it to those girls, don't I?"

Peterson held her eyes.

"Not the media," Gloria said. "But if I'm asked to testify in court, I will."

As they passed back through the house, Peterson stopped.

"I just thought of something that might play into this investigation. I'm not sure how, but you never know, and something tells me that you still have the elevator key that bypassed the teen floor."

The question caught Gloria off guard. "I do."

"I'd like to take it with me," Peterson said.

Gloria raised her eyebrows but retrieved it anyway, from a china teacup in a hutch in the dining room.

"It's just a feeling," Peterson said and pocketed the key.

CHAPTER
FORTY

Bernie was carrying a folder with the results of her search on the girls' names Peterson had given her. The Hargrove girl had overdosed two years ago in a boarding house in the ass end of the city. She was D.O.A. The other one, Mickey MacKinnon was a seventeen-year-old from St. Thomas, Ontario.

"A runaway a little more than three years ago," Bernie said. "Off the map for six months, then she turns up here, a squeegee kid that goes wild in a condemned building down-town. A cop stepped in, called social services, and they had her evaluated at Stoddard."

They were walking the boardwalk behind a condo com-plex and a couple of waterfront restaurants. It was a shirt-sleeves fall evening, still early enough for late season tourists to be strolling about.

"Underage and her parents didn't want her back," Bernie said. "Can you imagine?"

Peterson said nothing.

"She spent a month in Stoddard, then was discharged," Bernie continued. "Disappeared again for almost a year. She didn't have much going for her."

"No," Peterson said. "What else?"

"She got nabbed in a crack house three months ago. No charge. According to the report, she's well known in the neighbourhood near the Commons and strolls outside a pub in the north end. Some mornings she turns tricks for johns on their way to work. Uses the back seat of a Chevy Impala. I have a picture of her."

Peterson thought of Bony Walker's story about the girl stoned out of her mind in a junk Chevy in a backyard, spilling about T-Fi and a bloody scene that was somehow connected with the Drop Zone. Another girl saw it all.

They stopped under a light standard at a jetty. Peterson sat on a bollard and compared his photo of Mickey MacKinnon off the flash drive recording to the one Bernie now showed him.

"Tooka didn't leave much," Peterson said, more to himself than to Bernie. "Use them up and throw them out. Sell her to the highest bidder. Who's the pimp now?"

"A guy named Vance Sheppard, twenty-two, with a long record for break and enter and living off the avails."

Peterson shook his head. They walked out to the end of the jetty and watched a loaded container ship sail past.

"Anything on Tiffany Banks?" he asked.

"You think she's the body on Airport Road."

"I'm sure of it."

Bernie pulled another photograph from the file folder and handed it to Peterson. "Fredericton, New Brunswick. The photo's from her high school year book. Alcoholic parents. They never bothered to report her missing over three years ago. And there are no records of her coming here or living here."

"What about Stoddard Hospital?"

"Nothing."

Peterson was astonished, and Bernie saw it in his face.

"You know otherwise?"

Peterson nodded. "A nurse supervisor said Tiffany Banks was at Stoddard, and that Karl Bettis was her doctor. Who did you talk to?"

"Someone in PR or something, a Heather —"

"McBride."

"Yeah. She checked and there was no record of Tiffany Banks or anyone named Banks for that matter."

"Someone yanked her file," Peterson said. He rested his elbows on his knees and folded his hands under his chin. "Someone didn't want it linked to Stoddard."

"You want me to dig a little deeper? I got a cop friend in Fredericton."

"Careful inquiries," he advised.

"Tippy toes," Bernie said and handed him the folder. Peterson slipped the photographs of Mickey Mac and Tiffany Banks into it.

"Thanks," Peterson said. "I heard someone else thinks you're a detective."

"Connecting one shooter in two cold cases played well up the chain of command."

"You getting my job?"

"It's possible."

Peterson tried but failed to hold back the smile. "Watch out for Danny. He's looking for love."

Bernie looked the comment off. "You need anything else?" she asked.

"Yeah," Peterson said. "I could use a backgrounder on Dr. Karl Bettis."

He had the strong sensation of someone on the prowl, someone stalking him from the shadows of the tall buildings along the waterfront. From the time he had parked his car in the underground lot to his meeting with Bernie on the boardwalk, he'd felt he'd been tailed. And it was there on his return, toying at his cop sense like a cat with a mouse. He had slipped Andy Miles long before, but that didn't mean Miles hadn't caught up. And yet he hadn't noticed anyone to arouse his caution. It was just a feeling, paranoia, a byproduct of his suspicious nature.

He mentally noted the passing faces of pedestrians and the vehicles parked across from the piazza of retail tourist traps. The only thing that caught his eye was a dark green Chevy pickup, idling outside the entrance to the underground parking lot. One person was in the cab, the driver. The long hair offered no guarantee it was a woman.

Peterson descended the concrete stairs, then slid between two parked cars to his black Jetta. He waited before opening the door. Listening. Breathing the oily, gassy stink seeping from the walls. He heard the dull sound of soft-soled shoes on the concrete stairs come to a halt then retreat back up, stop again, then come back down. A young woman emerged from the stairwell, smiling, looking over her shoulder, and calling for someone to hurry. Within seconds her boyfriend clattered down the stairs and caught up with her. Arm in arm they negotiated their way to an Austin Mini.

Peterson got into the Jetta and followed the Austin up the exit ramp to the street. The green Chevy truck was gone.

He drove the four-lane away from downtown, passing what little traffic there was at that time of night, checking his mirrors and seeing a vehicle that was keeping up. He jumped a traffic light, turned left, gunned it for half a dozen blocks, then turned right onto a side street and killed the lights. He quickly pulled into a driveway and cut the engine. He waited. Two seconds. Five. Questioning his instincts at the ten-second mark.

Then he smiled as headlights flashed around the corner and up the street and passed him by. It was the green Chevy truck, now with a man riding shotgun.

Peterson let the truck get far enough away before backing out and driving in the opposite direction. He hung a left and then a right onto a main drag and pulled into a 24/7 supermarket, where he parked the Jetta in a cluster of other cars. He shut the engine down and followed a couple of late-night shoppers into the store.

✦

After midnight, he paid Mickey MacKinnon a visit at her place of work, a corner in a low-rent neighbourhood that had been struggling for years to make ends meet. He parked on a side street with a clear view of Gainer's Pub and of

Mickey Mac hustling tricks in red stretch pants that showed off her spindly legs and a light-coloured V-neck sweater that she could quickly pull off.

He sat and watched her for more than an hour, watched her climb into a Dodge Caravan rental, the sweater up and over her head before it drove off. She returned less than a half-hour later, juiced and stumbling in spike heels, flagging a hand at the passing cars.

She went into the pub for a short time, then came out with a drunk on her arm. She led him down the side street where Peterson was parked and behind a set of flats to the Chevy Impala. Within ten minutes, she had the drunk off and went inside the pub with him. She was soon back on the corner prowling the sparse 1:00 a.m. traffic on its way to the suburbs.

Peterson kept watching. Then he spotted her pimp arrive and start to keep tabs from across the street. An iPod pumped a driving beat through ear buds and into the pimp's loins. Baggy jeans hung off his ass, and a flat-brim ball cap was cocked at an angle on his head. He was street-level muscle for a girl who had been rolled out as bait and fleeced of her teenage body.

After a few minutes, the pimp crossed over to Mickey Mac and collected what she had earned. He counted it right there on the street. No shame. No worries. She must have mouthed off, because he offered her a backhand but didn't deliver. Then he walked off and around the corner.

Peterson climbed from his Jetta and walked over to the pub. He needed to see Mickey Mac up close; not to talk, talk had already shortened one girl's life. He just needed to see if anything sparkled in her eyes, or if her youth had all been hacked away.

She was strutting her ass and hailing potential johns as he drew close. She turned and lifted her drug-racked face to him. Her eyes were unfocused, neither here nor there, her hair wispy and dry, her voice raspy with all that life had made her swallow.

High beams swept across the shabby street and across the bleak look she gave him. He held her look too long, distressed by the dark circles around her eyes and by her misshapen jaw.

"I'm selling," she said, indignant and looking him straight in the eyes. "You buying?"

He didn't answer. He simply stood there, breathing in the stink of the street and the sour–sweet smell of sex. Then he shook his head and entered the pub, ordered a draft, and grabbed a corner table, sitting down with his back to the wall.

The pub reflected the worn look of the people it served — scuffed and scabby. Beaten-down men and women working off the ass end of an EI cheque or too troubled with demons of their own to make their way home.

Mickey Mac pushed through the door and made straight for the ladies room. After a few minutes, she lurched out, wobbled against a table, then stumbled through the door. Something up her nose or in her arm, Peterson reckoned.

He did the math. Two tricks an hour, ten hours on her feet, four on her back. Cranking up repeatedly, and stretching her veins like wet yarn. Skin like tissue paper. Likely sleeping in an unmade bed in a crummy room.

He knew the score on Mickey Mac, like he knew the

score for most of the runaways on the street — forty before they're twenty, buried under a junked-up life with a load of horse leaking from their arm.

His breathing quickened and his eyes flared. He gripped the table with an urge to fling it just anywhere. Then his cell phone fired a hole in his heart, and his spirit collapsed at the silence on the other end. Fingernails clawing at an open wound.

CHAPTER
FORTY-ONE

Peterson drove the bridge across the harbour to a small park that commemorated the first settlers on this side. He read the memorial plaques, then found a bench and watched the boat traffic. Now and again, he glanced down the street to where the green Chevy truck was parked. There had been no sign of Andy Miles in the dark sedan, not today, not yesterday. Danny arrived ten minutes later carrying a briefcase. He plopped down beside Peterson, opened the case, and handed Peterson a Colt automatic.

"I hope you know what you're doing with this," Danny said. "It comes with a toe tag, courtesy of the drug dealer I took it from."

"I'm just playing it safe," Peterson said. "My entourage is growing. The green Chevy pickup."

Danny didn't look. He had spotted the pickup before he had entered the park. "You run a licence check?"

Peterson shrugged. "I know who they are."

"Worried?"

"Not yet."

Danny pulled a folder out of the case and passed it to Peterson. "Bernie did the trace on Bettis."

Peterson opened the file and scanned the contents.

"Not the first time," Danny said. "Calgary, Niagara Falls, Windsor. He even did consulting work in Detroit."

Peterson stopped reading. "You'd think somebody would've discovered this."

"Medical profession," Danny said, "walled city. They're good at keeping bad news among themselves."

Peterson waggled the file. "Complaints but no charges."

"Nothing solid to stick him with," Danny said. "Staff won't speak up."

"Gloria Melanson will."

"Until some white coat stuffs a rag in her mouth, or a lawyer plays it out as ex-nurse with a grievance. I doubt he'll get a slap on the wrist."

"Plays out like that too many times. You have the flash drive?"

Danny went back into the case and handed him the copy Billy Bagnall had made of the video.

"What if we could show that the background on this matches the inside of Bettis's house?" Peterson said.

"That still might not be enough," Danny warned. "Loose connections won't make it, not with the high-priced lawyers he'll drag in. We need something airtight that links Bettis, and whoever else, to abusing these girls."

"And murdering Tiffany Banks."

"That's a long shot," Danny said. "You don't know they're connected. Anyway, we may be close to confirming she's the body on Airport Road. Bernie's cop friend in Fredericton chased down the parents to a house outside the city. The father wanted nothing to do with talking. He walked out. The mother wouldn't talk either. But Bernie had asked the Fredericton cop to get a cheek swab if the parents were willing. With the father outside, the mother agreed. And she signed off on the DNA test so she'd know if her daughter was dead."

"And?"

"And what? We're lucky if we get DNA results in a week."

Peterson watched a sailboat tacking in from the harbour mouth. He spoke without facing Danny. "Let's suppose there is a match and that Tiffany Banks was the murdered girl. How do we link her to Bettis?"

"No hospital records," Danny said.

"Not in the administration files. But what if Bettis keeps his own files?"

"Where? Home? Office?"

Peterson leaned over his knees, eyes still fixed on the sailboat. "Bettis said something at Stoddard about video recording all of his patients when they first arrived. He studies the tapes. That's what he said. And he offered to show us some. What if one of those patients was Tiffany Banks? That would make a direct link to Bettis."

"We'd never get a search warrant."

Peterson smiled. "I'm not a cop."

"That's break and enter!"

"Only if I get caught."

"It doesn't matter. Whatever evidence you get can't be used in court."

"No longer my worry."

"I don't want to hear that. You get caught, and time on the job will increase the length of sentence. A judge won't listen to your lawyer's request for minimums, not for a former cop. You know what they do to cops in prison, and the guards let them do it."

"I get in and out during visiting hours."

"Except that visitors need an escort to the top floor. Not to mention the guard on the door and security cameras throughout the building."

"I'll think of something," Peterson said. He reached into his jacket pocket and showed Danny the elevator key. "And I don't need an escort to the top floor."

"And if you come away empty-handed?"

"Then we're out nothing. I go back to cornering Bettis and giving him the third-degree, the old fashioned way."

"You'll need something solid to make him talk."

"We've broken suspects with less."

"If he doesn't break, you've shown your hand, and any evidence there was will be gone."

"We run the same risk with waiting," Peterson said. "I've been talking to people. If it gets back to Bettis that I've been pumping Heather McBride, Gloria Melanson, and two security guards, we can kiss any chance of nailing him goodbye."

Danny disapproved, but he still pulled a small voice recorder from the case. "Billy sends his compliments."

Peterson smiled, but Danny saw only worry. "An unwarranted recording won't hold up in court. Even a ten-cent lawyer will eat it up and spit it out."

"Still not my worry," Peterson said.

"Which means what?"

"I'm not sure. Something I've been thinking about since we found Teabag and Debbie Wilson. While I was punching holes in my house."

"I've been thinking too," Danny said. "It's a can of worms. You open it and if some spreads on Tooka, his boys will unzip you like Terry Sylvester."

CHAPTER
FORTY-TWO

Peterson shook off the Chevy pickup by twisting through a maze of side streets. Then he took the highway out of town, gunned it to 140, turned sharply off the first exit ramp, and doubled back over the bridge on his way to Stoddard.

He circled the hospital property a couple of times, noticing a service road that ran between the north side of the hospital and a field of high grass and knotweed. Then he drove through the main gate and parked in one of the empty visitor spaces. A grey SUV pulled in beside him and an elderly couple got out and headed for the building. Peterson followed them in.

Visitors and patients with passes stood outside a small coffee shop, talking. Staff and visitors walked through the lobby in both directions. The elderly couple made for the glassed-in security booth to register their visit in the log book that was propped on the counter in front of the security guard. There were three teenage girls near an elevator, two of them saying their goodbyes to the third. A white coat waited at the elevator beside the one the teens were waiting for. The door opened and the white coat walked in, taking a key from his coat pocket and slipping it into a slot in the panel on the right side of the door.

Peterson waited for his turn to register, reading patient names over the shoulders of the elderly couple and recording the times earlier visitors had signed in and out.

"You ever worry the visit won't go well?" Peterson asked the couple, loud enough for the heavyset security guard to hear.

The man looked up at Peterson. "Every visit," he said.

"My first," Peterson said, "and I'm getting cold feet."

"Are you a patient's father?"

Peterson put on a forlorn expression that he made sure the security guard saw. "Uncle," Peterson said. "My brother won't visit, and he won't let his wife. And right now I don't think I can."

Peterson started to turn away, then stopped and asked the couple, "You think I could go upstairs with you?"

"Of course," the elderly man said. "It might make it easier for you."

Peterson thanked them and edged closer to the booth to sign in. He checked out the monitors for dead spaces in what the cameras saw. The one on the parking lot covered the driveway and the visitors' parking spaces but fell off before it reached the sides of the building. The front-door camera was aimed straight at the double doors and caught the faces of anyone coming in and the backs of their heads going out.

The lobby camera had a narrow field of view that included the coffee shop and security booth, but only one of the elevators, the one used by visitors and patients with passes. Floor cameras viewed the nurses' stations and hallways, and the one on the administration floor had wall-to-wall coverage.

Peterson signed the name Archie Marcuchie and printed a patient's name, Lori Campbell, from one of the names someone had visited earlier.

The guard turned from watching the monitors. "It's not that bad," he said to Peterson. "Most of them appreciate the visit."

Peterson forced a smile and followed the elderly couple into the elevator.

"I hope it doesn't happen again," the woman said to her husband.

"It won't," her husband assured her. Then to Peterson, "There was a lockdown during our last visit. We couldn't leave the social room for almost an hour."

The elevator door opened on a female security guard sitting at a small metal desk beside a locked door that required a magnetic key card to open. There was another log book to sign. Then the guard lifted a stick with a magnetic card taped to one end and touched it to the keypad to buzz open the door.

The three entered. Nurses' station to the left, padded room to the right, and a long hallway straight ahead with a cuckoo's nest of teens in various stages of dress and undress pacing the floor or hanging out in doorways on either side of the hall, making friendly or goofing off. A few patients remained in their rooms, curled on their beds, facing the wall.

Peterson stood at the nurses' station watching the show.

His attention was drawn to a girl with a tomboy look and a side-mouth irritation. The girl could have been his daughter, with glassy eyes and a face full of bad mood.

The elderly woman watched him watching. Followed his eyes to the tomboy. "You really don't know what will come of it," she said by way of encouragement. "But it's worth the risk."

Peterson shot her a look that bordered on panic. Then he turned back to the door, caught the security guard's eye, and nodded that he wanted out.

"Short visit," the guard said.

"Yeah," Peterson said and pressed the black button for the staff elevator.

"That one's for staff," the guard said. "You need a special key to go down." She pointed to the elevator nearest her. "This one goes to the lobby."

"The patients can't go upstairs?" Peterson asked.

"A pass or a phone call from one of the doctors will get them up, but they have to sign out."

"And they can't go to the lobby on their own?"

The guard nodded. "They can if they have a pass."

By 7:30 p.m., fog had rolled in from the harbour mouth and a light rain had started to fall, blurring the windshield and forcing him to keep the engine running and the wipers going. From a community college parking lot across a busy four-lane, Peterson was watching Stoddard. Most of the administration staff had filed out of the hospital and into their cars hours ago. He raised his binoculars and squinted through the blur at the remaining three office lights on the fifth floor. By the cars still parked in the administration lot, these office lights belonged to Dr. Barbara Coughlin, Dr. Hamlin, and Dr. Bettis.

Peterson waited. Passed the time raising the binoculars and lowering them. His mouth was dry and his nerves strained by weighing duty against the thought of doing two to six for break and enter, being a former cop in medium security where other inmates would make sure he did hard time. He thirsted for some courage, but he held back from reaching for the mickey in the glove box. Anxious to get doing. Thinking it through. Thinking about what he was after and why.

His cell phone sounded. He dropped his head back and rolled his eyes. Then he answered the phone and opened the image he hated to see. Same unmade bed in the same filthy room. A dirty needle on the floor.

His stared at the hospital across the four-lane so as not to look at the image on his phone. Then he did.

After a long moment of silence, he said, "We're living it the same way, Katy. Getting even. That's what it is. I doubt it's what we wanted for a life. I doubt we'd stand in line for the chance to live like this. But this is what we're doing. Probably because of who I am. Not much of a father. I know I wasn't much good for your mother. But what about you, what you're doing to yourself? That's what matters now. That's what really matters. Your life. It matters to me. Oh Christ, Katy, it matters to me!"

The image disappeared as the connection broke. He kept talking to the blank screen. "I missed your growing up. I missed it all. But it doesn't mean I didn't . . . It doesn't mean that. I just . . . I couldn't let it go. And I couldn't bring it home. What I lived on the street didn't wash out."

He swallowed hard and turned his head to the hospital. "I still can't let it go. Twenty-something years on the job and I'm sweating it, and for what? What?"

He shut the phone off and shoved it into his jacket pocket. Waited some more, then, when there were only forty minutes of visiting hours left, one of the three remaining office lights snapped out. He scoped the front door, timing the elevator on the two-minute clock in his head, and saw Bettis exit the building and walk across the lot to his car.

Hamlin and Coughlin's cars were still in the lot. Peterson watched for a few minutes more. He couldn't wait. Not with the edge starting to blunt and his deep unwillingness to drink it back. He decided to chance it and swung the car from the community college lot and across the four-lane to the service road behind Stoddard. He parked and reached into the back seat for a small shoulder bag. He checked his watch. Thirty-five minutes to get in and out under the cover of visiting some messed-up teen.

His shoes and pant bottoms got wet as he negotiated a small hedge, passed through a thin stand of birch, and came up the side of the hospital, out of view of the camera on the parking lot. As he entered, he hid from the front door camera by pretending to wave to someone standing outside the coffee shop. Then he angled to a quarter profile for the lobby camera as he walked to the security booth to sign in. He used the same names for himself and for the patient that he had used earlier.

The guard from earlier in the day must have been pulling

the second half of a split shift. Coffee'd out. Eyes working the monitors and not the incoming visitors.

Peterson kept his head low and stepped to the elevators, outside the guard's view and into the camera's blind spot. With key in hand, he pressed for the staff elevator. The doors opened immediately and he slipped in without the guard ever looking his way. He inserted the key, pressed five, and pulled out a white lab coat from the shoulder bag. He quickly put it on over his green jacket.

The fifth floor hallway was ablaze in fluorescent light. The offices along the front of the building were dark, except for the two at either end, Hamlin's and Coughlin's.

He took his time walking down the hallway, reading the nameplates on the office doors. He had his lock pick in hand like it was a key. But when he tried the door to Bettis's office, he found it unlocked. He slipped in, closed the door, and clicked on a small LED flashlight. He cross-beamed the room. Ikea wall-to-wall. Desk and two chairs, credenza, file cabinet. Two abstract paintings on the wall facing the desk. Peterson made no effort to figure them out. Diplomas and medical certificates on the wall behind the desk above the credenza. He didn't bother to read them either. But he did take a close look at a large photo of a two-masted sloop under sail on the open water, and another of the same sloop, Bettis at the wheel, beaming, right hand cocked in a proud salute to camera. A third photo featured the sloop at anchor against a brilliant sunset, its name a stand out on the stern — *Jelly Fish*.

The desk was more a workstation with a cheap veneer top set on solid legs. An iMac was on top, twenty-seven-inch screen. The desk had a drop-down shelf in the centre for a keyboard and mouse.

Peterson pulled out the shelf and hit the power button at the back of the computer. The single tone of the iMac turning on sounded loud enough to raise the dead. He waited for the computer to load and run its opening sequence. Then a prompt window appeared, asking for a password.

Disappointed, he crossed the room to the three-drawer file cabinet and slowly pulled open the top drawer, looking for what was more his speed — paper files. The drawer was crammed with folders organized by year, but they all dated back to before Bettis's tenure at Stoddard. He started on the middle drawer, then stopped and went back to the iMac.

He remembered how he and most other cops worked the passwords to access department files, which had to be changed every week by order of internal security. Random combinations of numbers and letters that most cops couldn't remember. So they wrote the passwords on Post-It notes or masking tape they stuck on the backs of computers or the undersides of keyboards.

Bettis wasn't even that clever. Surgical tape on the front edge of the keyboard shelf bore an eight-digit number. Peterson entered it and the hard drive was at his command.

He clicked the Document icon in Finder and scrolled down the folder list: office schedules, hospital committees. One named "patients." He opened it and second from the top of file names was Tiffany Banks. "Goddamn," he muttered, now knowing for sure someone had pulled her file from administration records.

He read it quickly, paraphrasing the clinical jargon in

his head: A twenty-year-old runaway jungled up in a crack house was flamed out and baby talking on the street until she faced a strung-out moment of good sense and walked into Stoddard on her own.

Next came a lot of psychological mumbo jumbo that Peterson reworded as well: a mentally fragile young woman who was desperate for affection and prone to long bouts of depression. She had responded positively to antidepressants and psychiatric counselling, and she was discharged to continue counselling as an outpatient under the care of Dr. Karl Bettis.

Peterson pulled out the flash drive Danny had given him and inserted it into a USB port. Then he copied Tiffany Banks's file to the flash drive.

He scrolled down to the file for Michelle MacKinnon. A crackhead squeegee kid living on the street until a good cop wrangled her into social services, which signed her into Stoddard for thirty days of observation. He copied Mickey Mac's file to the flash drive.

Then he pulled the scroll bar to the bottom and found a patient's file without a name. It read pretty much the way Bettis had described Molly's condition when Peterson and Danny had interviewed the executive staff in the boardroom. He copied it as well.

He scrolled back through the files, looking for a title that stood out. A word that rubbed him the wrong way. A highlight. Bold lettering. Something unusual. A personal reference. Something private. He found nothing.

He ejected the flash drive then settled the flashlight beam on the credenza. He checked his watch. Fifteen minutes until visiting hours were over.

The credenza housed a single drawer and open shelves holding a scanner, printer, medical journals, and a few medical texts. He played the light over the titles, then opened the drawer. Inside were two rows of DVDs, each with a patient's name. They were in alphabetical order. He pulled the one for Tiffany Banks and set it aside, more proof she had been a patient of Karl Bettis. He found the one for Mickey Mac and pulled that too. He did not find one with no name.

Half a dozen flash drives were scattered in the space behind the DVDs. Not labelled. He selected one and slotted it in the iMac. Double clicked the video titled "Med. Conv. '12" and hit play. Ten seconds and he knew what it was, the keynote speaker at a medical convention moaning about the urgent need for government commitment to programs for mental health.

Peterson tried another flash drive. Different year, more of the same. He was digging for a third when he noticed an external hard drive on its edge at the back of the drawer. He set it on the desk beside the iMac and connected them with the USB cable from the scanner in the credenza.

He clicked the hard drive icon and entered the same eight digit number written on the surgical tape. It was incorrect. He squeezed a curse through his teeth. Stared at the hard drive as though daring it to show him what was hidden inside.

An office door opened and closed. Peterson cupped the flashlight and listened hard as someone walked to the elevator and waited. Then the elevator door opened and closed. From the sound of their voices, a teenaged girl and a woman greeted each other, then walked down the hallway and stopped outside Bettis's door.

"Do you want a Coke or something before we start?" the woman asked.

"I'm good," the teenager said.

The consulting room was directly across from Bettis's office, and now the door to it opened and they went inside.

Peterson listened. He checked his watch. Five minutes to closing. He shut down the iMac and tucked the two DVDs and the external hard drive into the shoulder bag. He cross-beamed the office for anything left out of place then listened at the door. Just voices coming from the consulting room. He exited Bettis's office and nonchalantly walked to the staff elevator. Once inside, he removed the white coat and stuffed it into the shoulder bag. He used the elevator key to override stops at the other floors, reached the lobby, and joined a young woman and two teens at the security booth to sign out. He used them to block the lobby camera as he made for the main door.

The rain had stopped and the parking lot was glazed with light. He stood for a moment in the portico, heaved a big breath, and retraced his steps along the side of the building and through the hedge to the service road where he'd parked.

The first thing he noticed was the broken window on the driver's side. Then the dark sedan parked across the service road, blocking his way out. Then Andy Miles stepping from the shadows and around the dark sedan. Walking forward. Dark jacket and a Blue Jays ball cap.

"What's in the bag, Peterson?" Miles demanded.

"Dirty laundry," Peterson said, changing shoulders with the bag so his right hand hung close to the pocket with the Colt Automatic.

"Drop the bag and I'll save you the cleaning bill." Miles narrowed the gap between them.

"It seems you clean up a lot of things," Peterson said.

"Maybe I don't like a mess."

"Your friends do."

Miles sneered. "Then it's a good thing it's me here and not them."

"Otherwise what? Choking a gun barrel like Teabag and the girl? Or stretched between two trees like Terry Sylvester?"

"Either way turns out bad for you," Miles said. He reached behind his back and his hand came out with a 9mm Sig Sauer. "So put the bag down and back off," Miles ordered.

Peterson didn't move.

"You said yourself, you're a certified screwball," Miles said. "I caught you sneaking from Stoddard and you went berserk." He stepped closer. They were five feet apart.

Peterson pointed his chin at the pistol. "One shot fired from department issue brings down a whole lot of investigation."

Miles snickered. "Like you said, I'm good at cleaning things up. Now drop the bag."

Peterson held the bag out between them, reaching deep inside for the nerve to keep his arm steady and not show the fear that was churning his guts. "You want it?"

Miles hesitated. "Just drop it, and we both go home."

"I hate going home," Peterson said. He dropped the bag and kicked it at Miles's feet.

Miles quickly stepped back, slipped on the wet road, and, as he did, Peterson lunged and grabbed the Sig in his left hand. He quickly reset his feet to throw a punch and landed a crunching right cross to the side of Miles's head.

Miles buckled but held the gun tight. Out of shape but strong as an ox, turning Peterson's hand and the gun to point at Peterson.

The gun exploded beside Peterson's ear. Then again. Panic took over. He dug his right thumb into Miles's eye. Pushing until Miles screamed wildly. Miles wrenched his body and pulled free the Sig. He had to re-grip to fire it.

In that split second, Peterson reared back and slammed his forehead against Miles's nose. Blood blew from both nostrils. His arms dropped, and Peterson yanked the gun free, flicked the barrel against the cop's cheek, then locked his hands together and snapped his forearm like an uppercut into Miles's jaw. Miles toppled to the ground face first. Peterson dropped onto him, his left knee landing on Miles's collarbone. Peterson heard the crack.

Gasping for breath, Peterson rolled to his feet, then quickly shoved the nine mil into his waistband and dragged Miles to the side of the service road. He fished car keys and an iPhone from Miles's jacket. He ran to the dark sedan, started it, and swung it to the side of the service road. Then he tossed the keys deep into the copse of birch trees, removed the SIM card from the phone, pocketed it, and tossed the phone. He ran back and grabbed the shoulder bag, climbed into the Jetta, cranked it, and peeled off.

CHAPTER
FORTY-THREE

He felt it. Tasted it. The adrenalin that suddenly drains from the muscles and nerves and leaves the body a wreck and the stomach coated with fear.

It was all he could do to wrestle the Jetta into a strip-mall parking lot, where he stopped and bowed over the steering wheel. His eyes blistered like a madman's and his thoughts raced, treading air, dithering and blathering, his body shaking like a blender at high speed.

Ten minutes, fifteen. He was still frayed but settling down. Forcing his breath to slow and his belly to unclench.

Twenty minutes later, he started the car and backed it up. Focused on what he still had to do and the time he had left to do it before Miles rattled a warning. To who? Tooka? Not likely, Peterson thought, gunning it out of the parking lot. Miles wasn't one to squeal on himself. He eased up on the gas and took it slow through the bridge toll. Licky lips for the whisky in the glove box. Dared himself to tough it out.

At 9:55 p.m., Peterson was standing in an alleyway across from the address Danny had given him. It was a two-storey red-brick Georgian, with a centre front door, two windows each side. Bettis sat behind one window, draped in lamplight, his back straight, legs crossed, reading and sipping what Peterson counted as his second drink in the last half-hour.

The wind had swung from southeast to west, blowing crisp fall air and rain into the city. Wet leaves covered the sidewalk and street.

Peterson unzipped his jacket, undid two buttons on his shirt, reached inside, and turned on a digital recorder strapped around his midsection. He buttoned up and pulled on a pair of latex gloves. He crossed the street, climbed the stairs, and hammered the front door. The bell would have been too polite.

Bettis glanced out the window, recognized Peterson, and came to the door. His welcoming smile was a little too welcoming.

No handshake, not on Peterson's part.

"Isn't it a bit late, detective?"

"Late for what?" Peterson said, pushing through the front door. "I have a few questions that can't wait."

Bettis led him to the room he had been sitting in, one filled with time-tinted oak and mahogany, and offered him a chair, which Peterson did not take. Then Bettis sat back where he had been sitting, beside a round parlour table under a portrait of a Victorian lady. Peterson prowled around two tilt-top tables and between two Windsor chairs with scrolled arms and stencilled seats, looking for something similar to the background in the video.

"This furniture as old as it looks?" Peterson asked, fingering a heart-and-star inlay in a work table.

"I collect art and antiques," Bettis said. He watched Peterson make his way about the room and stop before a dish dresser being used as a sideboard.

"I collect things too," Peterson said.

"Really?"

"I thought maybe you could help me with a few items I collected."

"I'll do what I can."

Peterson took the photos out of his jacket pocket.

"Here's five," he said. He passed one to Bettis. "This one you know, the girl who sliced her wrist in the Broken Promise. Her name is Molly."

"Molly?"

"Yeah, Molly, from Newfoundland."

Peterson passed Bettis another photo. "And this one is Michelle MacKinnon from St. Thomas, Ontario. You probably know her as Mickey Mac."

Bettis looked at the photo. His face was empty of expression. "I'm sorry, but I don't know her."

"She was one of your patients," Peterson said. "Hospital records have her down as one. According to some nurses at Stoddard, she was one of your favourites. The private consultations in the room across from your office weren't enough, so you discharged her to the street, where she's been screwed, blued, and tattooed. She's now loading her arm and turning tricks in the back seat of an abandoned car." Peterson moved close to Bettis and leaned into the psychiatrist's face. "Is that part of the cure?"

Bettis recoiled. "I don't appreciate the insinuation."

Peterson pointed at another photo. "What about the Hargrove girl, remember her?"

Bettis held Peterson's eyes, refusing to play Peterson's game of show and tell.

"You didn't look," Peterson said.

Bettis still held Peterson's eyes.

"Five of your favourites," Peterson said. "How many others were there?"

Bettis handed back the photos. "I'm sure there's a point to all of this."

Peterson took the photos and walked out of the room into the hallway. The door opposite was closed. Peterson marched in and flicked on the overhead lights.

Bettis was close behind. "You can't barge into my house and do what you want!"

Peterson turned on him. "I'm just checking out your collection and comparing it to mine." He unzipped the shoulder bag and stowed the photos. "You don't want to show me, I'll leave. But I'll come back, next time with a warrant."

"A warrant for what?"

Peterson ignored the question. He'd just seen what he had come to see. This was Bettis's showroom. "Funky," Heather McBride had called it. "Psychiatrist weird." Abstract paintings on the walls. Sculptures on the floor and on pedestals.

"It's déjà vu," Peterson said, standing back from an abstract painting like an art critic.

"What is?" Bettis stuck close.

"Being here. I've never been in here before, but it looks and feels so familiar. Like this painting, I'd swear I've seen it before."

"I doubt you have," Bettis said. "It's an original Gabriel Adair."

"Yeah, but you're a shrink, you know the feeling I'm talking about. Like I've been here or seen it before. Like the glass case with the knick-knacks —"

"Those are hardly knick-knacks."

"But I've seen it before. Up here, I guess," he said, pointing at his head. "Out of focus, you know, when the camera's aimed at something else and the painting or glass case just gets in the shot."

"Why are you here?" Bettis asked. Cold smile, sharp eyes.

Peterson ignored him. He eyed a couple more paintings and the sculpture of the earth mother with the big boobs. "I'd swear I've seen this before."

Then he saw a group of framed photographs that took him by surprise. There were six in all, one within a circle of five. They hung above a mahogany sideboard. The five photos, taken from various angles, were action shots of a two-masted sloop cutting the water like split. It was the same sloop as in the large photograph on the office wall at Stoddard, the *Jelly Fish*.

The centre photograph was of Bettis at the wheel. It was taken from behind to show off the masts and rigging, the polished deck, and spray over the bow. Bettis was shirtless and looking back over his shoulder at the camera, beaming. On his shoulder was the tattoo of a ram.

Peterson turned slowly from the framed photo to Bettis. "Your boat?"

"Yes."

"It must make you proud owning something like that."

"My pride and joy," Bettis said. "Most important thing I own."

"Good name," Peterson said, without taking his eyes off him. "*Jelly Fish.*"

"Would you mind telling me what this is about?" Bettis demanded. Firm voice. Uncomfortable eyes that travelled from Peterson to the photos on the wall.

Peterson turned back to the photo, tapped it. "A tattoo like that is special, right?"

"Original design."

"That's special. That's what I mean. A man with a special tattoo. It means something. It's a ram, isn't it?"

"Yes."

"And you're the only one with a tattoo like that?"

Bettis lost the charm. "What is this about?"

Peterson took the flash drive from his pants pocket. "One of your patients, Molly, the girl in the Broken Promise, she had this when she killed herself. I think it's yours. I think she lifted it the last time she was here."

Bettis stared. His left thumb flicked across his fingers.

"She was fifteen, maybe sixteen years old," Peterson said. He started to sit in the stuffed armchair, but he changed his mind and remained standing. "There's about fifteen minutes of video on this. Child pornography. All of it shot in this room. You know where this is going?"

"No, I don't." Bettis's voice had lost all self-assurance.

"Someone edited the video but didn't do a very good job," Peterson said, watching Bettis's reaction. "He left in one frame of one scene, a girl leaning over that chair. This guy was on her and going to town doggie style. The guy was naked. And on his left shoulder was a tattoo just like the one in that photograph."

Bettis looked at the photograph on the wall. He didn't answer. He barely breathed.

Peterson shoved the flash drive back into his pants pocket. Then he dug into the shoulder bag for the hard drive. Taking a chance. "The photo makes a good case," Peterson said, colouring his voice with certainty, "but seeing you in action makes a better one."

"What are you talking about?"

"The passwords we pick," Peterson said. "Something easy to remember, mother's name, dog's name, something we own, our pride and joy — something like Jelly Fish."

Bettis's jaw dropped.

"It was like playing a lottery number and hitting the jackpot," Peterson said, bluffing his way, talking about evidence he hadn't seen. He had done it before, pounding a suspect with nothing to go on but a feeling. "Home movies. Dirty details."

"How did you —?"

"Some things are easy to find. More than enough to bring charges."

Peterson had seen it many times before, the sudden defeated look of a criminal: the jittery, unfocused eyes seeking refuge, the mouth suddenly dry, the tic in a cheek, the body shivering with tension.

He had him. Peterson knew it and so did Bettis. And all of a sudden the loathing Peterson felt for this man came to a head. His insides churned to bust the man. And in that churning, he saw Molly's tortured face. He saw her blood spurting, the flayed flesh, and her wrist sliced to the bone. He saw the drug-racked face of Mickey Mac, and he saw other girls naked to this weasley man, stoned and weakened under his weight.

"I saw how you like it rough," Peterson said, pressing his luck. "Hurt them a little, maybe a lot? Teenage girls. Younger. You know what that makes you behind bars? Word gets around prison and you know what they're going to do with you? They're going to make it hurt. Oh yeah! And inmates know how to hurt."

There was fear in Bettis's eyes.

"This time you don't walk away from it," Peterson said. "Not this time. No simple complaint from a psychiatric patient. No hand slap. Not this time." He held up the hard drive. "This time there's real evidence, and staff willing to testify. You'll get four, maybe five years with time off. That's a long stretch behind bars. Day and night looking over your shoulder, wondering all the time which one of those motherfuckers is going to make you his wife. You're going to pay for the hurt you gave those girls. You're going to find out what it's like to get it up the ass."

Bettis caught his breath. His legs gave out and he clutched a chair back to steady himself and dropped into the seat.

Peterson grabbed a wooden chair and set it close to Bettis. He sat and leaned forward so Bettis could feel his breath.

"That's what they do to pedophiles in prison. Everybody gets a turn. Humped over your bed in a jail cell. Up and down the line until some big dude says, 'You're mine!'"

"Stop!" Bettis cried.

But Peterson didn't stop. "Any of those girls beg you to stop? Or did you have them too drugged up to feel a thing?

But you'll feel it! A candy ass like you will be wishing you could draw glass across your wrist."

Bettis whimpered.

"Hard evidence. People that will testify. It's over." His voice lowered. "It's over."

Bettis mumbled something and his head fell, as though he had lost the strength to hold it up.

Peterson knew the body language of a criminal when he breaks, a man weakened by what he has been doing and now relieved that it is over.

Peterson turned Bettis's face so they were eye to eye. "It's time to talk. Get it off your chest. The hard drive tells the story, but now for the details. I want names. I want you blowing cover for the big shots you share the girls with. And I want the ins and outs of your arrangement with Tooka."

Bettis started to shake his head, but Peterson tightened his grip on his face. "You get it nine ways to Sunday in the Big House, or I can do you a big, big favour. Ball's in your court!"

Bettis didn't take long to think about it. He nodded and gave Peterson what he was asking for. Three names. Big shots. David Heaney, CEO of Edgar-Eco Resources; James Williston, sitting senator from the Conservative Party; and Richard Pratz, CEO of Blatch, Collins, and Werner Pharmaceuticals and board member at Stoddard. There were several others, but none of them had the prestige and political and social clout as those three.

"Years," Bettis said. Vacant eyes. Desperate to tell it. A craven begging to pardon himself. "Fifteen. More. Alone. Keeping it to myself, until . . ."

"Until someone caught on to what you were doing," Peterson led him.

"Yes."

"Nurses?"

Bettis nodded. "Changing hospitals. And then it got so involved."

"By including others?"

"Pratz wanted them. He had friends. A club he called it. A private club."

Peterson sensed where Bettis was going. More players, more girls, more risk, which meant taking the sleazy games outside the hospital.

"Did you go to Tooka, or Tooka come to you?"

Bettis swallowed hard. "I went to him."

"How did that happen?"

"I asked around. You learn who to ask. Then I got a visit."

"From Tooka?"

"No. Someone else."

"You asked for young girls?"

Bettis didn't have to answer. His face said it all.

"How young?" Peterson demanded.

Bettis shook his head.

"How young?"

"Early teens," Bettis said. "Pratz wanted them younger, but I didn't."

"What about the others? What did they like?"

"Williston and Heaney wanted them as young as they could get."

"And Tooka provided?"

Bettis buried his face in his hands.

"I didn't hear you."

"Yes."

"You tried some out in the hospital," Peterson said, struggling to control his feelings, forcing his voice to sound calm. "Closed door, private consultations. Then you discharged your favourites to Tooka. Pick of the crop. But Molly you couldn't discharge. So you walked her out the front door."

Bettis looked up, quick to shift blame. "Pratz wanted her too. It was his idea."

"But you went along."

"Because . . . the risk of it. The pleasure. Nurses outside the door. They could have heard it all, but I didn't care. It was like before."

"In the other hospitals?"

"No planning. No videos. A sudden urge. That's all. A need. A coarse need."

Peterson struggled to stay cool. He locked his mind on what needed doing. "So what happened to Tiffany Banks? You get too rough?"

"Not me!" Bettis screamed. "You saw the video. You saw it wasn't me!"

"I saw a guy slapping her around." Peterson made it sound true. "He looked like you."

"It was Williston!"

"And you recorded it!"

Bettis covered his face again. "She was dead . . . she was just dead."

"Who buried her?"

Bettis lowered his hands. His eyes were deep pools of fear. "We got the body and her out of the house. His car."

"Her? Another girl?"

"Yes."

"Which girl?"

"The photo you have, the one who killed herself in that bar."

"She was in the house?"

"And I panicked. Williston said he'd take care of it. He had connections. He called and the cop told us what to do."

"What cop?"

"A cop! A detective."

"What was the cop's name?"

"I don't know. Williston made the call. He knows."

"What did he tell you to do?"

"He told us where to take it. But it wasn't safe there."

Peterson cocked his head. "Where wasn't it safe?"

"Across the harbour. A warehouse. A . . ."

"The Drop Zone?"

"It wasn't safe." Bettis was shaking his head in distress. "Tooka said it wasn't safe."

"So you moved the body," Peterson said.

"Not us. Tooka moved it. Buried it."

Peterson let the silence have its time, then he held up the hard drive. "You recorded how many girls?"

Bettis shrugged.

"Why?"

"To watch."

"And the flash drive?"

"For when we travel."

Peterson pointed at the chair across the room. "We swab that chair for DNA, how many girls we going to find?"

That shocked Bettis. His eyes went to the chair. "Each of us had our favourites."

"How many?"

"I wasn't cruel to them. I tried to make it personal."

"How many?"

Bettis whimpered. "Ten. Twelve. I don't know. I just don't know!"

"More?"

"Yes, more."

Peterson tried to unclench his fists. "What were their names?"

"I only knew the older ones, the ones I had as patients," Bettis said. "I didn't know the others."

"Where did the others come from?"

"Tooka."

Peterson put it together. The older ones were the psychiatric wrecks. The others were . . . "How young were the others?"

Bettis hung his head.

"Early teens, pre-teens?" Peterson pressed.

Bettis nodded.

"Younger?"

"No! Not younger."

Peterson lowered his voice. "But you wanted them younger."

"Not me." Bettis was sobbing.

Peterson wanted to sink inside himself, to creep into a quiet place where he could not be found. But he hadn't finished. He kept his voice low, like a priest's during a confession. "Did these other girls have names?"

"No names. Tooka insisted on that. He gave them numbers."

"And you and the boys just loved where he tattooed the numbers."

Bettis didn't answer. Peterson leaned back, let the silence settle.

Another question suddenly occurred to him. How had the 911 caller known about Bettis and Williston taking Tiffany Banks's body to the Drop Zone? He shot forward on his chair. "The girl that killed herself in the Broken Promise, Molly, she went with you to the warehouse didn't she?"

Bettis nodded. "We forgot she was in the car. She was stoned. Out of it. Asleep in the back seat."

"But she followed you in."

"Yes."

"And saw you bury Tiffany Banks."

"I don't know what she saw. She was stoned."

"And you never told Tooka she'd been there," Peterson said.

"I knew what he would do."

"Is that why she was your favourite? Worried about what she might remember?"

Bettis closed his eyes and didn't answer.

"For months she was your favourite," Peterson said. "Did you ever talk about that night?"

"No."

"Not about the Airport Road?"

"I didn't know about it! Not until they dug up the body."

"How did you know? There was no ID made on the body."

"I didn't need an ID."

Peterson thought for a moment. "And she didn't need one, either."

"Not after Williston threatened her. He said he'd kill her too."

304

"When was that?"

"When she was talking gibberish. Nothing we gave her would keep her quiet. Then she . . . the drugs or whatever . . . she just went wild. Screaming about the baby, the baby. Williston, he . . ."

"He what?"

"He hit her."

"The way he did the other girl?"

"Yes. Yes. And she was screaming. And Williston was beating her. I grabbed her. I didn't know what to do. I grabbed her and opened the door and threw her out."

Bettis bawled. Peterson waited.

"Then what?"

"I called Tooka."

"You called Tooka?"

Bettis nodded. "She was outside in the cold. Crying. And I was afraid Williston would do it again."

"So you called Tooka."

"They came for her."

"Who came for her?"

"Tooka and two others. They took her away."

Bettis shook terribly. Peterson waited until he settled a little.

"What did they do with her?"

Bettis looked at nothing. "I was afraid."

"What did they do with her?"

"Dumped her."

"On the Strip?"

"Yes."

"Tooka told you that?"

"He said no one would believe a crazy bitch like her."

Peterson got up and circled his chair. He wanted to pound his fists into Bettis's face, the way he had pounded holes in the walls of his home. He sat back down. "What about Stephen Emery?"

Bettis dropped his head. His lower lip trembled. "I didn't want . . . But Tooka said there was a problem. He needed to make an example."

"And you just happened to have a patient that could help."

"I didn't want to."

"But you did! You opened the door!"

Bettis said nothing.

"Tooka tell you the problem?" Peterson asked.

"He said someone had talked too much."

Peterson stood again and walked over to the sideboard. "His name was Terry Sylvester," he said, as though hearing the name would make what happened more real for Bettis. "You know what Tooka did to him."

Bettis nodded.

Peterson opened his shirt to show Bettis the voice recorder. Then he switched it off.

"Simple scenario," he said. "I go to Tooka, tell him about the hard drive. Then I play this back so he knows what you said. Then Tooka pays you a visit. If you're lucky, you won't be alive when he cuts you open."

Bettis covered his face. He couldn't speak. He couldn't cry.

"You own a gun?" Peterson asked.

Bettis shook his head and the shaking seemed to release his voice. He howled.

Peterson took out the Colt Automatic, chambered a round, and eased down the hammer.

"Here's the big favour I offered," he said. He set the gun on the sideboard and started for the front door. "All you have to do is pull the trigger."

CHAPTER
FORTY-FOUR

Peterson drove straight home to download the digital recording of Bettis's confession onto his computer, then dump it to an eighty-gig iPod.

His hands were still shaking from what he had heard, and they shook even more from picturing what he was about to see. He needed something to calm down. But he refused to give in to the craving. Wrapped his arms around himself to hold back from giving in. It helped steady him.

He clicked the icon for the hard drive and entered the password: Jelly Fish.

The video came up and started playing automatically. Close up images of male and female body parts squirrelling against each other. Then the zoom pulled back to reveal the slick bodies of Bettis and two nymphs going at it on a throw rug on a hardwood floor. The ram's head tattoo was clearly visible on Bettis's shoulder.

Peterson moused over the timeline. There was more than two hours of video. All the players, all the girls, all the positions. Ten minutes of viewing was more than enough for him. He scanned the rest until he saw Senator James Williston beating Tiffany Banks to death.

He left the den for the dark kitchen, where he splashed cold water on his face and stood for a few minutes, staring out the window above the sink. Then he returned to the den and copied the hard drive onto his computer, then onto two more flash drives.

He paced the den and living room, worrying around the edges of what he was about to do, about what he had kept from Danny, about the green Chevy truck.

The truck had tailed him for days. He'd lose it when he needed to and let it tag along when it served his purpose. It had been parked a block away from Bettis's house and was now in the Shopper's Drug Mart parking lot at the end of Peterson's street.

He had seen the driver up close more than once, a bruiser with hair to his shoulders. He hadn't needed a clean look at the passenger to know who it was: Dickie Palmer.

Peterson phoned Danny and told him all that had happened at Stoddard, with Miles, and later with Bettis.

"You didn't give Bettis a lot of choice," Danny cracked. "Face Tooka, swallow a bullet, or blow the whistle on himself."

"We get the same results," Peterson said.

There was a short silence then Danny said, "You don't

have to go there. The hard drive blows this whole thing wide open."

Peterson didn't answer. Long silence. Then Danny said, "If you're worrying about me, don't. I'm still good."

Miles's Sig Sauer was on the dining-room table. Peterson removed the clip, checked that it was loaded, and snapped it back. He pulled on latex gloves and wiped the gun down with a cloth napkin. As he shoved it into his jacket pocket, he looked at the remaining framed photograph of his wife and daughter on the wall above the sideboard. He removed the gloves and traced their faces with a finger. Then he reached into the sideboard for a bottle of London Dock. He poured half a glass and took it to the den and sat in the leather recliner.

He held the glass in both hands and shut his eyes. His thoughts played hard against his feelings. It felt as if his nerves had grown on the outside of his skin. He sat there, thirsting for a drink but not giving in, for a little more than twenty minutes, then he carried the glass to the kitchen sink and dumped it. He checked his watch, patted his pockets for the iPod, the flash drive, and the Sig, and he left the house.

He drove across the bridge to the Strip, trying not to think, not to worry, but keeping track of the Chevy truck in his rear-view mirror.

The Posse worked out of a backroom at the Flame, a raunchy two-bit lounge off the Strip. It was nearly 2:00 a.m. when he turned into its parking lot. He put on a fresh pair of latex gloves and, from under the driver's seat, retrieved the cat's paw and slid it up his jacket sleeve. Then he clipped the expired badge onto his jacket and walked over to the main door of the Flame, pausing just long enough to see the Chevy truck swing into the parking lot.

CHAPTER
FORTY-FIVE

Two guys in black leather coats were sitting on stools at the crescent shaped bar. Both were hard bodies. One wore shades despite the low light, and the other had a lot more muscle. Behind them was a door to a backroom.

The tables across from the bar were all empty, but a young woman and two men were in a booth near the front door. From what Peterson overheard as he walked in, the men were trying to negotiate a two-for-one deal.

The bartender was another of Tooka's muscle. He wore a dark red shirt and black apron, and his head was shaved. Peterson was certain that he had seen him shaking down pimps along the Strip.

Peterson reached the bar and the bartender snapped down a coaster bearing a stylized image of an Olympic torch.

"You drinking?" he asked, nodding at Peterson's badge.

"Talking," Peterson said.

"Talking's not on tap."

"You're not the one I want to talk to. Tooka is." At the mention of the name, the two heavy hitters swivelled his way. Peterson made sure they saw the badge, but he didn't need to. By the looks he got when he came through the door, they'd already pegged him as a cop.

"He's busy," the guy with shades said. His voice sounded familiar.

"Tell him to get un-busy," Peterson said. "I got something for him."

"What you got?" The same guy asked with a hitch in his voice that took Peterson back to the night in the hospital district when two guys had laid a beating on him.

"I don't play show and tell with the hired help," Peterson said.

The muscle man got off his stool, showing his size.

"The badge make you tough?" Muscle man challenged, his voice croaky, like the voice of the man who had clubbed Peterson from behind.

Peterson smiled without warmth. Hearing that voice made him want the guy even more. "The badge just makes opening your skull legal."

The muscle man's grin gleamed with menace. "Lose the badge, I'll fuck you up!"

"Don't let it slow you down."

They faced off for a second or two then the bartender intervened, saying, "No trouble!"

Peterson broadened his grin for the muscle man. "Somebody yank your chain?"

That did it. The muscle man shifted to his back lag to get

his weight behind his fist. But Peterson had already dropped the cat's paw down his sleeve into his hand. He brought it up hard between the muscle man's legs.

The muscle man grunted and bent over. He hit the floor after the cat's paw came down once on his shoulder and once across the back of his neck.

Peterson quickly turned to the bartender and to the guy with shades to make sure they were staying out of it. He pulled his cell phone from his jacket pocket and punched in a ten-digit number. "I'd like to report a bar fight at the Flame," he said to the man who answered. Then to the threesome in the booth near the door he said, "Time to leave."

Then the backdoor opened and a guy with dreads and wearing a white shirt with a vest and pants from a pinstriped suit came out. "What the fuck's going on?"

Peterson nudged the muscle man with his toe. "Somebody thought he was Mike Tyson."

"A cop," the bartender announced.

The guy looked at the muscle man on the floor and then at Peterson. "Did you get your badge back, or you just faking it?"

"The man with the inside track," Peterson said. "That would make you Tooka."

"What are you after?"

"I have a message from Karl Bettis."

Tooka looked back down at the man on the floor. "Is this the message?"

"This is just the envelope."

Tooka gestured with his head for Peterson to follow him into the backroom. Once inside he gave an order, "Out!"

A girl in bra and panties jumped up from a black leather

couch, hastily gathered her clothes and left by way of a door to an adjacent room.

The office was all black leather and chrome. A couch and half a dozen leather armchairs, a big-screen TV, and a chrome and glass table that held an Xbox, PlayStation, and Bose sound system. There was a stocked bar in one corner and a desk in another. Tooka's suit jacket hung from a high-back swivel chair.

Tooka slid behind the desk and lowered himself into the chair, opening a top drawer as he went down. The move wasn't lost on Peterson.

"What's the message?" Tooka asked.

"I'm reaching for it," Peterson said. He still held the cat's paw in one hand. With the other he reached into his shirt pocket and came out with the iPod. He went over to the Bose and, without taking his eyes off Tooka, docked it.

Tooka picked up a remote off his desk and pressed play.

Peterson remained standing. They stared at each other as they listened. Both expressionless, neither willing to give anything away.

When the recording stopped, Tooka leaned back and studied Peterson. Then he said, "You think you got something?"

"There's more. A hard drive with lots of sex. And one murder."

"Nothing but bullshit, man. Chump change for a lawyer to eat this up. So where's it going? I mean, what are you after? You got a number, tell me the number."

Peterson took one of the chairs. "That sounds like worry."

Tooka smiled. "The price I'll pay for peace of mind."

Peterson gave him the smile right back. "I got nothing for sale."

"Out-of-work cop, alone in a big house, decent neighbourhood. A few extra in the wallet goes a long way to paying off that mortgage."

"Like Andy Miles?"

"Nickel-and-dime cop. Errand boy."

"A fixer," Peterson said.

"I get a ticket, the man comes across."

"Like a double murder in the old military housing or a guy strung up and gutted."

"What language is that? I don't understand a word you're saying."

Peterson held the smile. He undid the buttons on his shirt to show he wasn't wired. "Let's talk about you. Big operation, pimp business here and out west, and I'm the one holding a way to cramp your style."

"You got nothing that'll stick," Tooka said.

"It doesn't have to stick, not to you anyway. But I have more than enough to stick it to Bettis and his little band of perverts."

Tooka lost his smile. Then he flattened his hands on the desktop. Careful. Unsure.

"I have photos and video of the big-time players doing dirty things with little girls," Peterson said. "And one of them, a mucky muck in Ottawa, getting carried away with his hands. The kid died. Somehow it gets on the internet, then the media runs with it. The public scandal will have the cops scrambling. Your name is bound to come up, and then they'll ride your ass, while an unnamed source leaks information. Steady flow. Word gets out where you work, where you play, the kind of dirt under your nails. A week, maybe two, they shut you down and choke off your supply. Then the same source leaks it that Tooka is willing to cop a plea. And then all of a sudden Tooka has to answer to his biker friends."

Tooka's surprise showed. "You a crazy motherfucker to bust in here and rag my ass with bullshit. I mean what the fuck, huh? You don't make it to the front door."

Peterson rose from the chair, pulling out the pistol as he stood. "This should get me out."

Saying it like that, with the gun in his hand, and Tooka twitching at hearing it, sharpened all his senses. He could smell the stink of beer and whisky from the lounge and the girl's perfume still hanging in the room. The shadows stirred beyond the edge of lamplight, low voices and music seeped through the closed door, and the rumble of traffic on the Strip shivered the window. Tension grew in the space between them. And the urge that had propelled him to this moment slowly unburied its ugliness.

They stared at one another, Tooka sizing up the options, Peterson's insides clenched with anger.

Then Tooka said, "You won't shoot me on a childfucker's say so."

"That, and two girls you whored out," Peterson said. "One opened her wrist in the Broken Promise. The other swallowed a Glock 20."

Tooka held up his hands in mock surrender, trying not to show the sweat. "Nothing points the finger at me about those girls!"

"This ain't a finger," Peterson said. A sweat bead ran down the side of his face.

"That'd be ice-cold killing." Tooka looked frightened. "You a man that can do that?"

Peterson didn't answer. He just looked down the barrel of the gun into the other man's eyes.

"I sweet talk them," Tooka said. "Serve them dinner when they hungry and horny. Pimp them out too, man. You know what I'm saying? Candy don't make them run away from home. Those girls are already broken in pieces when they come to me. I'm just using the garbage people like you throw out on the street."

Peterson's thoughts took him someplace else for a moment. The gun in his hand lowered a bit.

Tooka saw the chink in Peterson's resolve. "You know what I'm saying," he said. "I got ears to the Strip. I know about the cop that drinks his face off. Yeah, the one standing right here with a sorry-ass look that says he put his own trash out on the street."

Tooka's hand on the desktop inched closer to the open drawer. "You dumping down on me for what you fucked up. But it wasn't me that shut the door on your girl's coming home."

Peterson raised the gun, his finger on the trigger. His mouth was dry and his hands were wet.

Tooka swallowed, moved his hand back, and dropped his cool-ass swagger.

"Life fucks us up, man. Before long we working the only jobs the man let us do. We don't even get to drive the trash truck. Why else we pimping whores and selling whatever else we sell on the street? Ain't me that put me here."

Peterson felt not an ounce of sympathy. "I cap you now, you'll die in wet pants."

Tooka's eyes widened, unblinking as he watched Peterson's finger on the trigger.

"Misunderstood street rat is just sucking wind to my ears," Peterson said. "Make it self-defence."

Tooka choked off a cry and moved his hands farther away from the open drawer.

"You shoot me, they come for you," he said.

"Not if the gun that drilled you belongs to Andy Miles."

Peterson raised the gun a half-inch higher. The trigger felt good against his finger. Even better was the sight of Tooka across the barrel, covering his face with his hands, his voice squeaking like a child who's been forced into a corner.

Peterson's smile broadened as he backed up to the lounge door. With the hand that held the cat's paw, he reached behind for the doorknob.

Tooka looked dumbfounded.

"You're just well-dressed scum and not worth the bullet it would take to kill you," Peterson said. "Besides, I like knowing someone else will make a bigger mess."

He cracked the door and called into the lounge. "Danny!"

"I'm here," Danny called back. "Everybody's sitting tight. But the one on the floor still hasn't moved. Bernie kicked him, and he didn't budge."

"What the hell is she doing here?"

"Partners," Bernie called back.

Peterson snickered and backed into the lounge, and the three of them backed out the front door. Peterson gave Danny the digital recordings before they separated in the parking lot, Peterson making for the Jetta and Danny and Bernie for a Ford sedan. Peterson hesitated before opening the door, looking hard across the parking lot to the passenger in the green Chevy truck. When he'd got Dickie Palmer's attention, he nodded at the front door of the Flame. Then he climbed into the Jetta and drove away.

CHAPTER
FORTY-SIX

Peterson drove straight home. Danny and Bernie paid Bettis a visit and found him crouched in a corner beside the sideboard with his hands over his head. The Colt was where Peterson had left it.

By 10:00 a.m., Bettis had signed a lengthy statement based on the digital recording Peterson had given to Danny. The lawyer at his side had advised him against it, told him that the recording would not stand up in court. Bettis signed it anyway. He wanted it over and was relieved that it was. His lawyer bargained on Bettis's behalf, agreeing that his client would turn Crown witness in exchange for a lesser charge of sexual assault.

The story went viral on the internet a couple of days before making it to the CBC and CTV nightly newscasts. Local and national newspapers ran it over the following week.

There were no names at first, but within a few days, they made the front page. There was much from the hard drive the broadcast media didn't show, and much that it did. The internet was less discriminating. A police investigation found Bettis's pals had hard drives with the same content. Within a week, the RCMP laid charges against David Heaney, Richard Pratz, and Dr. Karl Bettis: sexual assault, sex with minors, unlawful confinement, and a dozen others. It took another two days for the RCMP to confirm DNA results. That's when they charged Senator James Williston with murder.

Then an unnamed source leaked more information about a criminal ring that trafficked young women back and forth across the country as sex slaves. That brought the RCMP farther into the act, had whores and pimps ducking for cover, and had the brass in cop shops in every big city in every province scrambling to crack down.

✦

Vindictive was how Overton had described Tooka. Hot tempered. Quick to get even. Peterson had expected Tooka to hit and hit soon. When he still hadn't after a week, Peterson figured he had dropped out of sight to avoid the pressure. Still he stuck close to home, the Sig Sauer on his hip or well within reach. At night he roamed the dark house, peeking from the windows. Danny and Bernie came by regularly, keeping watch.

Peterson stayed clear of Anna. He couldn't face her after what he had felt while threatening Tooka, the urge to see the man's face melt like gum on hot pavement. Tooka could have gone down without him going face to face. But he needed it then, the way he needed it now. He needed to freeze that moment with the gun in his hand, pointed at Tooka's head. That was his life.

It was another grey afternoon with a coming storm darkening the sky. Peterson spent it raking leaves. Then going inside for a beer. One beer. Weaning off. Dozing in the recliner.

His head filled with faces, girl's faces. Ones with false smiles on the street and others fear-stricken among the shadows. He saw them all at once, turning tricks in alleys and in fleabag rooms with unmade beds and wallpaper peeling away. He saw them hustling the passing traffic. He saw them as wet leaves kicked along the gutter.

Then Anna slipped into his thoughts. She was standing across from him in her kitchen. "I won't live your life," she was saying. "I won't let myself. Do you understand?" Then she turned from him and left the house, on her way to some place he knew he could never go.

He sank deeper and dreamed of blisters of coloured lights and splintered planks boarding up empty warehouses with graffiti-scarred walls. He heard the wind rattling the window and his cell phone ringing somewhere far away. His mind drifted back to where he was dozing in the recliner. He opened his eyes. The phone was still ringing. He reached for it.

"Daddy!"

His breath caught at the sound of her voice. Tears flooded his eyes, and his voice squeaked. "Katy!"

After a long silence, she said, "I want to come home."

"Yes! Oh God, yes."

"Open the door," she said. "Daddy, open the door. I want to come in."

He looked across the living room to the front door.

"Daddy! Daddy, please!"

He scrambled from the chair and was across the living room and at the door. Opened it to the wind and to a young girl in a grey hoodie.

"Katy!"

The girl lifted her head. Her dark eyes were empty. Then she raised a .22 calibre Smith & Wesson and fired.

The first shot caught him in the chest and drove him backward into the house. The second blew apart his left knee as he hit the floor. The third pounded into the ceiling, as Danny slammed the girl face-first into the doorjamb.

Danny ripped the gun from the girl's hand and threw it aside. Then he rocked her head against the jamb again and flung her into the house, where she crumpled to the floor.

He whipped out his phone, told the dispatcher a police officer was down, and where. Then he dropped to his knees beside Peterson and hugged him, begging his friend to hold on. He heard Peterson mumbling his daughter's name, felt his friend's choppy breaths, and listened for the sirens.

CHAPTER
FORTY-SEVEN

He watched leaves floating down a slow river, then swirling around a big rock into a deep pool that lay beneath a branch. A boy was gripping the branch, afraid to let go. Afraid of his shadow on the water, afraid of what lay hidden beneath it. His mind slipped away.

He sensed a shape beside him. Felt a hand in his hand, fingers stroking his. A voice calling him back from where he had gone.

He opened his eyes. There was no one there at his bedside, just an IV pole haloed in white light.

After surgery, he was two days in ICU with an endotracheal tube down his throat and a ventilator whooshing air in and out of his patched lung. Another pump sucked residual air and blood from his chest cavity. Then the tube in his throat was gone and the whooshing stopped. He could hear voices but sensed they were not speaking to him.

He was two more days mostly in a cloud of thoughtlessness, but thankful for Danny and Bernie's three-minute visits, which a nurse timed to the second.

"She waited with me during surgery," Danny said.

They had moved Peterson from the ICU to a semiprivate. He was still groggy on painkillers, but clear-headed enough to know who Danny was talking about.

"She visited a couple of times when you were in ICU. Prayed over you, like you had a soul or something. I had coffee with her. A funny duck. She likes you, Peterson, but I'll be goddamned if there's anything in it for you. This whole mess, the Broken Promise, you getting shot, the whole goddamn thing, has screwed her up. She said she was going back to the convent. How do you deal with that?"

Peterson turned his head away.

The next day the nurses had him sitting up in a chair. He was fussing with a bowl of soup and a chicken salad sandwich when Danny and Bernie came in.

"You look a hell of a lot better than when I left yesterday," Danny said.

Peterson forced a smile. "I heal fast. Nothing but scars, inside and out."

"I could have gone easier with news about the nun, but when the hell did we ever hold back?"

"Skip the hearts and flowers. Who's the shooter?"

Danny looked at Bernie, and Bernie said, "A seventeen-year-old junkie working the street."

Danny added, "I broke her cheek bone. A kid. What the hell's a seventeen-year-old girl doing with a handgun? City Hall brags about it getting better, about the crime rate going down. If they only knew. If they only fucking knew."

"What's her name?"

Danny lifted a package of crackers from Peterson's tray and opened it.

"Michelle MacKinnon," Bernie said. "Mickey Mac."

Peterson heaved a breath and the pain brought him up short.

"I thought that would make it hurt," Danny said. "Tooka went after your weak spot and used a shooter you'd never expect." He pulled out a cracker. "What's the long-range forecast on you?"

"Big hole, popped lung. I won't be on the dance floor any time soon. They want another go at my knee."

Danny looked out the window to a courtyard where several patients were walking about. He turned back to Peterson, a big grin on his face. "Miles got called on the carpet. No hard evidence, but there's enough innuendo to keep him sitting behind a desk until he retires."

Peterson scowled.

"Yeah, I know," Danny said. "But I heard auditors are screening his accounts for large cash deposits. Maybe something will turn up."

A nurse entered the room, saw Peterson had visitors, and said she'd be back.

"Should I tell him?" Bernie said to Danny.

"Be my guest," Danny said.

"There was a fire at the Rendezvous while you were in ICU," Bernie said.

"Somebody muscling in," Danny added. "At least that's what's on the street. Everyone's guessing, but nobody knows who they are."

"Nothing but ashes," Bernie said. "How timely was that?"

"What do you mean?" Peterson asked.

"It came two days after somebody busted up the Flame," Danny said. "They did a number on Tooka's boys, but no one's talking."

"What about Tooka?"

"He wasn't there," Bernie said, "at least not when the police showed up."

"An undercover thinks whoever busted up the place took him for a ride," Danny said.

"I'll bet they did," Peterson said.

"My guess is they'll dump him where he won't be found. But who's looking? No one's reported him missing, and it's not a homicide until a body washes up."

Peterson toyed with the soup. "And you're not looking."

Danny smiled. "Budget cuts."

They held each other's eyes, both thinking the same thing, both unwilling to compromise the other by saying it.

FORTY-EIGHT

In his mind, the knee brace and straight-legged walk made him a cripple. The cane made him look old. The two young women who cleaned his house once a week made him feel even older. Ushering him from one room to another while they worked. Then talking to each other as if he wasn't there.

His doctor had said he'd lose the cane in a week or two, and the brace once the deep healing was done and his leg muscles strengthened. A couple of months. Maybe more. It depended on his dedication to therapy and willingness to exercise. "That knee won't bend the way it once did," the ortho doctor had said, "and you won't be running any marathons, but you should obtain a full recovery with some minor restrictions."

Driving was out of the question until he regained some

flexibility in the knee, and that felt like a prison sentence. Taxis were a pain in the ass. So was asking for help. Self-pity made him want to drink, and wanting it and denying it put the lid on his self-imposed confinement, turning it into a tomb.

On Saturday morning, Danny dropped by with a cold case file for him to have a look at, strictly on the Q.T., boosting Peterson's spirits. But he kept it to himself and shrugged off Danny's gesture.

Danny knew the game, but he was too tired and over-worked to play it. His face showed it. His slumping shoulders did too.

Peterson nosed at the file. "Is this a fee-for-service deal, or am I working off an IOU?"

"If you're going to be a smartass, I'll take it back," Danny said.

Peterson pulled the file to his side of the dining-room table.

"Crack it and I'll get you another," Danny offered.

"Who does the leg work?" Peterson asked.

"Billy's coming by to juice up your computer. Bernie said she'd help. That's the best I can do. Besides, you got legs. Use them."

"I can't drive."

"Take a bus. You're pensioned off. On Tuesdays old people ride for free."

Peterson let it go and opened the file, a sixteen-year-old male, Nicholas Rafferty, shot dead in a public park. High school basketball player taking a shortcut on his way home after practice. The thick file was a few months old, lots of interviews, no suspects.

Danny dropped a legal size envelope on the table. "I got a call to pick this up for you. Can you imagine hand delivery in the age of instant messages? It's from the once-a-nun friend of yours."

Peterson kept his eyes on the murder file.

"Bernie got her the girl's full name and the town she came from in Newfoundland. Closure, right." Danny rolled his eyes. "So your friend went up there and talked with the girl's mother. She called it a summing up before she went back into the convent. There's a letter in there for you."

Peterson glared at Danny.

"What?" Danny threw up his hands in feigned protest. Beaming. "I'm a detective. I'm supposed to be nosy."

Peterson went most of that day without opening the envelope from Anna Gray, pretending he was uninterested, but his curiosity thickened by the hour. It was mid-afternoon when he set aside the Rafferty murder case and opened the envelope. He emptied the contents on the dining-room table: a note addressed to him and nearly a dozen photographs. He poured himself a Coke and settled at the table. He read the letter first.

Dear Peterson,

I have never written a letter like this. I have never felt such tenderness, and, at the same time, I have never experienced such violence. My heart has been torn over you, and I am as confused and split apart now as in any other time in my life. I am Humpty Dumpy all over again, and I pray God will put me back together.

Our lives are so different, so at odds. We shared a traumatic experience, and I have come to realize we share little else. A girl's violent and tragic death bound us to one another these few months, but that is not a secure basis for a deep personal relationship.

I needed to put that experience behind me. If I am to make the most of my life, I needed to settle that horrifying night in the Broken Promise. That is why I went to Elbow Harbour to visit Molly Gornish's parents. I believed it was the only way I could come to terms with a teenage girl bleeding to death in my arms. I believed it was the only way I could reconcile a grief that seemed irreconcilable.

Her parents were heartbroken by their daughter's death, yet unforgiving about the murder she had committed. They refused to accept Molly's mental health as cause for killing the priest at St. Jude's. Her mother said Molly often had fits of wild behaviour. And yet her mother could not accept the poor girl's mental state as cause for her daughter's strange behaviour. Several times, their priest caught Molly in church playing with candles before the statue of the Blessed Virgin and crying about having her period. They punished Molly each time Father Garrity brought her home.

My efforts to console them were rejected, and I returned even less settled than before I had left, still stricken with a private grief and deep sense of guilt that I cannot explain.

After much contemplation and professional encouragement, I am returning to the convent and placing my life, once again, in the hands of the Lord.

We never exchanged expressions of love, but I can assure you that I will always hold you dear to my heart.

Anna

PS. The photos of Elbow Harbour are for you. I thought you would want to see where Molly grew up. Several are of the new church the community built. The old one caught fire more than two years ago and burned down. They salvaged the statue of the Blessed Virgin from the ashes, and that has been a source of village pride. Father Garrity guided me through the church. He was so proud of the statue and of the stone floor the village men cut from a nearby quarry. I thought it all so beautiful and wanted to share it with you. Knowing more about the girl who died in our arms offered me some consolation. I hope it offers some comfort to you.

Peterson drained the Coke and squirmed for something stronger. He thumbed through the photos to one that pictured Elbow Harbour as a village of wood-frame houses with blistered paint in a rainbow of colours. There was a shot of the newly built church and one of a four-room schoolhouse. Another depicted an outcrop of rock in the foreground and a path dipping to where four houses crouched beneath a stony bluff. One of these houses was featured in another photo. It had dark blue paint peeling from the clapboard siding. A man and woman he took to be Molly's parents were standing behind a weathered picket fence in front of this house.

He spread out all the photos. Glanced at them. Reread Anna's letter. Glanced back at the photos. He pounded the table then pushed himself away, hobbled to the front window and looked out onto the street. He realized it was Saturday as soon as he saw his neighbour teaching his youngest, a six-year-old girl, how to ride a bicycle. He watched the girl wobble unsteadily on the bike, while her father gripped the back of the seat.

Peterson rubbed his face. A nagging impression. Something about the photos. Something familiar. Something he had seen before.

The little girl fell off the bike, and her father helped her up, encouraging her to get back on.

Peterson turned from the window. Twisting on his bum leg. Feeling pain shoot up to his spine. He stood still until it passed, then returned to the table and leaned over the photos. One of them caught his eye at once — an interior of the new church featuring the statue of the Blessed Virgin.

Seeing that statue had him gripping the table edge for support. The statue's face and hands were black from when the previous church had burned to the ground. In her right hand the Blessed Virgin was holding the world. In her left was a rod of flowering lilies carved in ivory, the top of which was the letter P over a cross — a Chi-Rho.

His thoughts went back to St. Jude's Church and the dead priest in the sacristy and the blood pooled before the blackened statue of the Blessed Virgin. He remembered the rag doll placed at the statue's feet as an offering. He was deep in that memory when his cell phone rang. He fumbled for it in his pocket, got it on the third ring.

He saw the same shabby room. Heard the same silence. Felt the same remorse. Begged again for his daughter to say something, anything. But there was no response; just the ambient sound in that fleabag room on the other side of the continent.

He listened harder and detected her breathing. As he listened, his eyes strayed back to the photo of the Blessed Virgin. Then he looked at the photo of an old priest standing at the transept gesturing broadly as if showing off his church to the camera. Grey hair. Stooped shoulders.

Peterson fingered this photo aside, revealing a photo of the stone floor before the charred statue of the Blessed Virgin. He jerked his eyes back to the one of the old priest. He cradled the phone with his shoulder and listened to his daughter's silence as he grouped together the photos of priest, floor, and statue. He focused on the burned statue holding the flowering rod of lilies with the Chi-Rho on top. Then, as he had done the night of the murder in St. Jude's church, he shifted his gaze from the Blessed Virgin to the stone floor. He leaned closer and saw that bright speckled stones had been shaped into stars and inlaid in a circle around a single Greek letter — Alpha.

He looked back and forth from the circle of stars and the letter Alpha set in the stone floor to the old priest and blackened statue. Two churches, he thought, two priests, the past and present confused in Molly's disturbed mind. Then he gathered the photos and set them aside as he realized the motive for her ritual and for her outrage at St. Jude's was tangled in gibberish and in madness.

Then his daughter hung up, and his mind emptied.

ACKNOWLEDGEMENTS

Thanks to the late B.J. Grant for always nudging me in the right direction, to Patrick Murphy for his encouragement, to Karen for her patience, to Cpl. Mike Sims and Dr. Gary Carson for their insights, to Dinah Forbes and Laura Pastore for the spit and polish (errors are all my own), to the hundreds of overheard conversations on public transit, and to the railway car knocker who was coupling air hoses between freight cars when he said to me — life is a crap shoot.